OTHER B

T

SEEKER'S FATE

SEEKER'S WORLD, BOOK THREE

K. A. RILEY

For all the readers out there in need of an escape:
I've got you.

PREFACE

Over those first few days in Fairhaven, Callum and I spent almost every minute together.

During the daylight hours, our lives were as close to perfect as anyone's could possibly be.

But when night fell...

Everything changed.

DARKNESS

MONDAY, *August 24th*
  Shortly Before Dawn

CALLUM WAS LYING in my bed, his features highlighted by the faintly glowing streams filtering in from the streetlight outside. His chest rose and fell with the pulse of his gentle breathing.

He was dressed in an old cotton t-shirt and a pair of shorts that had once belonged to my brother Will, and his light brown hair was mussed from an uneven sleep.

Staring down at his face, I wondered how I ever managed to resist the constant temptation to kiss his perfect lips, his neck, his jawline.

Then again, there had been plenty of times when I'd given in, my desires taking over and drawing me perilously close to further dangerous temptation.

Right now, though, I had other things on my mind.

I hardly dared to speak for fear of waking him. But I didn't have a choice.

The lie had gone on too long already.

"Callum," I whispered, nudging his shoulder.

I watched, guilty, as he stirred.

"Mmm?" he moaned. "What's going on? What time is it?"

"It's really late. And…also really early," I said, noting the change in the sky's color from navy to violet as dawn threatened to break. "There's a Waerg on the street outside. Watching us." Holding my breath, I added, "Watching *me*, I think."

At that, Callum's eyes popped open. For a second, he stared at me, his irises flickering with the defensive flame of the dragon who lived inside him—the creature who clawed away at his insides each night as he tossed and turned. I could see the enigmatic beast staring out at me as if trying to assess me. Hoping to figure out once and for all if I was friend or foe.

Since our arrival in Fairhaven, his dragon had become restless, aggressive. Late each night, when Callum finally managed to drift to sleep, his skin flared hot, as if a vicious fever was attacking him from the inside. He tossed and turned for hours, muttering words I couldn't understand.

It was like the dragon was taking advantage of his unconscious state, trying to steal his body and mind away from him while he was at his most vulnerable. All because *it* was coming.

The day they called the Naming.

It was Niala, my closest friend at the Academy, who had first told me about the day when dragon shifters truly came of age. The day the beast who lived inside them turned one hundred years old and revealed its true nature, free from the constraints of a human's control.

The change killed some dragon shifters and drove others to madness.

There was no way to know what it might do to Callum.

But now, awake and alert, he seemed to shake the powerful dragon off, his irises fading to their usual shade of exquisite blue. Suddenly energized, he jumped to his feet, stepped over to the window to look out to the street below, and said, "I'm going out there."

"I'm coming with you."

He spun around, and for a second, it looked like he was about to protest. But when he saw my face, he seemed to change his mind. "All right."

I grabbed my sheathed silver dagger from my nightstand, fastened it around my waist, and, together, Callum and I raced downstairs and out the front door.

But by the time we reached the street, the Waerg had disappeared.

"He must have gone into the woods," I said, gesturing to the edge of the forest at the end of the cul-de-sac where I'd lived all my life.

I was about to head in that direction when Callum grabbed my arm, holding me back.

"How long?" he asked, his voice sounding parched with tension.

"How long what?"

"How long since you first saw the Waerg?"

I bit my lip as I contemplated a lie. But I thought better of it.

He knew me too well.

"I saw him the first night we spent in Fairhaven, and he's come around every night since."

"Why did you wait until tonight to tell me?"

"I've been worried about you, especially at night. Lately, you've seemed so..."

"You don't need to worry," he interrupted, his tone tinged with the hoarse growl of something not quite human. "I'm fine." A brief scowl flashed across his features before he relaxed again and looked toward the woods. "And right now, I want to focus on finding the Waerg you chose not to tell me about."

"I'm sorry for not telling you. I really should have."

"Yes, you should have." With a heavy sigh, his shoulders relaxed. "If something happened to you, Vega—"

Disarmed by his shift in tone, I smiled and took his hands in mine. "I'm careful. Nothing will happen to me."

Callum narrowed his eyes and smirked. I knew that look. It was his not-so-subtle way of reminding me that over the last several weeks, I'd suffered through an ill-advised series of near-death experiences that no *actual* careful person would ever endure.

I'd managed to get imprisoned in the Usurper Queen's dungeon in the Otherwhere. I'd led a contingent of Seekers into a trap that had gotten one of us killed.

And more than once, I'd stared into the eyes of giant wolves who were salivating as if they couldn't wait to tear my head from my shoulders.

All right. So maybe he had a point.

"Fine," I said. "I'd like to amend my statement to *Nothing will happen to me as long as you're with me.*"

"Good. See to it that you keep me with you when you leave the house—at least at night. And maybe you could tell me when, oh, I don't know, you see any stalker-like mortal enemies staring up at your bedroom window."

"Fair enough. Now, let's go."

I pivoted and looked toward the forest, suddenly struck by the realization that I had no idea where to start the search for the aforementioned mortal enemy.

Multiple trails led into the woods, some more established than others. Most had been carved out over years by the neighborhood's more adventurous kids.

"I'm sure he's in there," I said. "But I'm not sure *where*, exactly…"

Callum's certainty was unflinching. "He's gone down the path to the right."

"How do you know?"

"I can smell him."

I shot him a look of surprise. He'd never mentioned before that he could pick up the scents of Waergs like a tracking hound.

He shrugged. "What can I tell you? My sense of smell has become a little more acute lately. It's one of the few benefits of having an overly active dragon living rent-free inside my head."

"Cool." I drew my dagger, sliding it out slowly enough to muffle the whisper of steel against the leather sheath. "I'm going to move into my Shadow form."

"Good. I'll fly overhead so I can get a look at the woods."

"Fly? Are you sure that's...safe? Your dragon is..." I didn't want to say the words out loud. That his dragon was becoming more erratic, more willful. It wasn't like he didn't already know that the day was coming when he would change forever.

"Keeping him imprisoned inside me will only make him more restless than he already is. It'll probably be good for me to free him for a little and let him think he's in control."

"But what if someone sees you?"

"No one will—at least no one we need to worry about. You, on the other hand, *should* worry about being seen, at least by the Waerg. Make sure you stay hidden from him, no matter what. This is a reconnaissance mission only."

I nodded. "Don't worry. I have zero interest in being spotted by a slobbering wolf who looks like he's itching to devour my liver with some fava beans."

Laughing, Callum backed away as we reached the trailhead, and with a quick, brilliant flash, he took off, his massive golden wings propelling him into the air.

A pang of wistful regret tore at my chest to watch the nameless dragon lunge skyward. He was easily the most beautiful creature I'd ever seen...aside from Callum himself.

I was fond of the dragon, which was odd, considering that he could decide any day now to char-broil me. Or worse, he could steal Callum away from me forever.

I sent a mental thought out to the majestic beast as I watched him disappear over the trees. *You're a part of Callum. Believe it or not, that's enough to make me love you.*

For now.

With a hard exhalation, I turned to focus on my own ground-level mission.

My transition into Shadow form, as always, was excruciating. But I'd grown so used to it that I almost looked forward to the brief injection of pain. It was like the searing ache of a good workout—a throb deep within my muscles and bones. Something I knew was good for me, that made me stronger, safer, all but invincible.

When the pain dissipated, I began the hunt.

The scent of damp leaves clung to the air as I glided, unseen, between the trees. It was too dark to make out much of anything, other than the scattered silhouettes of ancient oaks and maple trees. But after a time, I spotted something moving in the distance: a figure with the unmistakable gait of a wolf.

For a time, I followed my prey, my blade clenched in my right hand. After a few minutes, I was close enough to see him outlined against a bank of white-barked birch trees. His sleek coat was a dark charcoal gray over top of rippling, powerful-looking muscles.

He stopped to sniff the air, turning to look behind him as if he was vaguely aware of an encroaching threat.

When I caught the bright flash of his eyes, I gasped.

His glowing irises flickered silvery-blue in the moonlight. In a flood of horrific memories, I was reminded of a certain intolerably cruel, shape-shifting warlock I'd encountered in the Otherwhere.

But no. This Waerg wasn't Lumus. He was tame by comparison and far less frightening than the silver-haired monster I'd had the misfortune of getting to know.

The monster who'd killed a fellow Seeker and had all but torn my soul from my chest in the process.

For whatever reason, the wolf I was looking at now seemed more mischievous than destructive. He exuded a surprising sort of gentleness—if there even was such a thing as a gentle Waerg. He didn't feel like a killer, which I supposed explained why I hadn't felt compelled to tell Callum about him on the first night we'd spent in town.

The Waerg was a Watcher, perhaps. Possibly a sentinel sent by the Usurper Queen to keep an eye on me and report back, in case I appeared to be on the verge of discovering the location of the next Relic of Power.

Whoever he was, I needed to keep an eye on him, so I decided to get a closer look. I needed to study him, to memorize his face, so I could describe him to Callum in detail.

But as I slid silently around the broad, rough trunk of an ancient tree, I cursed under my breath.

He was gone.

SPOTTED

SOMEWHERE IN THE DISTANCE, the distinct, percussive snap of a dry branch echoed through the silent forest.

I ran toward the sound, careful not to slam face-first into any of the tree trunks blocking my path. I may have been little more than mist, but I was no ghost. It wasn't like I could run through solid objects. And the last thing I needed was to knock half my teeth out in a moment of excessive confidence.

When I finally found myself emerging into a small clearing, I was surprised to find my eyes meeting Callum's. He was breathing heavily, no doubt winded from trying to maintain control over his dragon.

I pulled out of my Shadow form, struggling to keep myself from crying out with the pain of the change. "Did you...is he..." I sputtered as soon as I was able to speak, but I stopped myself. I didn't have the courage to ask if he'd actually *killed* the Waerg. Somehow, the thought of drawing blood here in my hometown was more gruesome than doing so in the Otherwhere.

To my relief, he shook his head, his fierce blue eyes dancing with red and orange flames that pierced through the darkness. His dragon, it seemed, was still very much awake inside him.

Callum tilted his head toward the sky. "I saw him from above the treetops, standing right here. It was the weirdest thing…"

"What happened?"

"He shifted into his human form."

"Why would he do that? He had to know he was being watched. Why make himself vulnerable?"

"Honestly, I have no idea. He spun around a few times before he ran off—he even glanced upward at one point. Some part of me thinks he *wanted* me to see him, though I have no idea why."

"Did you get a good enough look that you'd be able to recognize him on the street?"

"That I did," Callum replied with an impish grin, stepping over and pulling me close even as the last vestiges of his dragon faded from his irises. "I know his face now, both in human and wolf form. Not to mention that I'm all too familiar with his scent. I'll be able to track him to anywhere in town. Though I suspect I won't have to look very far."

"Why do you say that?"

"He's young. Seventeen, maybe eighteen. Tall. Very good-looking, too. I suspect the girls at your school will go mad over him."

"Wait—you think he might be a student at Plymouth High?"

Callum nodded. "It's a definite possibility. Even if he hides from us for the next several days, we're bound to run into him once school begins. He'll stand out in a crowd, that one. He's not exactly your average teenage boy."

"Sounds like another not-so-average teenage boy I know," I chuckled, relieved to be done with the Waerg for the time being. "Well, I hope you're right about finding him. He was freaking me out, and I'd love to give him a piece of my mind. I'm not crazy about being stalked."

"Yeah, well, I still wish you'd told me about him sooner. I don't like the idea of someone watching you. Unless it's me, of course."

"I told you why I kept it to myself." I bit my lip, unsure if I should say anything else. "But…I'll admit part of it was pure selfishness. I didn't want to ruin our time together. We finally get to sleep in the same bed every night, and, well, getting to spend nights with you without worrying about waking up at dawn to get my ass kicked in the sparring ring is quite a luxury, you know. It's not something I wanted to give up. I just wanted a few days of normal."

"I suppose that's fair. Normal can be quite nice sometimes, though I think you or I would wither and die if we were to suffer through a lifetime of it."

"I guess the good news," I said, "is that this little night-time adventure wasn't entirely unpleasant. For once, I got to stalk a Waerg, instead of the other way around. I think I could really learn to enjoy the rogue assassination game. I mean, if the thought of actually assassinating anyone didn't make me sick to my stomach."

"I'm glad to know I'm not dating a *total* psychopath," Callum replied with a chuckle. "Anyhow, I'm glad you enjoyed it. You're the primary protector of this town now, you know."

"Protector," I repeated. "I like the sound of that. But we both know *you're* the only real protector. My only job is seeking the rest of the Relics of Power." With that, I sighed. "I just wish I knew where to start."

"Don't rush it," Callum said before planting a soft kiss on my lips. "Remember what Merriwether told you."

"*The clues will come to me in their own damn time,* you mean?"

"Yeah, I'm not sure he put it exactly like that."

"Ha. Well, it's not that I'm eager to find them today or anything—I'm in no hurry to end my time as a Seeker. It's just…I feel a little lost right now, like I'm waiting for something to happen, but I'm not sure it ever will. Like you and I are living in a state of limbo where nothing about our futures is certain."

"Most things in life aren't certain. But you *can* be sure the clues will eventually come your way. Remember, this *is* your fate."

"Yeah? Well, in my limited experience, fate is a total bitch."

"It's not so bitchy once you figure out you can control it yourself." Callum shifted his eyes to the sky, which was just beginning to lighten, "Speaking of which, it seems that my particular fate is to be hungry. How about if we head home, get cleaned up, then go find somewhere to have a nice, greasy breakfast?"

"Actually, Mr. Drake, as fates go, that sounds just about perfect."

A CHANCE ENCOUNTER

BY THE TIME we'd each showered, dressed, and headed down-stairs, it was a little after eight A.M.

Light streamed into the kitchen through the large window above the sink, washing away any residual apprehension or anxiety our strange night had inflicted.

"There's a place on High Street called the Crescent Diner," I told Callum as we perched on the tall stools by the kitchen island. "Liv and I used to go there for breakfast pretty often."

"I know the place. A couple of blocks down from the Novel Hovel."

"Right, of course—I keep forgetting you lived in Fairhaven for a little while."

"Too little. I hardly had a chance to get to know you before you were called to the Otherwhere." Callum inhaled deeply, as if taking in the scent of my world. "I never expected to be back here, but it's nice, this. Spending some proper time here, I mean. It feels like the greatest luxury imaginable to have you to myself for days on end."

I smiled, partly out of pleasure, but also because it was nice to see him relaxing. His dragon, such a strangely nocturnal menace, was hostile enough that I often felt I was losing a piece of the Callum I knew so well during the dark hours of night.

It was a relief when he came back to me each morning.

He reached across the counter and took my hand in his. He really did seem like his usual self: bright blue eyes devoid of any traces of a fire-breathing beast. A warm smile that sent invisible waves of affection flitting through the air to leave a trail of goosebumps along my skin, just as his fingers so often did.

"I could get used to this kind of luxury," I said. "I could get used to the idea of you."

No matter how much time we got to spend together, I knew it would never feel like enough. Part of me still hesitated to tell him how happy it made me to have him with me here, so close to the beginning of my senior year of high school. To feel like we were more than just the frivolous summer fling so many teenagers bragged about each September when they returned to school.

He was mine, and I was his: heart mind, and soul. To call him my boyfriend seemed trivial and insufficient. But really, there was no word in the English language—no term for the love between a Seeker girl and a gorgeous, heroic dragon-shifter— that could possibly encapsulate all that he was to me.

Still, for the purposes of appearances, he *was* my boyfriend. The first boyfriend I'd ever had and the most extraordinary person I'd ever met, all wrapped up in one.

But he was so, so much more than that. And as frightening as it was to admit it to myself, I could no longer imagine living without him. I couldn't fathom returning to my mundane life. To the goals I'd once had: good grades, a part-time job, college.

Yet, as much as we'd managed to delay it over and over again, I knew the day would come when we'd go our separate ways. He would head back to the Otherwhere, just as my grandfather had done so many years ago.

I'd lose Callum. I'd pine for him for the rest of my life. I would stay behind to live a banal existence, devoid of the kind of magical wonders and deep love I'd come to know, to feel coursing through my veins.

The kind of love one only read about in dreamy, idealistic fairy tales.

Except for one thing:

What those fairy tales had failed to tell us was that it wasn't just love.

It was an *addiction*.

An addiction from which people never quite recovered, no matter what happened in their lives from that moment on. It was a chemical dependence that resided deep in their souls forever. And there was no cure.

"What are you thinking about?" Callum asked.

"Sometimes," I replied, choosing my words carefully, "I'm so perfectly content that it scares me. I know, I know—nothing is perfect. I know our lives are filled with uncertainty. But it feels so right, being with you. And I guess I feel like there's nowhere to go from here but down."

He nodded in agreement but said nothing. Instead, he took my hand and kissed it in a moment of quiet chivalry.

As he pulled his head up, his eyes met mine and instantly conveyed a thousand words.

It was reassuring to remember that he felt it, too.

The cruel, wonderful addiction that might one day destroy us both.

It was nine A.M. before we finally left the house and headed to the diner. We chose to walk, despite the fact that my ancient, rust-addled but perfectly functional Toyota was sitting in the driveway.

My brother Will had left the car I'd since named the Rust-Mobile to me when he'd moved out to California, and as much as

I appreciated the gift, I enjoyed wandering the meandering streets of Fairhaven too much to want to be confined to the interior of a vehicle.

Hand in hand, Callum and I headed toward High Street, savoring the early morning breeze and the hints of autumn wafting on the air.

For a few seconds, I felt like a normal teenager with a normal life.

Well, except for the fact that my boyfriend was anything but normal. Tall, magnificently handsome, with an accent no one could quite place and a wisdom that no one who looked eighteen should possess.

"I feel like I've been keeping you all to myself ever since we arrived in Fairhaven," he said as we walked along under the morning sun. "Tell me, are you looking forward to seeing your friends again?"

"I'm excited to see Liv. I feel guilty I haven't called her yet. But she's really my only friend. I mean, there are other people at Plymouth High, but I didn't really hang out much with any of—"

My words were cut short by a shrill voice shouting, "Vega?" from somewhere behind us. "Callum!"

I spun around, snapping my hand away from Callum's to see Liv, her sleek, dark hair swept up in a ponytail, sprinting toward us at full throttle.

"Speak of the devil," I laughed as she leapt at me with a force that nearly knocked me over.

"I saw you out my window and had to come catch you!" she cried. "I just got up."

I looked her up and down to realize she was dressed in a silk camisole and shorts.

"I can see that," I said. "Didn't feel like throwing a bathrobe on, huh?"

"No time. Besides, it's hot as butt out here, even at this hour.

And not all of us like covering ourselves like the nuns of some ancient order, Sister Vega."

"*All* nuns cover themselves. Not just the ancient-order ones," I said, self-consciously pulling at the hoodie I'd put on after my shower.

"Face it—you're a hoodie addict," she replied. "I guess old habits die hard. Pun intended."

She had a point. I reminded myself to go through my clothes and find something that made me look less like I wanted to hide from the world. It wasn't like I was the same self-conscious girl I'd been a couple of months ago. I was a Seeker now. I'd been to hell and back, and I'd lived to tell the tale.

Not that I could ever tell Liv about a single second of my otherworldly misadventures.

"Where have you been, anyhow?" she asked, thankfully changing the subject. "I got back from our road trip a week ago and not a peep from you. Didn't you get my texts?"

I shot Callum a quick, panicked look. "I…no…I'm so sorry. I was away and didn't have internet. I'm a little behind on all that stuff."

"Away, huh?" she asked, glancing at Callum as a knowing grin painted its way across her lips. "Oh, right. Will said you were camping. But I thought he said you went with *friends*, plural. Not one solitary *hunky male friend*." She gave Callum a teasing punch to the arm. "It's good to see you again. You look even better than last time, if that's possible."

"Thank you?" Callum answered with an uncomfortable grin.

"Wait a minute—you said you talked to Will?" I asked, ignoring her over-the-top flirtation—something that was usually reserved strictly for my older brother.

Not that it bothered me to see her compliment Callum. After all, she was the one who'd first set us up, and Liv was too good a friend to make any kind of serious move on him.

At least, I *hoped* she was.

"Yeah. I called his cell when I couldn't find you. He sounded good. Happy. Naturally, I told him I'm still mad at him for moving out West. How am I supposed to marry him if he's so far away?"

"He'll come back for holidays," I assured her. "Don't worry. You'll have plenty of time to entrap him into a lifetime of domestic horrors."

"Good, good," she said, curling her fingers and tapping their tips together like an evil arch-villain. "Sooo, you say you two were camping?"

"Yes, in a manner of speaking," Callum replied, glancing at me sideways as if to say *I'll field this one.* "In a very large tent. Like, circus-size. So big it had towers and courtyards and a giant library. It was so big, in fact, we slept in totally and completely separate rooms."

Liv rolled her eyes. "Yeah, I *totally* believe that."

"It's true," I insisted. "And we went on some nice hikes. Saw some very interesting birds, and even a wolf or two." I threw Callum a conspiratorial smile.

"Wolves?" Liv said. "Where the hell were you, the Rockies?"

"No," I said. "Not exactly. We were close to Fairhaven. And yet, not so close. It's…hard to explain."

"Actually," Liv added, ignoring my reply, "Devin—you remember him from English class—told me the other day he was sure he saw a wolf on the West Side. I didn't believe him. But if you guys saw some, maybe he wasn't lying after all."

"There are quite a few in the woods around here," Callum said. "They just like to keep themselves hidden. They're not overly fond of people."

"Huh." Liv looked like she was already losing interest in the topic. "Oh hey—a bunch of us seniors-to-be are headed to the beach at Castle Hill Lake tonight, for a bonfire. You two should come!"

Callum and I exchanged a look, and I knew we were thinking the exact same thing.

Our Waerg friend might be there.

"Yeah," I replied. "That sounds great. What time?"

Liv shrugged. "Eight or nine, I think. I'll meet you there?"

"Sure."

"Great! Wear something less stuffy than your usual nun's habits, would you?"

"I'll try my best."

She gave me a squeeze and whispered, "I can't believe this is working out so great for you and Callum! Just make sure you still make time for me. I've missed you."

"Of course I will," I whispered back.

When she'd started jogging back toward her house, I finally let out the deep breath I'd been holding in ever since I'd heard her call my name.

"That was so crazy," I told Callum. "The last time I saw her, I was…"

"…freeing her from my sister's dungeon," he replied.

"She doesn't even know," I moaned. "She doesn't remember. I mean, I'm glad she's not suffering from the trauma of it, but…"

Callum turned toward me and slipped his hands onto my waist. The warmth of his touch was a soothing balm on my mood.

"Are you okay?" he asked.

"I'm fine. I just wish I could talk to her about it. About everything. I feel like I'm going to be living a lie for the next year. Or possibly forever."

"I know that feeling."

I looked up at him and smirked. "Yeah. Of course you do." Pulling in close, I pressed my face to his chest, savoring the sensation of his arms enveloping me, a shield against my own sadness. "This is going to be a weird autumn, isn't it?"

"Mm-hmm. In ways we can't yet imagine."

I let out a chuckle. "You sound so much like Merriwether sometimes. All doom and gloom."

"Hey, I didn't say anything about gloom."

I pulled back and looked up at him. "Oh, good. Only doom, then."

"Well.... maybe a *little* gloom."

"As long as we face it together."

"Vega Sloane, I would go to Hell and back with you."

"Let's hope it doesn't come to that, Callum Drake."

After a quick kiss, we turned and continued our walk to the diner.

THE BONFIRE

WHEN WE GOT HOME after a long, relaxing breakfast, I phoned Will, relieved when he apologized for not calling me sooner. We'd exchanged a few texts since I'd returned from the Otherwhere, but this was the first time I'd actually managed to get him to answer his phone.

I hadn't heard my brother's voice in so long that I'd almost forgotten what it sounded like. Once or twice over the course of our conversation, listening to his deep, familiar lilt, I found myself getting choked up.

The awful memory of seeing him trapped was assaulting me in waves. Images of his lifeless body, suspended in the Usurper Queen's demented dungeon, kept materializing in my head.

It was good knowing he was truly safe and under the watchful eye of Merriwether's allies.

Not that Will knew anything about that.

Still, I missed him. I wished he was here, so I could hug him tight after everything that had happened to both of us.

I wished he could meet Callum and get to know him a little.

But more than anything, I wished I could tell him the truth about our grandfather, about where we'd come from and about who we really were. I felt he had a right to know about the strange world beyond our own, the one I could access with nothing more than my mind and a magical key.

"Life in California is a little busier than I expected," he told me with a laugh. "I got a job at a restaurant, and I've even managed to make a few friends. Not that that's any excuse for not calling you instead of just texting. I've been delinquent. I know. It's so weird…I've been meaning to call you for days and days, but…"

"But what?"

"It's almost as if I forg—"

I smiled when he cut himself off and offered up a guilty-sounding, "I'm sorry—I…I don't know where that came from."

But my feelings weren't hurt.

I knew perfectly well there was no way Will could ever forget about me. Not without the intervention of a powerful magic-user. There was no question that Merriwether—or someone else—had somehow gotten into my brother's mind from afar and deliberately steered his thoughts away from me.

It was for Will's protection as much as for mine, and I was grateful for it. The last thing I wanted was for him to worry about me. It was only right that he should start a new life, just as I was beginning my own.

If he knew half of what I'd gone through over the last several weeks, I had no doubt he'd hop on the next flight back to Fairhaven, lock me in the basement, and throw away the key.

I couldn't begin to imagine what he'd do if he knew my boyfriend was a dragon shifter on the verge of a momentous event that might turn him into an incredibly dangerous killing machine.

Then again…

What he didn't know probably wouldn't hurt him.

AROUND NINE O'CLOCK THAT NIGHT, after a blissfully uneventful day, Callum and I headed to Castle Hill Lake, a smallish body of water tucked on the far side of the woods that surrounded Fairhaven. On its eastern edge was a sandy beach where Plymouth High's seniors traditionally gathered on the last weekend of summer. By the lake's shore, they transformed old furniture, obsolete textbooks, and kindling gathered from the nearby woods into an enormous bonfire.

The partygoers made out, consumed bottles of unidentifiable liquid they'd stolen from their parents' liquor cabinets, and generally wreaked self-destructive havoc at a safe distance from any of the town's adults, who apparently lived in a state of utter denial that any of this mayhem was unfolding so close to home.

A few months earlier—before I'd ever heard of the Academy or the Otherwhere—I would have come up with any excuse to avoid such an event. I hated big gatherings, particularly if they involved the very people I'd been avoiding for the past three years of high school.

It was ridiculous to think most of us had been together in some form or other since we were five years old, yet Liv was the only one that I actually called a friend. She was the only one who even remotely understood me.

And yet, here I was, attending the bonfire like any regular, sociable teenager. Vega Sloane, outcast extraordinaire, the girl who wore hoodies and shrank into a slouch in the corner when confronted with too many faces at once, had come out to party.

Then again, I was standing a little taller now than I had during my first three years of high school. There would be no more slouching. No more hiding. No fear.

I no longer felt like an ugly, orphaned little duckling.

I was a Seeker.

Whether anyone else knew it or not, I kicked butt. I could travel between worlds. I could disappear into a mist and summon objects and creatures that most people here in Fairhaven could never even dream of.

And it didn't hurt my confidence level to have my powerful, perfect boyfriend—the heir to the throne of the Otherwhere—walking by my side.

I'd followed Liv's advice and left behind my usual outfit of jeans and a hoodie. Those were the trappings of the old Vega—the one who concealed herself and hung her head in quiet shame for not fitting in with the crowd.

Instead, I was wearing an Indian cotton printed top with spaghetti straps and a pair of jean shorts, along with a pair of strappy, flat leather sandals. Not exactly an outfit out of a glamor magazine. But not something out of the garbage bin, either.

Callum, GQ-handsome in pretty much anything, was dressed in jeans and a white linen button-down shirt, both of which fit perfectly enough to show off his athletic body without making it look like he was *trying* to show off his athletic body.

As we approached the beach, it struck me how sophisticated and mature he looked in contrast with the bellowing, football-jersey-wearing teenaged boys from Plymouth High who called each other "dude" and "bro," and considered the volume and duration of their belches some kind of mark of social status.

When we stepped out of the woods onto the beach, much of the senior class was already gathered around the fire. Most were standing around, socializing with drinks in hand. Whether the beverages were legal or not, I couldn't tell, and I wasn't sure I wanted to know.

I scanned the area as we approached, eyeing the sea of familiar faces as they flickered with reflected orange flame.

"There's Liv," I said, pointing to the far end of the small beach. She was facing us, talking to a young man with curly black hair who looked at least a head taller than her. "Looks like she's chatting up some guy. Good for her. I almost don't want to interrupt them."

"Even so, I think we'd better," Callum said, taking my hand with a strange urgency and beginning the walk over. "I think we need to meet her new friend."

"Wait a minute—why do I feel like you know something I don't?" I asked.

He stopped, his eyes still locked on Liv and her companion. "Because this isn't the first time I've seen that boy."

THE NEW BOY

My eyes widened. "You're telling me the first time was…"

"Last night. In the woods."

My jaw threatened to unhinge itself, drop clean off my face, and land on the sandy ground below. "*That's* the Waerg?" I whisper-hissed, leaning in close.

"One and the same. Come on. Let's go find out why he's chosen to befriend the one person on the beach who's close to you."

As Callum pushed through the crowd, teenagers parted to make way like a flock of birds evading a predator. It seemed even those who'd never met Callum could sense the strange, exquisite power inside him. The way he walked—shoulders back, chest forward, chin up—gave him a half-regal, half-criminal appearance. Definitely someone you didn't want to mess with.

It took some effort to avoid chuckling.

"You're like a human battering ram," I observed as we moved easily through the throng of sweaty adolescents.

"Except it's not the human part that's making them back away."

"You think they can sense...*him*?"

He nodded. "Prey animals always know when there's a predator about. Even if they've never met the predator in question. Self-preservation is a powerful instinct."

The way he said it sent a frisson of excitement along the surface of my skin, though I couldn't decide if it was a shudder of fear or pleasure.

Wait, I wondered. *Am I prey, too?*

Somehow, the thought wasn't as frightening as it should have been.

How strange, daunting, and extraordinary to think my greatest ally and worst enemy both lived inside the same body and shared one mind.

I shook off the thought as we made our way toward the edge of the water.

When Liv saw us coming, her face lit up.

"You made it!" she squealed, bouncing up and down in a little half-dance as her companion turned to face us.

"Of course we did," I replied, glancing at the boy who was standing just a few feet from her. His eyes, light green against bronze skin, reflected the distant fire. His eyelashes were as black as the impressive mess of curls on his head.

Callum was right. He was gorgeous.

Exceedingly so.

I could see why Liv looked so giddy.

"Vega, this is Lachlan," she said, grabbing his arm with both hands like she was shackling herself to him. "Can you believe it? He's going to be in our class at Plymouth next month!"

I assessed the boy for a second before jutting out a hand to shake. "Good to meet you," I said with a smile. "This is Callum."

Callum followed suit and shook Lachlan's hand. As they made contact, I was pretty sure I detected the briefest hint of terror pass across the boy's face.

"Did you just move here?" I asked. "I haven't seen you around before."

He forced a smile. "My family moves around a lot. I'm a military brat."

I threw Callum a quiet look. The boy's accent, lilting and musical, was all too familiar to us both.

"Military, huh," I replied. "So, where are you from, originally?"

"That's hard to say. We've moved around so much that I'm not really *from* anywhere."

"Your accent sounds familiar, though," I added, unable to resist prodding him a little.

"Ah. Yes, well, it's a mix of many things. I've lived in France, Germany, England…"

"Oh, really? Which *part* of Germany—"

"Vega!" Liv chastised. "I'm sure the poor guy doesn't want to give you his whole history."

"Fair enough," I replied with a smile.

"Liv," Lachlan said abruptly, "Would you like a drink? I'm going to pop over to the cooler…"

"I'd love a Coke," Liv replied, and when Lachlan took off, she let out another squeal of delight and grabbed my hand.

"Isn't he the hottest?" she asked, looking at me, then Callum. "I mean, after your guy, of course."

"He's…very good-looking."

"I just met him, but I already feel like he's my soul mate."

"I'm not entirely sure he has a soul," I said under my breath.

"Pardon?" Liv said.

"I'm pretty sure Vega said that's *cool*," Callum interjected.

"Super-cool," I confirmed. "*Inhumanly* cool."

"Seriously, I couldn't believe he came over to talk to me," Liv gushed. "Usually guys like that hang with the Charmers, not little ol' me." With that, she nodded over to the trio of surly-looking, pretty girls who were eyeing us from the other side of the

27

bonfire, expressions of quiet rage in their eyes. The tallest of them, Miranda, looked particularly displeased.

"Nice to know the three harpies are still excelling at the sport of synchronized Resting Bitch Face," I said. "They seem as pleasant as always."

I had no doubt that Miranda hated me even more than usual, if only for standing next to Callum, who was currently draping an arm around my shoulders. I couldn't help but recall how she'd approached him at Midsummer Fest, eyeing him like he was something specifically designed for her to feast on.

"Well, maybe Lachlan can tell what an awesome person you are," I said, turning back to Liv. "Just...be careful, okay? Guys like that..."

"Guys like what? Handsome?"

"Guys like him..." I repeated.

"...are not to be trusted," Callum concluded.

"Oh, so you *do* mean handsome. Well, speak for yourself, hottie," Liv laughed.

Callum let out a chuckle just as Lachlan returned with two Cokes and handed one to Liv.

"So tell me, Vega," Lachlan said, narrowing his eyes at me just enough to convey a hint of menace, "Are you looking forward to your final year?"

There was no question in my mind that he'd deliberately neglected to add the words "of high school" to the end of the sentence. I glared at him with a *Was that a threat?* look.

"I'm planning to make the most of my senior year, if that's what you mean," I replied, narrowing my eyes back.

"Good for you. I'm sure you'll have your hands full. You probably have a lot on your plate."

"Yeah, well, it's amazing how much one can accomplish in a few months, let alone ten of them. I'm sure I'll do just fine."

"Yes, I'm sure you will. As long as you're not distracted by...

outside complications. There's a lot that can happen during senior year. Unexpected events. You know."

I had to restrain myself to keep from snapping at him in front of Liv. "Unlike some people, I can walk and chew gum at the same time, so I'm not worried."

"I suspect that what lies ahead is going to be a little more challenging than walking or chewing gum."

"What the hell are you two talking about?" Liv asked with a nervous laugh.

"Nothing," Lachlan replied. "I've just heard through the grapevine that your friend here is a bit of an over-achiever. She needs to pace herself, if she wants to meet her goals."

Lachlan's expression was unreadable. He almost seemed to be enjoying our snarky little back and forth. But I could see that Liv was getting antsy, as if she wasn't entirely happy that I was pulling focus away from her.

"Why don't we go for a little walk?" Callum asked, tightening his grip around my shoulders.

"Sounds like an excellent plan."

As we stepped away, I turned and threw Lachlan a final look to say *I know who and what you are, and if you mess with my friend, I'll take a garden rake to your smug face.*

I no longer cared if he knew I was on to him. The Usurper Queen had already messed with Liv once. There was no way I was about to let a Waerg—no matter how handsome he was, or how into him Liv was—do the same.

We were just making our way over to a series of open plastic coolers when Miranda, the queen of the Charmers, leapt out in front of us with all the grace of an alley cat looking for a mate.

"Callum Drake," she said smoothly, pressing a hand to his chest in a move that made me wish I could pull my dagger from the sheath tucked into my waistband and press it to her throat without getting arrested. "Where have you been? I haven't seen you in weeks. Not since Midsummer Fest."

"Yes, well," he said. "I've been a little...busy." He uttered the last word in a way that filled it with hidden-but-not-so-hidden meaning as he sent an affectionate glance my way.

"You've *got* to be kidding me," Miranda spat with all the surly percussiveness of the villain from a cheesy high school drama. "You've been hanging out with Sloane all this time?"

I couldn't help but laugh.

"What's so surprising, Miranda?" I asked. "You seem shocked to find out he has good taste."

"Yeah? Well...he hasn't tasted my lips yet," she replied, spinning around and storming back to her two friends.

"I don't think he likes faux-strawberry flavored petroleum lip balm as much as you suspect," I retorted loudly enough that I was sure she heard me.

"Don't worry about her," Callum said, tugging me back. "She's just a hyena, looking for a kill. And you should know by now I'm not particularly fond of hyenas."

"I never would have thought it was possible, but she's making me miss the Zerkers at the Academy," I said, watching the three Charmers turn and shoot me more eye-daggers as they muttered something probably not-so-flattering about me to one another. "Sure, they were jerks, and most of them wanted me dead, but at least they didn't blatantly try to seduce you in front of me."

"No one," Callum said, turning to place both hands on my waist in another obvious display of affection, "will ever steal me from you."

"But what if—"

Callum shook his head and put a finger to my lips to halt my doubt in its tracks.

As if to prove it to the world, he kissed me. A long, drawn-out, passionate kiss that every single senior standing around the bonfire could see, and one that would almost certainly be talked about for days.

"Wow," I said when I'd pulled back. "You're amazingly good at territorial kissing."

"You're not my territory—I would never lay claim to you. At least, not in that way."

"I'm yours, and you know it."

"And I'm yours. Remember that in the days to come, no matter what happens."

I smiled up at him, uneasy with the insinuation of imminent havoc.

"On another topic entirely," I said, finally shaking loose any dread I had about the future, "what should we do about...the Waerg?" The last two words were a mere whisper as I pulled my eyes to where Liv was standing, a possessive hand clamped on Lachlan's arm.

"We keep an eye on him. Figure out who and where his allies are. Waergs seldom work alone. But if they do, there's probably something amiss. Come on. Let's grab a drink and have a wander around. I want to see who else is here."

"What do you mean, who's here?" I asked. "It's not like you know any of these kids."

Callum nudged me along but didn't answer my question.

When he'd grabbed a root beer and I had my hands on a ginger ale, he guided me back along the beach until we reached the edge of the woods, where we stopped. Oddly, his eyes kept veering to the forest rather than the fire, as if he was expecting someone—or *something*—to come bursting through out of the woods at any second now.

"Why do I feel like you're about to surprise me?" I asked as I watched him skulk around.

"Because I am...at least, I hope I am. But they should've been here by now..."

"They?"

Just as I said the word, my eye caught two figures moving toward us down the same narrow path we'd taken to get to the beach. One was stocky and powerful-looking. The other was lithe, feminine, and moved with the familiar, smooth gait of a panther.

"No!" I said, my lips curving into a grin. "Seriously? Is that—?"

"It is."

OLD FRIENDS

SECONDS LATER, I was hugging Niala, my best friend at the Academy, and Crow, the only Zerker I'd ever known who didn't habitually stare at me like he wanted to send my head rolling twenty feet away from my body.

"Where's Rourke?" I asked, glancing around to search for Niala's Familiar, the shapeshifting animal companion who never left her side.

Niala smiled and gestured to her small backpack. I stepped around her to see a ferret's head poking out, his glossy black eyes staring at me as his nose twitched in the air. I moved my hand to his face, letting him sniff me before giving him the briefest chin scratch. "Don't worry," Niala told me. "No one else can see him—at least, none of the Worlders."

"I'd forgotten about that," I replied, recalling the strangeness of Midsummer Fest. It was the first time I'd ever laid eyes on the girl with the cat-like eyes as she'd stood some distance away, chatting with Crow and Callum. I'd pointed out to my brother Will that she had a ferret with her, but he'd been unable to spot the very prominent creature climbing on Niala's shoulders.

At the time, I'd wondered if I was losing my mind.

That was the night I'd begun to learn who and what I was. It was also the first time I'd come close to being murdered by a Waerg.

"I can't believe you two are here!" I exclaimed. "It's like two worlds colliding. But in a good way."

"I told you I'd see you soon," Niala laughed. "Though I didn't expect it to be quite *this* soon."

"How long are you staying?"

"Not long," Crow replied. "This is only a quick drop-in. I've been assigned to a patrol of Rangers in the woods beyond the Academy."

"And I've been developing balms and potions in the Academy's infirmary," Niala added. "Merriwether just wanted us to see to it that you two were settling in all right."

"How is he?" I asked, probably a little too enthusiastically. I tended to avoid talking about the fact that the Academy's Headmaster was also my paternal grandfather. And now, surrounded by Plymouth High's senior class, seemed like an especially bad time.

Not that it really mattered anymore. No one would be accusing him of favoritism, at least not now that every Seeker Candidate had been assigned the role of Chosen Seeker.

Changing the topic from Merriwether, I asked Niala how things were going in the Otherwhere.

"They're tense since you Seekers left," she confessed. "Like everyone is waiting for the other shoe to drop. The queen's forces have been quiet, which is never a good sign. It's like she's plotting and scheming behind closed doors. Hatching a new plan. The problem is, no one knows what it might be."

"Speaking of plotting and scheming," Crow said, "have you two had any trouble here in town? Any recent threats?"

"Well, we know of at least one Waerg," I said, turning to nod toward Lachlan, who was still standing at the far end of the beach, charming Liv thoroughly enough to have her on the verge of swooning into a faint.

"Yes," said Niala. "Rourke picked up his scent from a mile away. He doesn't hide his true nature well, that one. Not like some people we've encountered."

I winced. There was no doubt in my mind she was talking about Raff, the deceitful intruder I'd rescued from the queen's dungeons, only to discover he was the Usurper Queen's horrid son.

"Raff isn't a mere Waerg," Callum replied, reading my mind. "His father is a shape-shifter. Concealment and deception are the gifts of his bloodline."

"True," Niala agreed, her tone velvety soft but bitter. "They are a whole other breed of cruelty."

"Well, this one seems to be a Watcher, not a fighter," said Callum, nodding toward Lachlan. "We went to confront him last night, and he could have challenged us—for that matter, he could easily have broken into the house at night and attacked us. But he chose to run instead of fight. He seems to be here on a reconnaissance mission. He's an informant, most likely."

"They're always Watchers until they find a way to get their teeth into you," Crow replied. "Waergs *always* want blood. Maybe he's holding back for now, but he's probably just trying to lull you into a false sense of security by pretending to be docile."

"Yeah, well, we're not the only ones he's lulling," I said, nodding in Liv's direction. Her face was mere inches from Lachlan's, her fingers twisting her hair as she stared, mesmerized, at him. She appeared to be giggling, her feet doing a little happy dance in the sand.

The only time I'd ever seen her like this was when she flirted relentlessly with my brother, and even then, she normally retained some semblance of control.

Without having had a drop of alcohol, she looked like the most intoxicated teenager at this beach party.

"Is she a friend of yours?" Niala asked.

"My *best* friend, actually," I said.

"Wait—she's the one who was in trapped the queen's dungeon? That's Liv?"

"Yep. It's a good thing she doesn't remember any of it. Although, I sort of wish she did. It would make it a hell of a lot easier to tell her the boy she's flirting with is likely to crush her soul, let alone what he might do to her trachea."

"He won't risk hurting her physically. Waergs only go after humans in this world as a last resort, and he'd bring the wrath of the Academy down on him if he tried anything. The last time a Waerg actually killed anyone here—"

"I know when the last time was," I interrupted. "I'll never forget the day my parents died."

Niala stammered for a second and bit her lip. "I'm so sorry. I didn't mean to…"

"It's all right. I know you didn't." I let out a deep breath, shuddering briefly with the memory, and redirected my gaze to Liv. "To be completely honest, I'm not so worried about what our Waerg friend might do to Liv with his claws and fangs. It's what he might do to her emotions that scares me. Liv has been single forever, and most of her life she's been pining for my big brother, which is bad enough—but at least it's harmless. This guy walks into her life an hour ago, and it's like she's already planning her wedding. It won't end well."

"Still," Niala said, her eyes locked on Lachlan, "you might be able to use their budding romance to your advantage. Keep your friends close and your enemies closer, and all that."

"I'm not so sure I want to be close to *that* guy."

"Anyway," Crow said, rubbing his hands together, "Who's in charge of food and drink around here? I'm starving."

Callum clapped a hand on his shoulder. "Right this way, good sir," he said, leading Crow toward the series of coolers in the distance.

Niala and I followed, with Rourke leaping down and transforming into his tabby cat form to stalk along beside her. I noticed as we walked that his small paws left no tracks in the sand.

"It's still so strange to think no one but us can see him," I said, eyeing the Familiar affectionately. "He's basically a ghost."

"No one can see Crow's scar, either," Niala reminded me and pointed to an angry-looking slash mark on Crow's cheek. "Magical entities—as well as marks left by magical weapons—tend to hide themselves from prying eyes in your world. It's a good thing, too, because otherwise he and I would get a lot more weird looks. The last thing I need is to draw people's attention. I'm already odd enough."

Odd wasn't the word I would have used to describe Niala. She was remarkably beautiful, in the same way as a Renaissance painting—an image out of another time and place. Her bright green eyes and milky-white skin were striking in our world of sun worshippers. She looked like an artist's muse, her skin as translucent as watercolors splashed along a canvas.

"Well, I'll admit that I'm grateful for the ability to hide certain aspects of my own secret life," I said. "I mean, I've got one of the Academy's daggers tucked into my belt, and I'm glad you're reminding me no one's going to call me on it if I bend over."

"Even if they could see it," Niala said with a chuckle, "They'd probably just think you were some kind of badass."

I let out a loud laugh. It was so odd to hear Niala use anything approximating a curse word. She was the most dignified girl I'd ever met.

"No one at Plymouth High will ever think of me that way," I replied with a quick roll of my eyes. "I'm a pariah at my school. I'm the moody girl who never speaks to anyone but Liv."

"I dunno," Niala said, nodding toward Callum and Crow, who were rifling through a cooler on a hunt for sustenance. "I don't think anyone who walks around with Callum Drake will ever find themselves treated like an outcast."

"You may be right," I replied, noticing a group of girls turning to gawk at him. "God, I can't believe I'm dating the future prom king. Meanwhile, I look like the prom serf, at best."

"You're way too hard on yourself, Vega," Niala laughed. "You really don't know how pretty you are, do you?"

"You think I'm pretty?" I asked. It was a terrible, leading question. Either I expected her to say *yes*—which put her in an awkward position—or *no*, which put her into an even worse one.

"I don't just think it. You are objectively beautiful. Why do you think other girls are so hostile to you? You're gorgeous, brilliant, and talented. But I suppose it serves you well that you don't seem to realize it."

My cheeks heated. I had no idea how to take all these kind words, especially from the usually reserved Niala.

"Thanks?" I said. "I mean, it's not like I'm agreeing with you. I'm just trying to graciously accept the compliment. For the record, I still don't think I'm anything special."

"Maybe not. But *they* do," Niala said, nodding toward the three Charmers, who were still glaring at me like I'd killed their entire families with a spork.

FLAME

THE FOUR OF us spent most of the evening seated on a pair of fallen tree trunks ten feet or so from the bonfire. We were careful to keep our voices low whenever we spoke of the Otherwhere, though to my relief, Niala and Crow were more interested in plying me with questions about Fairhaven.

Had I always lived there? Was there even a movie theater? What was the town's population?

I answered the questions as well as I could, almost relieved when Liv tore herself away from her menacing new love interest to head in our direction. I braced myself as I watched her approach, trying desperately to think of a plausible explanation for the two strangers in our midst.

As it turned out, I didn't need to worry.

"Where's your man-friend going?" I asked her as I watched Lachlan head toward the path in the woods.

Liv shrugged, turning to watch him go. "He said he had to make it an early night. He has some family outing tomorrow, I think." She turned back to us, eyeing Niala and Crow, her eyes in a squint of deep concentration. "Have I seen you two somewhere before? You both look really familiar."

"Maybe at Midsummer Fest?" Niala said with a charming smile. "We're…"

"Friends of mine," Callum interjected before she had a chance to finish. "Old friends. Brother and sister. From…New York."

Niala and I threw him synchronized looks of amusement. *Really, Callum? A backstory?*

"Siblings. Cool," Liv said. "Are you just visiting, or…?"

"Yes! Just in and out for a quick visit to our old friend Callum," Crow replied, and I could tell by his tone that he was trying to sound jovial and friendly, which just made me want to snort-laugh. The Crow I'd known at the Academy was gruff. He was aloof. He was the furthest thing from approachable. "Yup, just visiting. We…visit pretty often, so you may see us around again sometime, depending on which way the wind shifts and the crow flies. And so on."

"Ah. Cool." Liv shuffled her feet, clearly suspicious about Crow's story but too puzzled or else too polite to say so. "Well, I'm going to go hunt for Jen Russell. You remember her, don't you Vega?"

"The head of the Drama Club? What do you want with her?"

Liv beamed. "I'm hoping to audition for a role in the school play. I thought maybe she could give me a few pointers before I go out for it next week."

"That's great!" I replied, my eyes lighting up. "I really, really hope you get the role."

Liv frowned. "Really?" she asked. "But if I get it, I'll be busy with rehearsals and stuff. We'll hardly get to see each other."

"Yeah, but…it would be really great, Liv. For you, I mean. You'd love it. You're a born actress. A total and absolute drama queen."

Of course, I conveniently neglected to mention that my reasons were also selfish. The more distracted she was, the less time she'd have to notice that I was constantly on the lookout for jagged-toothed creatures who wanted to disembowel me.

"Thanks for your vote of confidence, I guess," she said with a snicker and a bemused look. "So, I think I'll go talk to Jen now."

"Great idea. Good luck!"

As I watched her walk away, I felt wretched.

"I hurt her feelings," I moaned. "She thinks I don't want her around. I've *always* wanted Liv around." My shoulders slumped. "I'm a terrible friend."

"Well, to be fair," Niala replied. "You *do* have other things on your mind."

I let out a sigh. "Like saving the world."

"Some would argue that's actually pretty important," Callum offered, coming to my defense. "If it makes you feel better, she looks fine to me."

Liv was already in the midst of an animated conversation with the Drama Club president. Callum had a point.

Liv wasn't exactly the kind of person who wasted time worrying about things.

I turned to Niala and Crow. "Hey. Can you two stay in town tonight?"

"Not sure," Crow replied. "But probably not. It would mean finding a hotel room. I don't even know how your hotels work."

"Don't be silly. You could stay at my house," I said. "You can even share a room. You *are* fake brother and sister, after all."

Crow seemed to blush—an unusual sight, but an amusing one.

"What do you say, Crow?" Niala asked, shoving his shoulder with her own. "Should we stay here? Mom and Dad might get worried."

"Damn, you're right. We could get grounded," Crow said with a crooked grin. "Mom gets especially antsy when we stay out after curfew."

"She'll be up all night, baking anxiety muffins," I said, joining in on the fun.

"I told you kids, no venturing to other worlds until you've tidied your rooms!" Callum bellowed in his best dad-voice.

We'd just begun to invent detailed tales about their nonexistent childhood when someone shouted, "What the hell?"

I pulled my head up to see that the bonfire, which had been burning quietly but steadily, suddenly expanded, its flames growing like out of control tendrils that were beginning to flail in every direction. A series of flickering, unpredictable ribbons of searing heat leapt into the air, exploding like small fireworks.

Partygoers shrieked and scurried backwards, grabbing hold of one another for comfort.

"Why's it doing that?" someone asked.

As I watched, the fire began to dance blue, then green, then purple.

"What's happening?" a girl shouted. "Who's doing this?"

The crowd was panicked, frozen. Helpless to stop the mounting threat.

And for reasons I would never be able to explain, I rose to my feet, fixating on the flames as the other terrified teenagers exchanged baffled looks of fear and concern.

People were still backing away as the bonfire continued to expand, swelling and thickening like it intended to take over the entire beach. Its color altered every few seconds, like the flame itself had swallowed a mound of flashing, out-of-control Christmas lights.

Even as everyone else retreated, I stepped forward, mesmerized, moving closer and closer until I stood mere inches from the conflagration, which licked the air around me, never quite touching my clothes or skin.

The strangest part was that it wasn't actually hot.

In fact, I couldn't feel a thing.

It was as if all my senses were focused on the flame itself, my eyes searching for something I knew to be hidden within its ever-shifting folds.

"Hey!" a concerned voice said from somewhere behind me. "What are you doing?"

I held up a hand to silence the speaker, all my attention focused on the fire.

"Don't say anything," I muttered. "I need to concentrate. I need to look...closer...I...I see..."

A second later, Callum's deep voice barreled through my mind.

—*What is it that you see, Vega? Tell me. Please.*

I see... I replied silently. *I see a man.*

—*What is he doing?*

He's...he's looking straight through me.

Before I had a chance to explain it—to Callum or to myself—an explosion ripped through the air.

NEW FOES

THE VIOLENT FORCE sent me hurtling backwards as the surrounding crowd shrieked with horror. Callum leapt forward, catching me in his arms, and I managed to land more or less on my feet.

But my mind was reeling.

"What the hell happened?" a shrill voice shouted.

Somewhere behind me, I could hear a girl weeping.

The fire was already dying down to a red-orange, controlled blaze.

But what everyone had just witnessed was enough to traumatize them.

"Someone must've tossed something explosive in," Crow said, his voice powerful yet calming as he stepped forward. "Guys, you should've known it's a really bad idea to fling bottles of vodka into bonfires!" he shouted with a broad grin the likes of which I'd never seen from him before.

And just like that, the crowd erupted into peals of laughter. Boys high-fived each other, and girls chortled. The blast, they now agreed, was the most awesome thing they'd ever seen—a massive blue explosion that had sent Vega Sloane shooting fifteen feet backwards through space. A freak accident, but hey, no one was hurt, right?

Only I knew the truth.

At least, part of it.

"What exactly did you see?" Callum asked quietly, taking my shoulders and turning me to face him.

I stared up at him, trying to sort my jumbled thoughts. But I could tell from the look on his face that he already had a theory.

"It was him, wasn't it?" he whispered. "It was Lumus."

I shook my head. "No. It was a face I've never seen before. He had strange, deep eyes. Frown lines...like he was old, but I couldn't tell *how* old. I could feel him pulling me into the flame. Summoning me. Digging through my mind—looking for..." With the last few words, my voice began to tremble.

It wasn't the first time a magic-user had worked his way inside my mind, but this felt different.

The man I'd seen in the flame hadn't invaded my thoughts, so much as *skimmed* them. It was almost as if he was perusing my memories, looking through them as one might leaf through a dictionary or a deck of cards.

But what he was hunting for, I couldn't say.

"Oh my God, Vega, are you okay?" asked Liv, who was jogging over from the other side of the fire. "I thought for sure..."

"I'm fine," I said with a weak smile. "I guess I forgot the rules of fire safety."

"Yeah. Namely, don't walk straight into a raging bonfire," she laughed, reaching for me as if she was trying to make sure I wasn't broken. "Pretty sure they teach you that in kindergarten."

"True. I don't know what I was thinking. Anyhow, I really am fine. But I...I think I'd like to head home," I said to no one in particular. I still felt shaken and couldn't imagine hanging around close to the fire that had nearly consumed me.

Not to mention that the last thing I wanted was more attention.

Liv eyed me with a healthy dose of skepticism. "You're sure you're all right? Do you want me to take you home?"

"Don't worry," said Callum, slipping his arm protectively around my shoulders. "I'll look after her."

"I'm sure you will," Liv said with a cheeky wink. "Hey, Vega— why don't we go to Perks in the morning, after you've recovered? We can catch up. I've missed you."

"Sure…that would be great." A bout of nausea swept through me, and I clutched Callum's arm for support. I took his hand and squeezed hard as I plastered a smile to my lips.

"Great! I'll come by your place around ten."

"Great." I parroted weakly. "I'll…I'll see you then."

The last thing I remembered were fingers wrapping around my arm, and then I was fairly certain that Callum was guiding me toward the woods.

After that, my mind drifted into a state of oblivion, and the world went dark.

THE NEXT THING I KNEW, I was lying on the couch in my living room, my head spinning. I could hear Crow and Callum talking in the kitchen. I managed to turn my head to see Rourke's panther form was stalking around the furniture, sniffing here and there. Niala was slouched back in my father's old armchair, her eyes fixed on me.

"Did I pass out or something?" I asked, pushing myself up onto my elbows only to feel a swell of dizziness that prompted me to lie back down.

"No," Niala said. "But you weren't…entirely yourself on the walk home." She pushed herself out of the chair, stepped over, and crouched down next to me, examining my face. "You kept muttering things and swatting at the air like there was a swarm of gnats bothering you."

"I don't remember any of that."

"It's probably for the best. Tell me, how are you feeling?"

"I'm fine, Doctor," I said with a snicker. It was mostly true. I was already starting to feel more like myself. "I was a bit shaken up, that's all. That man…" I groaned. "It was probably just my imagination."

"Uh-huh. Don't forget I've had my own dose of the enemy. I know what some of them can do to people. They don't play around."

"Well, even if he was real, I get the distinct impression that whoever he was isn't in Fairhaven, so it's all good. Plus, he felt…"

"Felt what?"

"Like Merriwether," I said. "Isn't that weird?"

"You mean he felt like a wizard?"

"Sort of. There was something magical about him. Calming, even. I wasn't afraid, like I would have been if I'd seen Lumus. At least, not at first."

Unconvinced, Niala reached into her pocket and pulled out a small vial. She uncorked it and held it up in front of my face. "Here—drink this."

"What is it? Eye of newt or something?"

"Just a little concoction I came up with back at the Academy. It'll help with the dizziness. And it'll help you sleep tonight."

I did as she commanded. She was a Healer, after all, and a gifted one.

But more importantly, she was a loyal friend, and I trusted her with my life.

The moment I'd taken a sip, my head began to clear, and any residual feeling of nausea disappeared. I sat up and smiled with relief.

"See? All better," I said.

"You'll never be all better, as long as some conniving magic-user is in living rent-free inside your head," Callum said from the doorway. He was leaning against the frame, his arms crossed.

"He and others will probably live there until we find the Relics," I replied with a sigh. "That's my lot in life. But at least there's *one* encouraging thing I can tell you."

"What's that?"

"The man—the one I saw in the flame—I think he's afraid of you."

Callum smirked. "Why do you say that?"

"When I was walking toward the fire, it was like…like he was pulling me in. Reeling me, like there was a fishing line attached to my waist, and I had no choice. But just as I got close, I felt his gaze shift to you. That's when the explosion sent me flying."

"He didn't know you were there," Crow said thoughtfully. "Maybe your presence came as a surprise to him."

"Which means whoever he is, he doesn't have Watchers here in town," Callum pointed out. "It also means our friend Lachlan isn't working for him."

"Lachlan must be working for the Usurper Queen, then," Crow guessed. "She has countless Waergs watching the Seekers."

"Well, instead of worrying about any of it," I replied with a deep sigh, "I think we should all get some sleep. Crow, you can take Will's room, and Niala, you can sleep in my parents'…"

But Niala shook her head and threw Crow a look. "Actually, we're going to head back to the Academy and talk to Merriwether. Unless you want us to stay longer…"

"Oh," I muttered, disappointed. "No, no. We'll be fine here. Callum won't let anything happen to me. And like you said, I should sleep well tonight."

I looked over at Callum, only to realize the late hour was beginning to catch up to him, too. His face was going pale, his forehead glistening with perspiration.

His dragon was beginning his silent, nightly onslaught.

"As long as you're sure," Niala said, giving me a quick hug as Rourke rubbed his face against my leg.

"I'm sure. Really, thanks for everything. And Crow—thank

you for your quick thinking back at the fire. I didn't know how I was going to explain that explosion."

"It was nothing," he said. "Besides, most of those kids will have forgotten it by the time you see them again. It was Old Magic that caused the flame to grow. Worlders' minds deny the existence of such spells, just as they deny so many other aspects of our world. Memories of magical incidents—even ones they've witnessed—become foggy very quickly."

"Well," Niala said, "We're going to head off. The portal we came through may close up soon."

"You don't need a portal," I laughed. "Or have you already forgotten my special talent?"

I shut my eyes and called up a Breach—a door to the Otherwhere. Then, unclasping my dragon-shaped key from its permanent chain around my neck, I unlocked it.

"It'll lead you straight into the eastern courtyard at the Academy," I said.

"Thank you."

"No, thank you two," I said. I cupped my hand over my mouth, stifling a yawn. "Again. And thanks for whatever you gave me, Niala. I think I'll sleep like the dead tonight."

"Good. You deserve some rest."

When they'd left, I watched the conjured door vanish and turned to Callum, my chest tight.

"Are we going to talk about this?" I asked, looking up at his face, which was somehow both flushed and pale at once. His eyes were red, his jaw set tightly.

"About what?"

"About how every night you seem to develop a sickness that looks like it's about to kill you."

"You know perfectly well what it is," he replied. "We've already talked about it."

"Isn't there anything I can do? Anything Niala could have done to help you?"

"A Healer can't fix me," he said. "No one can. I need to face my fate, just as you need to face yours."

"I'm scared, Callum," I said, stepping forward and wrapping my arms around his waist. I pressed my head to his chest, which was so warm that I was grateful for the protective shield of fabric between his skin and mine. "I'm scared of what's going to happen."

"I know," he said softly, stroking my hair. "So am I."

He kissed the top of my head and took my hand. "Now come on. Let's get some rest. And no Waerg-chasing tonight, okay?"

"As long as you promise to convince that hyperactive dragon inside you to let you have a few hours' rest."

"Deal."

PERKS

The following morning, I was still lounging in bed when I heard a loud knock at the front door.

"Crap!" I shouted, leaping to my feet.

Next came Callum's muffled voice, followed by Liv's, and then the front door shutting.

It had totally slipped my mind that she was coming by this morning.

Bad friend.

Crappy friend.

Cursing my forgetful brain, I threw on some clothes. After I'd checked my face in the mirror to make sure it wasn't marred by streaks of dried drool, I raced downstairs to find Liv already sitting in the kitchen with Callum, regaling him with hilariously exaggerated stories from our youth.

"Liv was just telling me how you two used to play hide-and-seek in the woods at the end of the street," Callum said with an affectionate grin.

"Oh, yeah," I replied, pulling my mounds of curly hair out from the neck of my shirt. "We knew every hiding spot. The old fallen tree by the trail, the boulder by the creek..." I threw Liv a look, and we said in unison, "The Murder Shack!"

"The *what now?*" Callum asked.

"The Murder Shack," I laughed. "It's what we called this old rickety shed in the middle of the woods. It had all sorts of horrifying things inside. Hooks, chains, creaky planks, weird old newspaper clippings...I was sure for the longest time that it was where I would die. I was terrified of the place for years. It used to give me literal nightmares. But Liv was obsessed with it, and she'd drag me there every chance she got. It was like she was torturing me for sport."

"Vega and I even invented a murderer called Daryl the Psycho Killer," Liv added. "He wore a plaid shirt and filthy jeans, and he only had about three teeth. Oh, and sometimes, he had a hook for a hand."

"Daryl the Psycho Killer, huh?" Callum chuckled. "Tell me— did he ever show up and make your nightmare into a reality?"

"Of course not. We didn't know who owned the shack—we never saw anyone come or go. We just used to make up stories about all the people who'd probably been murdered there, and the circumstances of their untimely demise. We...had pretty gruesome imaginations."

"You don't say."

"It was all just fiction," I explained, slightly embarrassed by the unhinged morbidity of the tale. "I mean, the shack really is creepy as hell. But I think the newspaper clippings were just there to freak out kids like us. I'm pretty sure it's just an old hunter's shed."

"Sure. A hunter of *humans*," Liv said, her hands in the air, fingers curled like menacing talons. "The most dangerous game."

"Anyway, I thought we were going to head to Perks?" I blurted out, grabbing my small purse off the counter before Liv's storytelling had a chance to get totally out of hand.

"You two have fun," Callum said. "Don't get killed by any men wielding meat-hooks, okay?"

"You're not coming?" I asked, disappointed to realize I'd have to navigate a morning of Liv's questions alone.

"Nah, I think you two ought to have a girls' day of it. Or at least a morning. I think I'll hang out around here and contemplate my mortality."

"Girls' morning it is, then," I said, stepping over to land a kiss on his cheek. "Will you be here when I get back?"

"I hope so."

I studied him for a moment, assessing his eyes, his skin, his posture. He seemed to have recovered from the previous night's strangeness, at least. His dragon was dormant, his mood cheerful.

"Good," I said. "See you soon, then."

When I'd shut the front door behind us, Liv and I began the walk downtown, her with her usual bouncy giddiness and me trying not to think too much about what had unfolded the previous night.

Thanks to Niala I'd slept soundly, but the face—the one I'd seen in the fire—had come to me in my dreams. I'd heard the man's voice, low and soothing, as he'd prodded me with questions about my hopes, my dreams, and my fears.

Each time he'd asked a question, I'd resisted answering. It was none of his business, I'd said. He had no right to my memories, my feelings, or my losses. No right to dig into my trauma or my joy.

Yet he didn't stop. And when I remained silent, he took me by the shoulders and stared at me. I watched as his shadowed eyes reflected the most important moments in my life.

Birthday parties.

Trips with my parents.

The day they'd died.

Their funeral.

The day I'd met Callum.

For some reason, I was convinced the man wanted to take him from me.

"No! I won't let you have him!" I'd shouted, waking myself at four A.M.

Callum was lying next to me. It was only when he'd draped an arm around me that I'd managed to get back to sleep.

"Vega? You're a million miles away."

The voice was Liv's.

I snapped out of my thoughts, realizing where I was. "Sorry. I guess I didn't sleep so great."

As we wandered, Liv and I chatted a little about the party on the beach, about how some of the boys had grown into men over the summer.

Liv commented on how everyone at the bonfire had managed to enjoy themselves, despite the fact that Kevin Ramsey, the quarterback of Plymouth High's football team, had broken up with Sheridan, his girlfriend of four years, only minutes before the festivities had begun.

The one thing Liv *didn't* mention was the explosion that had nearly knocked me unconscious.

She really has forgotten...

Which means everyone else has, too.

Thank God.

"Isn't Lachlan amazing?" Liv asked after a time, twirling around on the sidewalk like a princess in a Disney film showing off her gown.

"He's...something else," I replied, scratching the back of my neck and twisting my mouth into a disingenuous grin. I wasn't the world's *worst* actor, but pretending to think highly of a Waerg was enough to push me to the limit of my meager talents.

"You really don't like him, huh?" she asked with a frown as we turned onto High Street.

"I don't know him, Liv." It was as innocent a response as I

could muster. "But if you like him, that's all that matters. It's just…"

"Just what?"

"Like I said, you should be careful around him."

"You think he's one of those bad seeds, don't you? Someone my parents would be upset about."

"You might say that."

She shouldered me gently. "You do realize that only makes me want him more, right?"

I fought off the grimace that was working its way over my features. "I just…don't want you to get hurt, you know? I don't think I could take it. I'm protective of you."

I'd already seen her hurt in ways she couldn't imagine. I'd seen her trapped in a timeless void. Suspended in a vat of strange liquid in the queen's castle, unable to see, hear, or think.

After all that, I didn't exactly have any desire to let a Waerg get his claws into her.

"I won't get hurt," she pouted. "You know, Vega, it sounds to me like you just don't want me to be with a guy as good-looking as Callum. I'm starting to regret ever saying anything to you about him."

"That's not it at all!" I protested. "I want you to find someone perfect for you. It's just that Lachlan—"

I winced and bit my tongue. There was absolutely nothing I could say that would convince her to stay away from him, other than *He might shift into a killer wolf and murder your family but hey, if that's your kink, go for it.*

"You know what?" I said. "You're right. It's your choice, and none of my business. I'm really sorry."

She half-shrugged. "So what about you and Callum? You two have gotten serious, huh?"

"Pretty serious, yeah." *If only you knew.*

"But I thought he was living with his parents. How is it that he seems to be sleeping at your place? Or are they the super-cool types who believe in liberating today's youth from the shackles of uptight parental units?"

"Parents…?" I asked.

"Yeah. You remember—his dad and mine work together. In my dad's law office."

I'd all but forgotten about the "family" Callum had allegedly been living with when I'd first met him—friends of Merriwether's who'd provided cover for the young man who'd just arrived in Fairhaven.

Great. Now I had to tell yet another lie.

"Oh, yeah. They're…very laid back," I said. "I guess they trust him. Besides…"

"Besides what?"

I found myself blushing. "Nothing…*forbidden*…has really happened between us. He sleeps over, but it's all very innocent."

Liv blew out a *pfft* sound. "Uh-huh. That kiss last night told another story, Little Miss Alleged Chastity," she said as we stopped in front of Perks. "Everybody was talking about it after you left."

"That kiss was only for show," I protested, stepping into the café as a hit of refreshing air conditioning hit my skin. "Miranda's been eyeing Callum for ages. I guess he wanted to show her where his affections really lie."

"Well, it did the trick. I have to say, I love that you're making Miranda so jealous. It's like you've defeated the final boss of our high school."

"I couldn't care less about Miranda," I muttered.

Liv gawked at me as she pulled the door open. "Really? Because she and her trio of ice-queens have been total hags to us for years. I would have thought you'd love making her squirm."

"There was a time when I would have," I replied. "I guess I have other things on my mind now."

Liv pressed her hands to her hips. "Really, Vega? Like what?"

Like saving the world, for one.

"Okay, fine. I mean, yeah, I guess it's fun to watch her suffer a little." I said with a forced laugh. "But honestly, I don't want to think about her. My relationship with Callum is...special. It's not just some tool to torment the Charmers."

That, at least, was the absolute truth.

But how could I explain to Liv how completely my priorities had changed—that *I* had changed—in the last few weeks? That the petty squabbles of high school students were insignificant in the face of the danger that surrounded Callum and me every day?

How could I explain that our friendship would never be what it once was?

CHIT-CHAT AND CHECKING ACCOUNTS

WHEN LIV and I had both ordered our drinks, we sat down at a table by Perks' long row of large windows.

"So I want to know one thing," Liv said as she took a sip of her caramel Frappuccino.

My hands tightened into fists under the table as I met her gaze. "What?" I asked.

"Who exactly performed the surgery?"

"What surgery?"

"The one to implant the stick that now seems to be living permanently up your butt."

I took a sip of my mocha, fighting back the temptation to roll my eyes. "There's no stick, Liv."

"You've been acting so weird, ever since I saw you yesterday morning. I mean, it's not like you're usually Little Mary Sunshine, but now you have this cloud over your head, like the world is about to explode and you're just waiting for it to happen."

Without thinking, I snapped, "Well, after what happened last night, maybe I feel like it *is* about to explode."

"What? What happened last night? You mean the kiss?"

"No," I said, kicking myself. *Be grateful she doesn't remember, Vega. Don't be stupid.* "Just…nothing."

I took another sip and pulled my eyes to the window. Fairhaven looked so normal right now, its pedestrians strolling along without a care in the world.

Nothing about our town had changed.

Except for me.

I probably did seem like I'd lost my mind, or at least my sense of humor. The truth was, I couldn't enjoy the things I once had. Simple moments like sitting in a coffee shop or talking about boys.

All I saw when I watched people living their very normal lives was the potential for all of it to come crashing to an end. Loss, pain, death, and destruction.

All I could think was *It's up to me to protect them.*

"If you say so," Liv muttered. "I'm just worried about you."

"You don't need to worry. I'm just going through some stuff, but I'll be fine." I forced myself to smile. "Tell me, what's going on with the Drama Club?"

Liv brightened and began squirming in her seat. Turning the topic back to her had always been a sure-fire way to get her to cheer up. "I thought you'd never ask! Okay, so they're putting on a stage production of *Our Town*. I'm going out for Emily. And Jen thinks I'll get the part. It would be so amazing—Emily's story arc is so dramatic and tragic and stuff."

"That's great, Liv! I really hope you get it."

"Me too!" She paused for a second before adding, "Don't be mad, but I…may have approached Lachlan about trying out for the role of George."

I almost did a caffeine-laced spit-take all over her. "What? Why?" I asked, cupping my hand over my mouth.

Liv shrugged. "I just figured if he was in the play, we could run lines together."

"Uh-huh. I'm sure that's all you were hoping for."

"Fine. It was so we could practice the kissing scene. A lot."

"That's very conniving of you," I said with a snicker. "So, what did he say?"

"That he's not into acting." Liv looked downtrodden for a second, but then added, "But he did agree to go out with me on Wednesday."

"Like on a date?"

"Yup. We're going to a movie. I don't even care which one. I'm just hoping it's terrible, so we have no choice but to sit in the back and make out."

I had to fight to keep from grinding my jaw. The idea of Liv sitting in the back row of a movie theater with a Waerg...

It was just *too* weird and way too scary to consider.

Why would he agree to a date with her? What was his motive? Was he hoping to keep tabs on me?

Of course he was. It was the only possible explanation.

Not that Liv was an unappealing date. She was wonderful. Bubbly, pretty, talkative, fun to be around. There was a reason we'd been best friends most of our lives...but still...

What the hell was he up to?

"Vega? Did you even hear me? I said we're going on a date!"

"That's great, Liv," I mumbled, preoccupied with theories, none of which quite made sense. "Let me know how it goes, okay?"

"Of course."

After finishing our drinks, we decided to spend the rest of the morning strolling High Street and perusing its shops as Liv pointed out a pair of shoes that she desperately wanted, or a sweater she was intending to buy the next time she'd saved enough.

On some level, it felt like the old days when our sole entertainment consisted of window-shopping and fantasizing about the future when we'd each run off and get married, buy quaint little houses next to one another, and have perfect, cherubic, fat-bellied little babies.

But everything had changed since then, and nothing would ever be the same.

My fantasies no longer involved cherubs, picket fences, or quiet lives in small town America. There was now a barrier between Liv and me—a wall of secrecy that could never be breached for any reason.

And I was the one who'd built it.

Even though I knew she'd never fully understand, Liv had made it abundantly clear that she felt it, too. It was like we'd outgrown one another in completely different directions, all in a matter of weeks.

After what felt like several minutes of uncomfortable silence, I turned to her and said, "Hey, um…I need to run a couple of quick errands before I head home. Do you want to join me?"

I hoped she couldn't read my tone or my facial expression. The truth was, I desperately wanted to be alone. To have time to think and process everything that had changed so dramatically in my life.

To figure out if I would ever be my old self again.

"You go ahead," she replied with what looked like a manufac-tured smile. "I need to get home and sort through my old clothes. I promised my mom I'd do some end of summer cleaning of my closet. It was the only way to convince her I need a new wardrobe."

"Okay. I'll see you around, then?"

"Sure. Maybe we can go pick out my wardrobe together."

"I'd like that," I replied.

But I wasn't entirely sure I meant it.

When Liv turned to head home, I made my way to the nearest bank—a monthly errand during which I stuck Will's pre-dated checks into my account in order to pay the mortgage and groceries for the next several weeks.

My big brother had looked after me for years now, always working overtime to support us both. He always insisted that I not look for work until I was finished high school, and so far, I'd reluctantly gone along with the plan. But every time I deposited the money, I felt wretchedly guilty, and part of me was determined to lighten his load by hunting for a part-time job.

I may have been a Seeker, but there was no reason I couldn't serve food or bag groceries, too.

I'd just begun to recite a mental list of every restaurant and shop in town that might be looking to hire when the bank machine spat out a receipt. I glanced at it, prepared to crumple and toss it into the nearest waste basket.

But when I saw my account balance, my eyes threatened to pop out of my head.

"What the—" I sputtered, staring at the slip. "This can't be right."

My heart racing, I headed over to the nearest teller and showed it to her. "Excuse me," I said, "there's...a *lot* of money in my bank account."

"Lucky you," she replied with a friendly, if slightly sarcastic, smile.

"No, I mean there's money that I don't think is supposed to be there. Like a *massive* amount of money. I think someone's made a mistake."

She asked for my bank card, typed a series of numbers into her computer, then looked at me.

"It's the right amount," she said. "Your account is exactly where it should be."

"What do you mean? I don't have that sort of money!"

"No, but your benefactor does, apparently."

"Excuse me?"

She sighed and swung her monitor around so I could see the screen.

"August 19th," she began, as if reciting a rehearsed speech. "A

Mr. Merriwether deposited a large sum into your account. As with any such deposit, the bank did a check on the funds before finalizing the transaction. Everything was legitimate. It says here that he's a relative—a caregiver. Is that right?"

"I...Merriwether? Yes, he's my grandfather...but..."

How exactly was I supposed to explain that the man who had deposited that vast sum was a wizard who lived in another world?

"Wait—you didn't know he was giving you two million dollars?" she asked with a grin. "Well, what I wouldn't give for a surprise like that. Like I said, lucky you."

"I had no idea," I replied. "I didn't know he could even..." I bit my tongue, grinned at her, and said, "Well, um, thank you for your help. I guess I'll have to talk to my grandfather about this. I'm not sure what kind of thank-you card to buy."

"A gold-plated one with diamonds around the edges?" the teller laughed. "Seriously, you should take him out for a steak dinner! Grandpas love steak."

"Yes," I murmured as I turned away. "I should definitely do that."

Right after I finish bouncing off the walls inside my head.

WHEN I GOT HOME and told Callum about my grandfather's deposit, he simply raised his eyebrows and said, "Hmm. Two million, you say?"

"I don't even understand how he did it," I sputtered as I paced the living room, adrenaline fueling my legs. "I don't get it. How...?"

"Merriwether is wealthy. Extremely so," Callum said. "All wizards are. People joke that they conjure the wealth themselves —that it's one of the many perks of being gifted with secret skills. Who knows? Anyhow, I'm not even a little bit surprised that he managed to deposit funds into an account here. He's got talents none of us have ever seen."

"No kidding," I shot back. "I mean, what kind of bank is willing to exchange Otherwhere currency—whatever that even is —for American dollars?"

Callum chuckled, stopped me pacing long enough to kiss me, and told me it would remain one of life's little mysteries.

And for some reason, that was enough to satisfy me.

SUMMER'S END

CALLUM and I spent the last days of summer in a quiet, lazy state of semi-bliss, partly as a result of an unexpected heat wave.

The temperature had gone from late-summer cool to the sort of humidity where you could almost see the air around you, thick with droplets of water just waiting to collect themselves into small, waist-high storm clouds and fall to the ground.

Something about the engulfing heat sapped our energy and fed a desire to lie together on the couch as a rotating fan blew gusts of cool air our way. We spent hours on end musing about our uncertain futures while we twined our fingers together into intimate braids. Perfect, happy hours, with ominous thunderheads forming so far in the distance that we were barely aware of them.

Even Callum's dragon seemed to have settled down somewhat. Nights were more restful, Callum's fevers shorter in duration and less intense. Human and beast seemed to have declared a silent truce, and I found myself hopeful that even if the Naming Day came soon, it would pass without incident.

"Tell me something," I said one afternoon as we were hanging out on the couch. His head was on my lap, my fingertips twisting his hair into playful bunches. "Are these the good old days?"

"The good old days," he repeated thoughtfully. "The days when things are simple and carefree. The days before responsibility and hardship start to take a toll on a person's spirit. At least that's what we'll tell ourselves years from now, when we're feeling nostalgic and missing the simplicity of the past. You mean *those* good old days?"

"Yeah. Is this, right now, as good as it gets? I'd live like this forever, if I could. I just want to know if it can possibly last."

"Liar," Callum snickered.

"Hey!" I laughed.

"You know what I mean. You wouldn't be happy if this was your forever, Vega. Sitting on the couch with me, doing little to nothing. You'd grow bored and restless, and you know it."

I thought about it for a second. "You're right. I guess I *would*, eventually. But for right now, it feels…"

"Perfect?"

"Yeah."

Callum pushed himself up to a sitting position and pivoted around to face me. "Well, my guess is that things can—and maybe even *will*—get even better." He turned his head and looked toward the windows along the far wall, as if a thought had begun to churn in his mind. "But they'll get worse first."

His tone shifted with the last sentence, and I braced myself.

He'd pulled himself out of the present and had begun to look toward the future neither of us wanted to talk about.

"What's going through that complex brain of yours, Mr. Drake?"

"You don't want to know."

"Try me."

Callum let out a hard breath. "I was thinking the days ahead will be hard for both of us." Without looking at me he reached out and took my hand. "I've always tried to promise you I won't keep anything from you ever again, that I won't hide what's happening to me."

"But?"

"But the truth is, I don't know what's going to happen—I can't know. I don't know if I can promise always to be there. Because if my being there puts you in danger...I may have to distance myself from you. At least for a little while."

Distance.

The word hit like a punch to my gut.

And just like that, my mood went from glowing warmth to icy cold.

"I get it," I said, yanking my hand away as if his words had scorched my skin. "You're saying you'll leave, just like you did when we were at the Academy. I suppose I should be grateful that at least this time, I'm getting a little warning before you desert me."

"No, you don't get it at all," he said, his tone soothing as he turned his head to look at me, his eyes the purest blue. "You think this is a rejection, but it's the opposite. If you only knew..."

"Knew what, Callum?" I swallowed what felt like a jagged rock in my throat. "You're telling me you may leave me again someday soon, whether I like it or not? I'm not sure how many times I can take this. Your sudden departures. The pain that comes with them. It's torture."

He stared at me, shaking his head slowly. "That's not even close to what I'm telling you. The *last* thing I want to do is be apart from you. It hurts just to think of a distance between us. All I want when I wake up in the morning is to feel your arm around my waist, your head on my shoulder. It's the greatest feeling I've ever experienced."

"So what are you telling me, then?"

"I'm saying I love you, Vega. So much that all I think about is how I can protect you from myself."

My body, which had coiled into a series of cruel, self-inflicted knots, relaxed as his words flitted through my mind like a calming drug.

We didn't use the L-word often. It was as though we'd agreed to pull it out only in emergency circumstances—like uttering it too often would mean a commitment neither of us could possibly make with any sort of honesty.

But hearing him say it now meant the world to me.

"I love you, too," I said. "You know that."

"I do."

"So believe me when I tell you I don't want you to leave. I don't want you to disappear. I want to help you—no matter how difficult it is for us both."

"I know you do." Callum stroked his fingers over my cheek—a gesture that invariably melted my heart and destroyed my ability to focus. "But there *will* come a time, before too many weeks have passed, when I need to be alone for a little. I can feel it coming even now. It's like the rush of an unstoppable tidal wave in the distance. Every day and every night, it draws nearer, and it won't stop, no matter how much I may want or ask it to."

I didn't reply. There was nothing to say, after all. His mind was made up.

He would leave me, and soon.

"But," he added, seeming to read the sadness in my eyes, "I need you to know that I will come back to you, when the time is right. I will not leave you for good. Not ever. You're my life, Vega. Whatever I have to do so we can stay together—whatever sacrifices I have to make—I will make them."

I leaned forward, cupped his cheeks in my hands, and kissed him deeply before pressing my forehead to his.

"Thank you," I said.

"I never want you to doubt how I feel about you," he murmured.

"I can't help it. My whole life is about doubting. It always has been."

"What can I do to convince you?"

I pulled back and looked him in the eye.

"Just...keep telling me you'll come back to me. Remind me as often as you can. It's the only way I can let you go when the day comes."

He nodded. "Of course I will. As often as I can."

PLYMOUTH HIGH

By the time the first day of school arrived, I had grown as restless as Callum's insatiable dragon.

To put it mildly.

As happy as I'd been for the last couple of weeks, I couldn't deny that the unrelenting draw of the Relics of Power had begun to weigh me down. I craved a hint. A clue. Anything that might lead me to the next relic.

I was supposed to be a girl on a mission.

The only problem was that I had no idea what that mission entailed, let alone where to begin.

All I knew was that sitting around my house wasn't helping. Which meant I needed to do something, and Plymouth High would, at the very least, provide me with some kind of distraction.

"I'd better find a clue soon," I told Callum as I sipped a cup of tea at the kitchen counter around seven A.M. on the first day of classes. "I'm feeling so useless right now. So much happened while I was in the Otherwhere, but since we got back to Fairhaven, I feel like I'm frozen. Static. Waiting for something slightly terrifying to happen."

My mind raced with the memory of the face in the bonfire by the beach—of the mysterious man who wanted to extract pieces of my memory for some purpose I couldn't yet discern.

"I get it," Callum replied. "Waiting for a potentially dangerous future to kick in is a pretty harrowing way to spend one's time. Trust me, I know."

"Right. Yes—of course you do." I smirked, grateful to have a sympathetic ear. Though I wished more than anything that he didn't have to live with an even more cruel dread than I did.

"Meanwhile," he said, his tone more cheerful, "you and I have classes to get to. I'm looking forward to learning something about this world of yours."

"It's going to be so weird." I laughed as I grabbed my silver dagger off the counter, lifted the right leg of my jeans and tucked the blade into a delicate leather sheath Callum had crafted for me out of a couple of my father's old belts. "To go back to a school that doesn't have sparring classes on its curriculum. Of course, you don't *need* to go to classes at all. You could just as easily stay here, or go back to work at the Novel Hovel…"

"Hey—I'm pretty sure my presence *is* required at Plymouth High. Someone has to keep you and the Charmers from breaking out the boxing gloves and slugging it out during lunch hour."

"Oh, I don't need boxing gloves for that. If Miranda tries anything, she'll find herself face to face with Murphy."

"Murphy?"

"That's my dagger," I said, pulling it out of its sheath and holding it up to glint in the sunlight. "I named him."

"Him? So…you two have grown close, huh?"

"Sort of. I mean, it's not like I ever actually stab anyone with him. But I like to know he's there for me if I need him. For instance, if the colossally annoying Miranda decides to make googly eyes at my boyfriend…"

Callum laughed. "Well, I promise if your arch-nemesis Miranda tries anything with me, I'll simply remind her I'm madly in love with the most beautiful girl in the universe, and that she's of no interest to me whatsoever. Though I'll admit I *would* love to watch you two pull each other's hair and let out some high-pitched squeals. You know, just for the spectacle of it."

"You're joking."

"Of course I am," he said, rising to his feet. "I expect at least a *little* slap-fighting, too."

As I joined him to head for the door, I punched him in the arm.

I DROVE us to school in the Rust-Mobile, if for no other reason than that it was the first time in my years at Plymouth High that I had the privilege of parking in the designated seniors' section of the lot. Not to mention that it gave me an extra chance to show off my extraordinarily handsome boyfriend.

Even better was the moment when Miranda pulled into the lot in the Lexus her father had given her for her sixteenth birthday only to discover that there were no spots left for her.

She glared out the driver's side at me just as I reached for Callum's hand. If looks were acid, her window would have melted into a smoking liquid mess.

"It's so strange now, to think how many years I let her intimidate me," I said to Callum as we walked away. "She drove me nuts. And now, she needs me, whether she likes it or not. My whole life is about protecting people like her from my *actual* nemesis."

"Funny how the tides turn. When you've faced war, petty matters become all the more trivial."

"That's very deep. You should write it in a history essay or something. Of course, the teacher would probably accuse you of plagiarism, because no teenage boy would ever say something like that."

"Don't worry. I intend to be completely and appropriately obtuse when working on my assignments. Maybe I'll write an essay about how the French Revolution took place in Australia in the prehistoric past."

"Excellent. I was worried that you'd get better grades than I would. I'm glad to see you're going for Fs."

When we stepped into the school's main foyer, the first people I spotted were Liv and Lachlan, who were walking toward the stairwell leading up to the seniors' lockers.

We followed them from a distance, careful to stay far enough back that we didn't appear to be stalking them.

When we reached the second floor, Callum and I wandered over to the lockers that had been assigned to us: 235 and 236. Liv and Lachlan were down the hall by then, chatting by the water fountain.

I opened the door to my locker, noting the remnants of old stickers inside and the marker-scrawled declaration of true love, "M.L. + J.R." that would remain eternally etched in the dark gray metal. Who the owners of the initials were, I'd probably never know.

I stashed my homemade lunch onto the top shelf and turned to Callum.

"What should we do about Lachlan?" I asked in a whisper. "We still don't know who he's working for or what his actual plan is, other than worming his way into my best friend's life."

"The best thing is to do nothing at all. We let him make the first move. Figure out what he's really up to. Let him slip up. We've been assuming he's working for the queen, but what if he's not? We need to find out what he's up to, and the only way to do that is to keep an eye on him."

"But what if he tries to hurt one of us?"

"Even if he wanted to, the likelihood that he'd succeed is pretty slim, don't you think?" Callum lowered his chin and threw me a look that said, *Have you met my dragon?*

"Maybe. But still, I—"

"What are you two commiserating about?" asked a perky voice from behind me.

I tightened and turned around to see Liv, a fat physics text-book squeezed to her chest, a backpack slung over her shoulder, and a smile on her face.

"Nothing," I said, looking around in an attempt to figure out where Lachlan had disappeared to. "I was just…warning Callum about some of the teachers here. They can be serious hard-asses."

"Oh, yeah," Liv agreed. "Mr. Moore especially. Geography. A walking nightmare. He'll make you feel like a war criminal for not knowing the capital of Botswana."

"Will had him in senior year," I replied with a nod, "and he hated him."

Just then, the school's infamously deafening bell rang loud enough to vibrate the floor tiles under our feet.

"You headed to English first?" Liv asked me.

I nodded. "Mrs. Burns?"

"Yes! Oh, perfect. We can sit with Lachlan."

"He's in our class?" I blurted out before I had a chance to hide my disgust. "I mean, that's good, right?"

"Yeah, it's good! He switched classes so we could have the same first period. Romantic, right?"

"You two are getting serious, then?"

Liv sighed. "We haven't gotten *anything*," she admitted. "We've hung out a few times, but he doesn't…*do* anything. No kissing. No hugs, even. Just that adorable smile of his. I think he's playing hard-to-get."

Callum's eyes wandered up and down the busy hallway. "Well, much as I'd love to hear about your love life, Liv, I've got to head to History class. I guess I'll see you two at lunch?"

"Of course," I replied as he leaned in to kiss my cheek. "I'll see you then." As I pulled back, I threw him a desperate look, hoping he got the *Please save me from the Hell I'm about to endure* message.

"So it's just you, me, and my would-be-boyfriend then," Liv said, taking my arm and guiding me up the hall.

I turned around to throw Callum one final look, but he was already gone.

OLD FOES

WHEN WE GOT to our class, I made a beeline for the back of the room to sit in the corner by the window. It was a habit by now, putting myself in the greatest strategic position to keep a watchful eye out for enemies. Every time I entered a room, I was acutely and instantly aware of any potential threats. I assessed my position and plotted what defensive gear I'd summon in case of an attack.

Slowly but surely, I was becoming a reluctant warrior.

Even between the walls of my own high school.

Oblivious to the tension overtaking every inch of my body, Liv sat down to my right, slinging her bag onto the seat in front of hers. When Lachlan walked into the classroom, he headed straight for the seat she'd reserved, grinning an admittedly charming smile at Liv before throwing me a narrow-eyed look of warning.

Liv greeted him with a flirty wink. She lifted her backpack so he could sit down and then opened it up, only to curse under her breath.

"What's wrong?" I asked.

"Forgot my pencil case in my locker." Helpless, she turned my way. "Do you have any extra pens?"

"Sorry, no," I replied, gesturing to the laptop I was pulling out of my bag. "I've gone fully digital."

"Me too," Lachlan said, flashing another deceptively friendly smile. "But you probably have time to run to your locker before class starts."

"I know. I was just hoping…" Liv clammed up and bit her lip, then darted out of the room.

The second she disappeared, Lachlan turned to face me and leaned forward.

Any and all traces of friendliness were gone.

"Look," he whispered. "You know who and what I am. I know who and what you are. So let's not play any games, all right?"

"Who's playing games?" I hissed. "I'm not the one who stares up at a stranger's window at night like some insane stalker."

"You should be grateful that I do, Vega."

"Really?" I laughed. "Because I've actually been wondering why I shouldn't get a restraining order against you."

"Good luck getting a restraining order against a stray wolf that wanders out of the woods and hangs out on your street. I'm sure the cops would have a field day with that one."

"Good point. I should probably call animal control instead. They have some pretty high-powered tranquilizer guns. Though maybe if I told them the wolf has rabies, they'd show up with something more potent."

A crooked half-smile slithered its way over Lachlan's lips. "Look, I know you won't believe me, but I'm not the threat you think I am. There are people—if you can call them that—who want to hurt you." He lowered his voice still further as more students filed in to seat themselves around us. "They're closer than you think."

When I didn't respond right away, he leaned in even closer. "You must know you're not the only one looking for the Relics of Power."

"I'm well aware of that. There are a lot more of the Academy's Seekers, not to mention the queen's...*minions*, or whatever. That's not exactly a newsflash, genius."

"Oh, my God. You really don't know, do you?" he asked, furrowing his brow in a way that made me feel like he was trying to gauge my intellect.

"Know what?"

Lachlan looked as if he was about to reply, but just as he opened his mouth, Liv sprinted back into class and slid into her seat.

"What are you two talking about?" she asked, breathless.

I shot Lachlan a look, but he'd shut his mouth and seemed to have no intention of answering her.

Which meant I had to tell yet another lie.

"We were..." Unable to wrap my head around what he'd been telling me, I failed to come up with a plausible story for Liv.

It was Lachlan who saved me. "We were just discussing the importance of a good education. I was just saying knowledge is invaluable. I think Vega agrees."

"I...do," I replied, glaring at him. "Knowledge is, um...power?"

Liv looked back and forth between us like we'd both lost our minds. Shaking her head in an exaggerated show of annoyance, she rolled her eyes and turned her attention toward the front of the room.

Lachlan gave me a side-eyed glance I couldn't read before he turned away and joined Liv in focusing on the teacher.

I spent the next forty-five minutes completely *un*focused as I tried to figure out what Lachlan was up to.

What did he mean by *others* looking for the Relics of Power? Was that a warning?

Or a threat?

AFTER A SECOND PERIOD spent in Creative Writing class, I made my way to the school's first floor, hoping to find Callum in the cafeteria so we could eat lunch together.

I hadn't been able to stop thinking about what Lachlan had said about the relics. Questions kept raging through my mind.

Did I have an enemy I didn't even know about?

No. It was ridiculous. *He* was the enemy, and he was trying his best to scare me. Yes. That was definitely it. There was absolutely no reason for me to listen to a single word he had to say.

Distracted as I jogged along the wide, crowded hallway toward the cafeteria, I dropped my cell phone, which I'd been holding clumsily in my right hand. I reached down, picked it up, and kept moving.

But as I glanced down to make sure it still worked, I collided with someone.

"Sorry," I muttered as I tried to step around the figure—a tall, slender woman—without bothering to look at her face.

"*Are* you, though?" a strangely familiar voice said. "Sorry, I mean?"

I froze.

In one quick flash of horror, all the training I'd endured, all the experiences I'd had confronting enemies...just flew out the window.

I hadn't heard that voice—the lyrical timbre, the smoothness, the malicious purity of it—since the day I'd first found my way to the Otherwhere.

I drew my eyes up to the speaker's face, nausea slamming into me as I scanned a head of platinum white-blond hair and a pair of red lips curled into a smirk that smacked of abject hatred.

Even as my eyes met hers, the world around us stopped.

Students who'd been walking were frozen in awkward, gravity-defying one-legged stances. Locker doors stood slightly ajar on their way to closing. A girl a few feet away was in the midst of blowing a pink bubble that now looked as solid and fragile as glass. A boy, tossing his textbook in the air, stood under it as it hung weightless above him.

Silence filled the space around us like a vacuum.

"Hello, Vega," the woman said. "It's so nice to see you again. I've heard that you've made some progress since we last met. The Academy has always trained its people well, so I suppose I shouldn't be surprised."

"You," I replied, pulling my chin up as I regained some of the confidence that had temporarily deserted me. I yanked up the leg of my jeans to reveal the gleaming silver dagger I'd never successfully used against a single enemy, hoping it would be enough to convince her not to come any closer. "You heard correctly. I *have* made a lot of progress. For one thing, I'm not afraid of you anymore."

When I'd first met the Waerg woman in the Commons, Fairhaven's large downtown park, I'd fled from her, terrified.

The second time we'd met, I'd summoned a door to the Otherwhere and leapt through, escaping into a life I'd never dared imagine.

But this time, I had no intention of running.

I knew now that, for all her tricks and taunts, she was less powerful than I was.

She wasn't here to kill me. She wouldn't dare. Not in my school.

Not in my world.

Not after what she and others of her kind had done years ago to my parents.

"What are you doing here?" I snarled.

"Why, I'm teaching, of course," she replied, holding up a chemistry textbook. On its cover, written tidily in marker, was the name "Ms. Maddox."

"Chemistry? Great. Maybe you can start by teaching fourteen-year-olds to replicate that shade of lipstick out of pig's blood," I retorted with a sneer.

"If you think mocking my makeup is going to break me..."

"I don't give a rat's ass what breaks you," I snapped. "I don't want anything to do with you. I've told you before that I have no intention of helping the Usurper Queen. Who, by the way, is lucky I didn't kill her when I had the chance. So I suggest you stay the hell away from me, because I'm not feeling as generous now as I did that day."

The woman's eyes flared bright yellow for a moment, like a dose of jaundiced rage had shot its way into her irises.

It seemed I'd hit a nerve.

But after a few seconds, she seemed to settle down.

"You haven't found the first clue yet," she said, her body relaxing. "You're desperate. You don't know where to begin."

With that, she let out an irritating, velvet-smooth chuckle.

"You do realize there are a whole bunch of other Seekers out there looking for the Relics, right? There's no telling if one of them will find the clues before I do. So you're barking up the wrong tree."

You mangy mutt.

She shook her head and let out a frosty laugh. "We both know you're the Chosen Seeker, whatever ridiculous misdirection tactics that wretched Merriwether may be employing. Without *you*, the Seeking will fail, and the Academy will fall. You know it as well as I do, whether you admit it to yourself or not."

"You're wrong. Merriwether named the others himself. We all took the vow together. I'm no more the Chosen One than any of them."

For some reason, Ms. Maddox—if that was her real name—seemed taken aback by this. But after a second she shook her head. "No matter. You will all be stopped. If not by me, then by others of my kind."

"Well then. I suppose I'd better not let that happen."

She laughed. "It's not as if you have a choice. I am a Waerg.

You know I don't work alone. And my pack will keep you from succeeding, if it's the last thing we do."

"The *last* thing you do? Is that a promise?" I asked with a scowl. "Now, if you'll excuse me, I need to meet my boyfriend for lunch. I believe you've met him. Tall, good-looking, breathes fire?"

"Ah, your...boyfriend," she said, purring the words. "You've done well to hook him and tame him, but you know as well as I do that Mr. Drake will not stay tame for long."

"Keep his name out of your disgusting mouth!" I shouted, my hands curling into angry fists. I would have given anything to have the nerve to punch her right in the smug face. "Don't you dare pretend to know who or what he is. You have no idea how strong he is."

"Oh, I'm so very sorry. It seems he's a sensitive topic for you. Not surprising, given the circumstances. It must be difficult to see him growing weaker each and every day."

Tears began to rim my eyes, but I forced them back. I refused to let this woman—this *creature*—hurt me.

She didn't deserve my tears.

"I am a Shadow," I said. "And a Summoner. I have confronted the Usurper Queen and come out on top. And you will *not* injure me. You will not stop me. You will not win. I know perfectly well that you're powerless here. You may have frozen time, but you will not stop me. Not here. Not anywhere."

With that, I called on my Shadow form and raced down the hall away from her.

When I was some distance away, the world began to move again. Students continued on their way to lunch as if nothing had happened. Objects in mid-air landed in waiting hands, and locker doors slammed shut.

I turned to look back, only to see that the woman who called herself Ms. Maddox had disappeared.

But I had no doubt I'd be seeing her again.

AWKWARD

I PULLED myself out of Shadow form just as I stepped into the cafeteria, trying desperately to cover up the wince of pain I knew was written all over my face.

Seconds later, I was throwing myself into a seat at a corner table and pressing my head against the wall, my chest heaving more than I wanted it to.

Where are you, Callum? I thought. *Please, come. I need to talk to you.*

As if he'd heard my mental summons, he strode into the room a moment later, his piercing eyes locking instantly on mine.

"Vega?" he asked, seating himself next to me and taking my hands in his own. "What's going on? What's happened?"

"I had a run-in with a Waerg in the hallway," I replied under my breath. "With that blond woman…you remember her."

"I remember her, yes."

"Did you feel it? She stopped time. Froze everything for a minute."

He nodded. "I felt it—it's why I raced down here. I'm so sorry —I should have been with you when it happened. Damn it, I should have expected this. The whole reason I'm attending this school is to look out for you. I should switch my schedule so our classes are together..."

"It's all right. I can look after myself. I'm just...freaked out that she's here. She's *teaching*, for God's sake. At my school."

"She's probably trying to intimidate you. Hoping you'll give up the search before you've even begun."

"Yeah, well, I let her know it won't work. I'm not playing her mind-games. Besides, I don't see what harm she can actually do. It's not like she can prevent me from finding a clue, unless she kills me."

"Unfortunately, I'm sure she'd love to." Callum let out a heavy breath. "But she won't. She knows better than to shed a Seeker's blood on this soil—particularly the blood of Merriwether's grandchild."

"She and the others killed my father—Merriwether's *son*—near Fairhaven," I reminded him. "Not to mention my mother. It's not like they've never shed blood in my world before."

Instead of responding, Callum slipped an arm around my shoulder and pulled me close. I inhaled deep, then felt my entire body loosen under his touch as I pressed my head to his shoulder. "But you're probably right," I added. "If she—they—whoever—wanted me dead, they could have done it days ago. Instead, they're watching and waiting. It's what Lachlan's been doing, too, I'm sure. Waiting for his chance to get to me. He's one of them, after all."

"One of what?"

The voice was Liv's.

I turned and smiled up at her, only to see that Lachlan was standing by her side.

Well, that's just freaking great.

"Yes, Vega," he said. "What exactly am I?" he asked.

"Vega was just talking about sports," Callum replied when I once again failed to come up with an adequate lie. "She was saying that you're the sort of guy who should go out for the rugby team. Because of your build."

I nodded, probably a little too vigorously. "You know, one of those big, strapping man-types," I added with a smile. "You should totally go for it."

Lachlan replied with a sly look that told me he knew *exactly* what I was talking about. "Maybe I will. It could be fun. Full contact sports are kind of my specialty. I love taking others down."

"You can't go out for the rugby team!" Liv chastised, slapping him gently on the chest. "You're supposed to be in the play with me! Besides, you're too beautiful to die under a pile of meat-heads." She pondered the thought for a second. "Or maybe you *should* try out. You might just break a leg or something, which would mean you couldn't walk. That would be amazing."

"Just so we're clear here—you *want* me to fracture my femur?"

Liv nodded. "It would be totally great. I could nurse you back to health. Feed you chicken soup. Stroke your hair as you moan in gut-wrenching agony…"

"Well, I hate to ruin your plans for me, but something tells me I'd be just fine," Lachlan said with a smile. "I'm pretty inde-structible."

"Hmph," Liv retorted, apparently annoyed that he didn't intend to shatter his bones for her pleasure. She turned to me and shrugged. "Anyway, can we sit with you guys?"

"Um, sure," I answered with pained smile. "Of course."

"Lachlan and I were just making plans for this coming week-end," Liv gushed when she'd positioned herself on the opposite side of the table. "We're going to go hiking."

Threatening a minor coronary incident, my heart started hammering in my chest. "What? You…two? Hiking? Where?"

Give me the precise coordinates. Tell me where you'll be.

Tell me you'll bring a big knife.

"The Harper Trail," Liv said. "Wait—why do you look like I just told you we're going to take a chainsaw to a kitten?"

"Sorry," I chuckled awkwardly. "I just keep hearing about those wolf sightings lately. I want to make sure you two are safe."

"We'll be fine. I'll bring some lupine repellent or something."

"Which is a thing that definitely doesn't exist."

"Fine. I'll just spray myself with bitter apple. That always keeps my dog from chewing on the furniture."

"Don't worry, Sloane," Lachlan said. "I'll keep an eye on her."

Sure. But who will keep an eye on you?

AFTER THE DAY'S classes had ended, Callum and I drove back to my house in silence.

"You're very quiet," he said as we pulled onto my street. "You've hardly said two words since lunch. You okay?"

I nodded. "Fine. It's just...nothing feels like it used to, you know? My relationship with Liv is different. Walking down the hall, running into enemies who want me dead...everything has changed, and I don't...really know how to be."

"That doesn't sound fine, Vega. That sounds pretty heavy, actually."

I sighed as I pulled into the driveway, turned off the ignition, and pivoted to face him. "I mean, don't get me wrong—I didn't exactly love my old life. And I do love having you here with me. I was excited about going back to school, but right now it just feels so trivial in the grand scheme of things. It's hard to think about reading Shakespeare when my best friend seems to be dating one of the bad guys, and I can't figure out if he's planning to give her a hickey or chew on her carotid artery."

My attempt to lighten the mood with a joke fell flat.

"You're feeling lost. A rudderless ship. I get it."

"I just don't know where to look, what to do. I'm supposed to be a Seeker, but I feel like everyone is seeking *me*. Lachlan's been watching me. That Maddox woman—or whatever her real name is—is stalking me through the halls at school. Meanwhile, Liv seems to be wondering why I'm not paying more attention to her. I need to be able to look after my own needs. I have important work to do, but I feel like I can't even breathe without someone creeping up on me and trying to stop me."

"You know what I think?" Callum asked, opening his door and stepping out.

"What?" I replied as I followed suit and began to head toward the front porch.

"I think we should order some pizza and have a quiet evening, just the two of us. No talk of Waergs. No worrying about Liv or anyone else."

"That's another thing," I blurted out. "What happens if…"

"I said no worrying," Callum interrupted with a grin, pushing an unruly curl behind my ear. "Whatever Lachlan's mysterious motives, I don't think his plan is to do Liv any harm. Who knows? Maybe he actually likes her."

"You're right," I sighed, pushing the front door open. "I should calm down. Liv is great, and of *course* the new guy likes her. See? I'm a bad friend."

"You're a great friend. You just have too many things going on in your mind."

"You don't know the half of it." I let out a sigh. "Now, about that pizza…"

MINI-BREAK

B Y THE TIME the end of the week rolled around, my mind had found its way to some semblance of calm.

I'd even managed to settle into something like a daily routine.

Each morning in class, I watched Liv and Lachlan exchange flirty looks while I tried to suppress the urge to either gag or punch Lachlan in the face. At lunch, I'd walk warily to the cafeteria and meet Callum, always relieved not to have had another confrontation with Ms. Maddox.

On Wednesday, I came close to colliding with her again as I rushed to an afternoon class, but she simply looked down at me and said, "Excuse me, Miss Sloane. My apologies. Have a good afternoon."

Unfortunately, seeing her behave like a relatively normal person only made her creepier.

B Y FRIDAY NIGHT, the excitement that had energized me at the beginning of the week was entirely gone. I still hadn't come upon anything like a clue to the next Relic of Power's whereabouts.

And to add insult to injury, senior year was beginning to feel painfully normal.

I felt naive and foolish to think I'd convinced myself that my last year of high school would feel different. As if my newfound confidence would make things simple and erase the last several years of my awkward, antisocial existence.

The truth was, I felt more like a stranger between Plymouth High's walls than I ever had. As if I'd grown beyond high school, beyond its petty concerns and its even pettier cliques. I had no desire to chat with girls about what they planned to wear on their next date, or to listen to gossip about who was throwing a contraband party this weekend while their parents were at their cottage in Cape Cod.

I just wanted to be left alone with my thoughts…and Callum, of course. Seeing his face at the end of the day was the one thing I looked forward to. The one reminder that my life had actually changed for the better—and not the worse.

As we sat together after dinner, I found Callum eyeing me with a cryptic smile on his lips.

I cocked my head to the side. "Do I dare ask what you're thinking?"

"There's…something I need to tell you," he replied. His tone was stolid, but his ongoing smile told me there was a twist coming. "Something deeply serious. Something intimate. Something that will blow your mind."

"Uh-oh. Is this going to turn into of those 'It's not you, it's me' conversations that teenage boys love to have with teenage girls?"

"Nope. This one is more like an 'It's not you, it's not me…it's *him*' conversation."

"Him?" I asked, though I was almost certain that I knew who he meant.

Even as the word left my lips, Callum's eyes flared bright orange, confirming my theory.

"Ah. *Him*. You're talking about Mr. Dragon."

"You know he's restless inside me," he said. "More so than ever before."

I grimaced. "But I thought you were doing so well. You've seemed calmer, happier. I even hoped that maybe…"

"You hoped I could successfully fight him off? Convince him never to show himself again, to forget his Naming was coming at all?" Callum shook his head. "I wish it were so simple. It's true that I've been holding him back, but to be honest, it's taken a lot out of me. I'm beginning to think I shouldn't push back quite so hard—that I shouldn't hold him prisoner, not if I want to keep him happy. He needs to be able to trust me, and there's only one way to earn that trust."

"What do you mean?"

"He needs some time to be free—to fly, to spread his wings uninhibited, with no Waergs around who might go after you if I make myself scarce for a few hours. I've had a few flights around here, of course, but I never feel as though I'm allowing him the freedom he craves. Maybe if I actually *gave* it to him…"

"He would know you're not trying to control him," I said. "He would trust you more."

"Yes. It would show my faith in him. I don't want to confine him inside my body and mind any more than is necessary. It weakens us both."

"I understand. I think."

"So, with that in mind, I thought maybe you and I could take a little road trip. A mini-holiday. We'd leave tomorrow morning. Call it a celebration of our successful first week of school."

My mood brightened instantly. "Really?" I asked.

"You seem surprised."

"I am. I figured you were going to suggest taking a trip on your own or something. This is so much better."

"Good. So let's head to the coast. We can stay at a Bed and Breakfast. When night falls, we'll be right next to the ocean. And my dragon…"

"...can come out to play," I finished for him. "Over the Atlantic."

He nodded. "It gives him plenty of space to fly uninhibited, and you'll be safely away from Fairhaven and our stalker friend. Sound good?"

"Sounds great."

"Perfect. You'll love the place. It's very homey."

"Wait—you're saying you've already booked it?"

"I have."

"Well, that's very confident of you. What if I'd said no?"

"Then you would have missed out on a perfect getaway. Which means there was no way you would have ever said no."

"Well...thank you," I replied, throwing my arms around his neck before pulling back again to revel in his grin. "I'm excited. Though I have to admit, I'm grateful not to have to drive there tonight. Five days of high school have exhausted me in a way the Academy never did."

"Same here. I've spent far too much of the week in the library, researching the Cold War. What a dull conflict. There weren't even dragons involved."

"I can only imagine what sort of country this would be if giant flying lizards who breathe fire had been in our arsenal over the centuries."

"I prefer the term giant *gliding* lizards, thank you very much."

"My apologies," I replied with a laugh, easing down to rest my head on the arm of the couch, "to lizards everywhere."

THE FOLLOWING MORNING, I rose early to pack, curious about what the weekend would bring.

But by the time Callum joined me for breakfast, a nagging worry had crept into my mind.

"This inn," I said, "the one you've chosen for us—it isn't going to be a *bad* surprise, is it?"

"What sort of bad surprise?"

"Like, filled with dragon shifters. Or Seekers. Or something. I just want to be mentally prepared, in case it's not the quiet getaway I'm expecting."

"I think you'll find it very quiet. Something tells me you'll like the inn a great deal."

With a squeal of excitement, I raced off to leap up the stairs two at a time until I reached my bedroom.

While Callum was off doing his own packing, I texted Liv.

Hey—we're heading out of town for a couple of days. I hope your hiking date—or whatever it is—with Lachlan goes well.

A few minutes later, she wrote back.

~He canceled on me. I'm not sure why. He said he'd explain later.

I breathed a guilt-riddled sigh of relief, cursing the smile that settled over my lips.

Oh. That's too bad, I typed. *I'm sorry.* :(

~It's okay. He promised to make it up to me soon, and I plan to hold him to it. Have a good time with Mr. Handsome. Don't do anything I wouldn't NOT do.

That's a double negative, Liv.

~Yes. Yes, it is.

I chuckled and tossed my phone into my purse before throwing a few last-minute items into a bag.

I packed light—just a change of clothes, my toothbrush and a few other essentials. My dilemma came when I was trying to choose between a silky pair of pajamas or a flannel pair that screamed *CHASTITY.*

I had no idea what the weekend would bring or what Callum's expectations were—though I could only assume we were sticking to our one rule about physical contact:

Kissing only.

Anything more, we'd decided, was delving too deep into the

sort of dangerous territory that had landed my grandmother and Merriwether in serious trouble all those years ago.

Just to be safe, I packed both pairs of pajamas.

"Ready?" Callum called up the stairs a few minutes later.

"Ready," I replied, skipping down to meet him. "So, where are we headed?"

"Mabel's Cove. Right on the ocean. Waves crashing against a rocky coastline. Seafood restaurants. Souvenir shirts with cartoon lobsters on them. Every cliché you could possibly imagine."

"Sounds like you've been there before."

"I've flown over it," he admitted as we headed out to the car. "I remember thinking it would be a very nice place to bring the girl I love."

I looked at him over the car's roof.

"You did not," I said before climbing into the driver's seat.

"I *did*, actually." He slipped into the passenger's seat and fastened his seatbelt.

"Well then, that's very romantic of you."

Callum smiled, said nothing, and locked his hands behind his head.

Laughing, I pulled out of the driveway and let my phone's GPS guide me through the first stage of our adventure.

IT ONLY TOOK an hour or so to reach our final destination: a beautiful old wooden house on the coast, on the outskirts of the town of Mabel's Cove.

The house was dark purple, with painted trim of various colors decorating its gables and its large wrap-around porch.

Something about it felt instantly welcoming and comfortable.

"It's beautiful," I told Callum when we stepped out of the car.

"This is a strange thing to say about a house, but it actually reminds me of Merriwether."

"Me too," Callum said. "It's why I chose it."

"Wait," I called out as he started to walk toward the house. "He's not *in* there, is he?"

"Merriwether? No, I'm afraid he isn't."

"Phew," I sighed, though part of me was genuinely disappointed. I missed my grandfather, with his comforting voice and dry sense of humor. He always managed to make me feel better about my strange and terrifying destiny—a destiny that was currently a mystery desperately in need of unraveling.

I let out a grateful exhalation as I stared up at the house, outlined against the backdrop of Atlantic Ocean and the rocky coastline. The scenery bore a strong resemblance to Cornwall, and particularly to the land around my Nana's house. There was something wild and untamed about it—a far cry from the hyper-groomed lawns of Fairhaven.

Callum had somehow managed to find a house that was the perfect combination of grandmother and grandfather, all in one place.

It felt safe. Warm. Welcoming.

So why was I suddenly chilled by an overwhelming feeling of dread?

FREEDOM

As Callum checked us in, the woman standing behind the wooden desk in the foyer eyed us both with curiosity. She must have been at least seventy years old, and she seemed to be cultivating the look of a kindly grandmother, complete with reading glasses, a silk blouse, and an elegant strand of pearls around her neck.

I was grateful when she neglected to ask if we were married… let alone how old we were.

I was even more grateful that she didn't question the fact that we were paying with cash like fugitives fleeing the law.

"I'm Mrs. Robbins," she told us with a warm smile when she'd completed the check-in process, which consisted of writing our room number down on a scrap of paper and noting that we'd paid. "If you should need anything—anything at all—I'll be more than happy to help."

"Thank you," I said, my voice mousy as I watched her step out from behind the desk to guide us toward a twisting staircase of ancient oak. We followed her silently to the second floor, quietly poking one another to point at this or that old painting of stern, scowling figures.

"My family history is all over these walls," Mrs. Robbins said. The Smythes—those are my ancestors—have been living in this region ever since 1895. One of the oldest families in this town."

"That's…amazing," I said, though I wanted to laugh to think Callum had been alive almost as long.

"You two are very lucky," our hostess said, turning our way when she'd reached the top of the stairs. "The place is empty, except for you. Not a lot of people heading to B&Bs at this time of year, I suppose."

"Great!" Callum said before adding, "I mean, it's nice to have some peace and quiet."

I stifled a laugh. He probably didn't want to seem like a sex-crazed teenager any more than I did. But our attempts to demonstrate our innocence only seemed to make us look all the more guilty.

"Right, yes. Quiet is what you're after, I'm sure," Mrs. Robbins said with a knowing wink. She handed over a key and nodded. "Last room on your right, down the hall. You'll find there's a lovely balcony, overlooking the ocean. I think you'll be quite happy with the view. And the privacy."

"Thank you so much," I replied, eager to hide myself away from inquisitive eyes.

"Enjoy yourselves," she said. "Breakfast is anytime between seven and ten. There's a list of restaurants on the nightstand, should you choose to go out."

"Excellent, thank you," said Callum, and I got the distinct impression that he'd lowered his voice to sound extra-mature.

When Mrs. Robbins headed downstairs again, Callum and I raced down the hall across rickety floorboards, and he managed to unlock and open our room's door in some kind of record time.

"Thank God," I breathed as I leapt inside. "I thought she was going to regale us with tales from her youth or something. I don't know if I could have taken it."

"I wouldn't have minded, honestly," Callum replied. "She looked as though she might have some good stories to tell."

"Fair enough, I guess. I just didn't want to be scrutinized too closely. People tend to judge teenagers, in case you hadn't noticed. They think we're all constantly doing drugs and...other things."

"Yes, well, if she knew the truth about you and me, I suppose she'd be far more horrified."

With a laugh, I stepped over to a set of French doors covered in thin white curtains and pulled them open to reveal the balcony —which was far larger than Mrs. Robbins had let on.

"Wow, look at this!" I said, eyeing the spiral staircase that led down to a sandy white beach behind the house. "It's absolutely amazing."

"Shall we go down and have a look around?"

"Absolutely."

After dropping our bags, we headed down and walked hand in hand along the beach, each carrying our shoes so we could feel the cool sand under our bare feet.

The scent of the ocean filled the air, a potent blend of seaweed and salt. I was transported to my Nana's cottage in Cornwall, to the last time I'd seen her. The look on her face when we'd talked about Merriwether...and about my true lineage.

"For the first time in a long time, I feel genuinely calm," I said, inhaling deep to take in the delicious aroma of our surroundings. Looking out toward the horizon, I could see a wall of dark clouds building. "Though this could just be the calm before the storm."

When Callum didn't reply, I looked at him. He, too, was staring into the distance, his jaw tight.

"What's going through that head of yours?" I asked.

"Just that I think you may be right," he said. "A storm is coming. In more ways than one." He nodded toward the rolling, dark thunderheads on the horizon.

"It's okay," I replied with a smile. "I like unpredictable storms.

They keep things interesting. Plus, they're less dangerous than a lot of what we've dealt with recently."

Callum relaxed, turned to me, and took me by the waist. "I'm glad you like tempests. Because you've chosen to spend a lot of time with one."

"Like I said, it keeps things interesting. I never quite know what I'm going to get when I'm with you. What I *do* know is that you'll always look out for me."

"Yes. That's true. I'll always try to protect you."

Even as he spoke the words, I could feel a nagging worry building inside him.

"As soon as night falls," I said quietly, "you can set him free. You'll feel better for it. So set him free, then come back to me. It's simple."

"I only wish it were, Vega."

We sat down on a nearby log, worn down by the salty ocean waves, and Callum took my hand and brought it to his lips for a kiss.

"It's coming soon," he said. "I've told myself more than once that my dragon is waiting until I'm back in the Otherwhere, but I'm not so sure anymore. It's like I can feel him plotting, scheming. Hatching a plan inside me. I just wish I knew what it was."

"What do you think will happen when his time comes?"

"That's a very good question." He picked up a small rock and tossed it into the lapping waves. "When the Crimson King—my great uncle—went through his Naming, they say he disappeared for a time. But not before his dragon went flying through the mountains of the Otherwhere, causing avalanches and destroying dwellings before the king could get him under control again."

"What happened after that?"

"The king began to recognize the dragon's true nature for the first time. He learned his strengths, his weaknesses. The red dragon was volatile, but focused, and the king used that power to his armies' benefit for centuries. Weaponized him."

"You're still worried that you won't be able to do what he did."

"Many men before me have suffered brutal fates on the day of their Naming."

"What happens to them?"

Callum went silent, pulling his face away. "Their dragon takes them over. Steals away their humanity. Sometimes they disappear, never to be seen again. Some die. Sometimes, though, it's worse than that."

"Worse how? What's worse than disappearance or death?"

He didn't answer, and I didn't ask him to. I could only imagine the horror he must have been feeling.

We sat in silence for a while, staring out at the ocean, contemplating the grim possibilities.

Finally, Callum pushed himself to his feet.

"Come on. Let's go into town and have some lunch. I'd sooner think about battered cod than raging monsters. At least for a little while."

WE DROVE into town and found the main street, where all the businesses had wooden signs lovingly carved and painted in maritime shades of blue and white, with gold leaf highlighting the shops' names.

After a few minutes, we spotted a little restaurant that looked like it had once been a fisherman's house overlooking the ocean. Its walls were made of white wood siding, and the name "Salty's" was displayed in big, white wooden letters on its slanted black roof.

"Looks perfect," Callum said when I pointed it out. "I can already taste the fish and chips. And the lobster. And the steak."

I glanced at him, amused. "You're hungrier than I thought."

"What?" he said, patting his stomach. "I'm eating for two, after all. And you've seen my dragon. That guy can eat his weight in cow."

Laughing at the image, I parked the car and we walked the half block back to the restaurant. It was a nice change, being somewhere I didn't sense the presence of enemies. No Waergs, no nefarious Watchers. Nothing but a quiet, sleepy town with its ancient wooden houses and horse-drawn carriages painted in shiny coats of black and gold, tourists ambling lazily along the sidewalk without a care in the world.

When we'd consumed enough lunch to feed a small army, we wandered along the street, window-shopping for items we didn't need and would never use: carved wooden lobsters, decorative fishing nets, model fishing boats, itchy-looking wool caps, bars of soap in the shape of a whale, cinnamon-scented candles.

I had to admit, a small part of me was enjoying conjuring fantasies of a domestic life with Callum in which we'd decorate our happy home to perfectly suit both our natures. Comfortable furniture. Bright-colored art on the walls.

An arsenal of deadly weapons in the garage...

Okay, so maybe we weren't quite destined to be the typical suburban couple.

"This is what Kaer Uther once looked like, isn't it?" I asked, staring wistfully through the window of a candy shop. I hadn't thought of the ruined town in the Otherwhere in some days, but now, memories of its lost beauty came flooding back to me. "Welcoming, warm, friendly. I'll bet it was the most amazing place, before it was destroyed."

"It was beautiful, yes. Until my sister got her hands on it," Callum said bitterly.

"Your sister," I murmured. I hadn't thought of her in days, either. "She's probably sitting on her throne right now, trying to come up with ways to ruin my life."

"Possibly. But more likely, she's thinking about how to ruin *mine*."

I shifted my eyes to his reflection in the glass. I could see his sadness, the sense of profound loss eating away at him.

I sometimes forgot that like me, he'd lost a family.

Only I was fortunate—I still had a brother, not to mention grandparents who cared about me.

He had no one except for his sister, who despised him. I had no idea if his mother was alive, but I hoped for Callum's sake that she wasn't. I couldn't imagine surviving long enough to watch your children learn to abhor each other.

My parents may have been gone, but at least I could tell myself they'd loved Will and me until the end.

"Come on," I said as I grabbed Callum's hand, desperate to change the subject. "Let's buy massive amounts of fudge, then devour it."

With a crooked grin, he let me drag him into the shop, where I purchased a half pound of peanut butter fudge and another of Rocky Road, which the shopkeeper wrapped in wax paper and placed into a small white bag.

"This," I told Callum, taking a ridiculously huge bite as we walked out of the shop, "will cure what ails us both."

FLIGHT

WE LINGERED IN TOWN, meandering in and out of shops for a few hours before grabbing some take-out to bring back to the Bed and Breakfast for a dinner that we never ended up eating.

At eight o'clock, when the sun had finally set, we walked down to the beach and hiked far enough away from the old house that we were confident Mrs. Robbins couldn't see us.

Callum went quiet as we wandered, his eyes constantly seeming to focus on some distant, nonexistent entity or other.

I didn't need to ask what he was thinking or feeling. I could see from the beads of sweat on his forehead that once again, his dragon was pushing itself into his mind on its way to taking over his body.

"It's time," he finally said, turning my way as we tucked ourselves behind a jagged boulder. Waves were crashing against the shore now, clouds passing over the moon like a warning.

I nodded, silently concerned.

"Will you be okay here for a little?" he asked. "You can always go back to the room if you're not comfortable out here alone…"

"Take all the time you need," I replied with a smile. "I'll watch.

Or stare at the ocean and think about all the homework I'm not doing. My point is, I'm fine."

"I'll be quick, I promise. I just need to let him out. He's especially restless tonight, for some reason."

"I can tell. Just be careful, okay?"

"I will."

I watched as he walked toward the water.

In a quick burst of light, he shifted, and the sleek dragon took off for the clouds.

Curious, I glanced around to see if anyone else was on the beach. But it seemed I was alone.

Not that any observers would have been any the wiser, even if they were staring straight at Callum when the shift occurred. As Crow and Niala had reminded me, Worlders—the Otherwhere's name for people from my world—didn't believe in the existence of dragons. And their denial made them oblivious to the very real threat in their midst.

I almost pitied them for what they were missing.

Callum's dragon, as always, was exquisite to watch. Graceful, powerful, fluid, he was poetry in the air.

I watched as he banked and circled over the ocean, wings barely moving as he soared in a steady, even glide.

Callum still had control over the beast—I could see that, even from a great distance. But occasionally the dragon would lunge and lurch, as if trying to rid himself of the meddlesome human inside him.

I couldn't help but wonder what it felt like to be Callum in those moments.

I'd spent enough time around the golden dragon to understand that he was largely unreadable. At times, he seemed gentle, welcoming. I'd stroked a hand over his scales, and he'd never made a move to threaten me. But in the presence of enemies, he was a monster. I'd seen him shoot fiery projectiles in threatening bolts, neck arched as though he was prepared to incinerate the entire world.

Like the Crimson King who'd sat on the Otherwhere's throne before the Usurper Queen had taken it, Callum would likely have a long struggle ahead of him.

As I watched him soar above me, I recalled the prophecy I'd heard back at the Academy—the one that predicted the Otherwhere's rightful heir would one day find his way to the throne.

It was commonly accepted and understood that the heir was Callum.

But Merriwether had warned me that the prophecy went deeper than that.

He'd told me that the heir would also leave a path of death and destruction in his wake…unless he found his "Treasure."

The only problem was that no one seemed to know what this so-called treasure *was*.

Feeling frustrated and helpless, I lay down on the sand, my fingers delving into its coolness. My legs were outstretched as I stared up at the sky and savored the breeze that washed over me, cleansing all the fears from my mind.

Before long, I began to feel relaxed. Blissful, even.

"Everything's going to be fine," I mouthed. "There's no need to worry."

After a few minutes of calm, I sat up and looked into the distance to see that Callum's dragon was still soaring, still beautifully controlled. By now, he'd settled into a pattern of graceful gliding, broken up by the occasional slow flap of his massive wings.

In that moment, nothing about him was frightening. He was a beautiful, balanced entity consisting of two halves, both living in perfect harmony.

All was right with the world.

Hugging my knees to my chin, I let out a sigh of pleasure and closed my eyes to let my other senses embrace the smells and sounds of the Atlantic coast. I inhaled deep, seeking the pleasantness of the salt air.

That was when a familiar scent met my nose.

And it wasn't a friendly one.

My eyes popped open, and I pushed myself to my feet, grabbing the dagger in my waistband.

An immediate, prickly fear pierced my chest.

Someone—or something—was watching me.

ASSASSIN

AT FIRST, the silhouette remained still, like a craggy rock formation jutting out from the edge of the ocean.

I tried to tell myself it was just a bit of coastline I hadn't noticed before.

An ominous outline. Nothing more.

But I could just barely make out two shining eyes, blinking at me from a distance. I could feel them assessing me as if their owner was determining my weaknesses.

Which, just then, felt like too many to count.

A Waerg, I thought, my chest tightening. *But it's one I've never met before.*

I'd *smelled* him. Since when could I do that?

Or was it that he was so rancid that his odor had wafted all the way down the beach toward me?

All I knew was that I didn't particularly want to find out.

I glanced up to see Callum's dragon still high in the ever-darkening sky above.

A world away.

I turned just in time to see the Waerg's shadow had begun

moving toward me, skulking close to the ground like a stalking predator.

In the blink of an eye, it picked up its pace.

I called on my Shadow form, which overtook me immediately. Wincing from the pain of the transformation, I slipped away from the water's edge as the wolf broke into a full-on sprint, leaping toward the place where I'd just been standing.

I watched the beast's nose snuffle at the ground, its paws digging bits of sand up in a frustrated attempt to discern my location. As I backed away with my eyes fixed on its face, I wanted to retch at seeing the repugnant, feral froth dripping from its lips.

Its eyes were dark, a brown so rich that it bordered on red, and they glowed eerily in the moonlight.

The Waerg turned my way, focusing intently. Whether it could see me or not, I couldn't tell. But it sure as hell felt like the monster was looking right into my eyes.

With its nose pressed to the ground, he began to move toward me, sniffing in rapid huffs.

"Not cool," I half-muttered. "I'm not okay with this."

Tripping backwards over my own feet, I was reminded in a moment of horror that I wasn't *entirely* devoid of a physical body. In a clumsy pseudo-display, I went careening backwards, landing hard and scattering sand like a hard blast of air had assaulted it.

The wolf's head shot up, and I grew convinced it could hear the rapid thumping of my heart. As if to confirm my fear, it leapt at me, and I just managed to roll to the side before it tore at the patch of sand where I'd fallen a few seconds earlier.

I had a choice. Leave my Shadow form behind and hope I could fight the creature off with my blade—an extremely unlikely scenario—or run like hell.

But as it turned out, I never got a chance to choose.

As I stared at the Waerg, a blood-curdling howl tore through the night air...but it wasn't my would-be attacker who'd made the sound.

I looked around, my heart racing. I was using every ounce of my strength to keep myself hidden. But if there were two Waergs —or even more—my Shadow form wouldn't be enough to save me.

Surprised by the intrusion, the Waerg who'd lunged at me spun around and, spotting something in the distance, put his head down, raised his hackles up, and snarled a cold, deadly threat.

I was baffled.

Why the hell would two Waergs be challenging one another? Everyone knew they were allies. Not to mention that they were, without exception, bent on taking out Seekers like me.

I squinted into the darkness until I made out the shape of another wolf, padding slowly along the sand toward us. His head, too, was low to the ground, his eyes glowing silvery-blue in the moonlight.

"No," I thought. "It can't possibly be..."

I pulled my eyes to the sky, looking for Callum. Surely he'd heard the howl.

But his dragon was still soaring out over the ocean. He might have been a mile away, or ten...it was impossible to tell.

Stunned, I backed up several feet and pulled myself out of my Shadow form. I knew the risk I was taking. But I needed to know I wasn't imagining things.

"Lachlan?" I called out, baffled both by his presence and by his seeming desire to confront my attacker.

The charcoal-gray wolf's head twisted my way for a second, as if to acknowledge that he was indeed the boy I'd met in Fairhaven. The boy who seemed to despise me.

The boy who should have been miles and miles away.

I flinched, half-expecting him to leap at me and finish me himself.

But it was the other Waerg who turned my way and, wasting no time worrying about the new intruder, sprang toward me once again.

He was powerful. He was huge. And he was quick.

But Lachlan was faster. He charged at his opponent, tearing with savage ferocity at the fur and flesh around his neck, and the other Waerg returned the favor, gnashing his teeth, raking his claws along Lachlan's side as he flailed wildly.

A series of yelps and snarls told me at least one of them was being badly injured, but I had way of knowing who was winning.

Summoning all my strength, I circled around and stalked toward the two wolves, who were now so tangled together in battle that I couldn't tell where one ended and the other began.

With a flash of Lachlan's eyes, I deduced that he was on top of his opponent, who was fruitlessly snapping his jaws at Lachlan's neck.

But after a few attempts, he succeeded, biting deep into Lachlan's shoulder and extracting a tormented cry from deep in his throat.

"The enemy of my enemy is my friend," I muttered, grasping my dagger tight in my hand. I sprinted at the pair and leapt, jamming the blade into the side of the unidentified attacker.

When he let out a cry that sounded horrifyingly human, I pulled the knife back, sickened by the blackness of the blood under the pale light of the moon.

I stepped backwards, unable to think.

The enemy Waerg let out one final snarl then, pulling away from Lachlan's grip, twisted and sprang away down the beach in the direction he'd come from.

I dropped the dagger and collapsed onto the sand next to it.

Lachlan's wolf, breathing heavily, was staring at me, blood matting the fur on his left shoulder.

"You may as well kill me," I said miserably. "I don't think I have it in me to stab you with Murphy, too."

But instead of taking advantage of the perfect opportunity to take my life, he shifted into his human form and stepped over, reaching a hand up to staunch the bleeding on his wound.

"Are you all right?" he asked.

I looked up at him, frowning. "Are you serious right now?" I asked.

"Yes, I am. You nearly died." He pulled his gaze toward the far end of the beach, where the other Waerg's footprints disappeared into the distance. "I haven't seen a Sasser around these parts in a long time. They're...not like the rest of us."

"Sasser?"

"It's what we call Assassins. They travel alone. They're mercenaries, usually hired by the powerful to take down their enemies. In your case, he's probably been waiting patiently to find you alone."

"Who does he work for? Why is he here? Is he one of the Usurper Queen's servants?"

Lachlan shook his head. "No. She doesn't trust Sassers. Which is probably sensible, to be honest. But I did warn you—the queen isn't the only one hoping to get her hands on the Relics of Power."

As he spoke, I pulled my eyes up to the sky. I could still see the distant dragon, apparently oblivious to all that had just transpired on the beach.

"Callum will be back anytime now," I warned in the hopes Lachlan wouldn't get any ideas.

Lachlan let out a chuckle. "Yes," he said, following my gaze. "I can see him. I suppose I should leave before he finds me here like this. I don't think he'd be very happy to see me. I'll see you around, Vega."

He began to walk away, clutching his shoulder and sucking air in through his teeth.

"Wait—" I said, annoyed at myself for feeling even a morsel of sympathy for the enemy. "You're hurt."

He turned back to me, pulling his hand from the wound. "It's not that bad. Besides, I heal fast. I'll be okay."

"I don't get it. Why did you help me like that?"

"If I told you," Lachlan replied, "you'd probably want to kill me. So let's just say I owed you. Take care."

With that, he shifted once again before turning away to race into the darkness.

CALLUM LANDED A FEW MINUTES LATER, shifting into human form even as his dragon's feet hit the beach. He raced over to me, his eyes wild and glowing with flame.

"My God, Vega," he said, sniffing at the air as he looked around at the series of paw prints in the sand. "What happened? Are you all right?"

"I'm fine. But it was...so weird." I gathered myself and proceeded to tell him the whole story—from spotting the first Waerg to my terror when I realized he could detect me despite my Shadow form.

And how Lachlan had saved my life.

"He just...showed up," I said. "I don't know where he came from. He fought—like, really *fought*—the Sasser. He..."

"Wait," Callum said, "did you just say Sasser?"

I nodded. "That was what Lachlan called him."

"So, someone is sending Waergs from the Mordráth Wood."

"Do I even want to know what that is?"

"Probably not. Let's just say that none of its inhabitants are friendly. And all of them will kill for a price."

"Well, whoever sent the Sasser must have been paying well, because that thing was determined to take me down. If I hadn't stabbed it, I think it would have killed Lachlan. It's completely crazy to think he almost died for me tonight."

Callum looked down at my dagger, which was still lying in the sand. He reached down, wiped it on his jeans, and handed it to me.

"I'm so sorry, Vega. I should never have left you down here alone. I was a fool."

"I wasn't alone," I told him with a smirk as I sheathed the dagger. "I can't imagine why Lachlan would be following us like that. It's one thing to watch the house in Fairhaven, but we're miles and miles from home."

"I don't get it, either," Callum said. "What's in it for him? Why keep you alive? Who's he working for? Never in my life have I met a Waerg who's an ally to those at the Academy."

I shook my head. "I have no idea. All I know is that suddenly, I feel a desperate desire to crawl into bed next to you. I need some comfort."

"Of course," Callum said. Taking my hand, he led me back up the beach toward the house.

"I'm an idiot," I said as we walked. "I haven't even asked about your dragon. Your flight."

"It was…fine," he replied.

"Just fine?"

"Yes."

As we trudged through the sand, I bit the inside of my cheek hard, as if punishing myself.

I'd had the courage to stab a Waerg. And not just any Waerg— an assassin with glowing red eyes.

Yet I didn't have the courage to ask Callum to tell me the truth about what was happening to him.

BEDTIME

WE PLODDED up the spiral staircase to the deck outside our room. Both of us were exhausted and mildly defeated.

What was meant to be an escape had turned into something of a nightmare—and had set us both on edge.

"I'm going to take a shower," Callum told me as we stepped inside the room and locked the door behind us. "Will you be all right?"

I nodded before throwing myself onto the queen-sized bed. It was an antique, its headboard ornately carved of mahogany, its linens pristine white. If it weren't for the fact that I was feeling so vulnerable, I probably would have found a way to relish the opulence of it.

"I'll be fine," I said. "I'll shower when you're done."

Callum smiled and opened his mouth to say something. Then, seemingly thinking better of it, he turned to head into the bathroom and shut the door.

I lay back and stared up at the ceiling, contemplating everything that had just happened and everything that might be on the *verge* of happening.

In all the excitement of the last half hour or so, I nearly forgot that we were about to spend the night in a romantic Bed and Breakfast.

It was one thing for us to share my narrow twin bed in Fairhaven, or my tiny bed at the Academy. Even when we were pressed against one another, we somehow managed to keep a respectful distance—at least metaphorically speaking. We never let ourselves go too far.

But I was still wondering if Callum had expectations for tonight. This was the perfect setting for a romantic tryst, after all.

Well, if you didn't count the assassination attempt.

When he'd finished in the bathroom and I'd slipped inside, I found my teeth chattering with nervous excitement, goosebumps rising along my arms.

"Don't be silly, Vega," I muttered at my reflection in the mirror. "Nothing is going to happen. There are rules in place for a reason."

We'd promised one another never to let things escalate.

We were allowed to kiss. To hold each other. To sleep in the same bed.

"That's it," I told my reflection. "That's all you're allowed."

Or...maybe it was all Callum wanted.

Whenever I'd come close to losing control—to pushing things to far—it was him who'd stopped me. It was his idea to keep a distance, to maintain boundaries.

Maybe the simple truth was that he didn't *want* to go any further.

When I'd showered, brushed my teeth, and dried off, I threw on the soft white robe that was hanging on the bathroom door, tied its belt around my waist, and headed back into the bedroom, nervously and uselessly trying to push my mounds of curly hair behind my ears.

"Tired?" I asked Callum, eyeing the alarm clock on the nightstand. Ten o'clock.

It wasn't even remotely late, yet it felt like three in the morning.

"I am," he said, leaning back on the bed with a warm smile on his lips.

He was wearing a pair of pajama bottoms and nothing else. In all our time together I'd seldom seen him like this. The definition of his muscles. The sheer strength of his body.

Forcing my eyes away, I walked over to the antique writing desk that sat by the French doors and fidgeted with the stationery on its surface.

"Aren't you coming to bed?" Callum asked.

"Should I?"

"Of course. Don't be nervous—it's not like we've never slept in close proximity."

When I turned and looked at him, his expression changed.

"Oh, I see. You're worried that I'm expecting something because we're away from home."

"It's not that. It's just..." I walked over and perched on the edge of the bed. "Is everything okay? Between us, I mean?"

"Why do you ask?"

"I just...can't always read you. At night, you usually fall asleep so quickly—which is fine. But sometimes I'm not sure if it's because you don't want..."

"...you?" he said, chuckling.

"Well, yeah. I mean, don't get me wrong, I know we have rules. I know we're deliberately holding back, and that's good. It's just..."

He reached his hand toward me, and I took it and slid over next to him, leaning my head on his chest as he slipped an arm around me. "You know I want to be close to you, Vega. Always. I love falling asleep and waking up next to you. It means everything to me."

"Me too."

"So let me be close to you. We don't need to do anything. We can just…be together. There's more than one way to be intimate, after all."

I smiled as I pulled my face up and looked into his eyes. Those perfect, expressive, ever-changing eyes that had blown me away the very first time I saw them in the Novel Hovel.

Kind one minute, angry the next. But always protective.

They were windows to two very different souls.

Grinning with an affection I couldn't hold back, I kissed him on the lips. Gently at first, to test the waters. When he seemed to relax, I pushed myself onto my knees and took his face in my hands, kissing him deeply, my head spinning with pleasure.

Almost immediately, I felt him tighten, then pull back.

"I can't," he said, recoiling against the headboard.

There it is.

"What is it?" I asked, trying to mask the pain in my voice. "What's wrong? Is it me?"

"No." He held up a hand, palm out. "It's this."

"Your hand?"

"Both hands. My arms. My legs. All of me."

"I don't get it."

"*He's* in here," he said, tapping his chest. "I fight him all day long. I struggle against a strength inside me that's almost too great for me to control. The last thing I want to do is invite you into the fight. And if I were to get carried away…"

"You're afraid of hurting me," I said quietly. "That's what this is all about?"

He nodded. "I've always been afraid of hurting you. But now…so close to the time when *he* comes into his power…the risk is too great. I can't take that chance."

"What if I want you to take it? What if I'm willing to risk it?"

"Vega—"

"Just let me try."

When his shoulders finally relaxed, I kissed him again. This time, he surrendered more readily, surrendering a little under my touch. His hands went to my jawline, my neck, my hair, even as I felt the heat from his body fill the air around us both.

Then, suddenly, his fingers were wrapped around my upper arms.

At first, the pressure was firm, but gentle.

But then, a searing, burning pain shot through both arms and I cried out in pain, yanking myself backwards in abrupt terror.

With a gasp, he freed me and leapt off the bed.

"Oh my God, Vega. I'm so, so sorry."

"It's okay," I said, holding up my hands to show him I could still move. "It's okay. I'm fine. I was just surprised, that's all." I pressed my back to the headboard, and gasped when I looked up at him.

His irises, dancing with wildfire, were alive with the beast inside him.

But that wasn't what frightened me. Nor was it the ache that hadn't yet subsided in my arms.

It was that his skin, too, had begun to glow. It pulsed with flame as if an explosion was building inside him, just waiting for its chance to erupt and blow through the walls...and through me.

Whether I could see him in his entirety or not, the dragon was in the room with us.

I could feel him. The air had turned heavy, the temperature rising to a nearly unbearable level. The nameless creature was taking over the space around us. Taking over Callum's body. He was thrusting himself between us, and I had no way of knowing if it was accidental or deliberate. All I knew was that if he wanted to, he could kill me with all the ease of taking a fly swatter to an insect.

Callum spun around and darted over to the French doors. Yanking them open, he leapt out onto the balcony.

There was a bright flash, and then he was gone.

A few seconds later, a knock sounded at the door.

"Dears? Are you all right in there? I thought I heard something…a cry of pain…"

"Everything is fine, Mrs. Robbins!" I called back, working hard to keep my voice from quivering. "I just stubbed my toe on the chair!"

"Do you need some ice? I can fetch you some."

I wanted to laugh. Ice would have turned immediately to water in this sweltering heat. To be honest, I was amazed the varnish on the furniture hadn't melted.

The open doors at the far end of the room had brought a little relief, but it was slow in coming.

If Mrs. Robbins entered the room, I'd have a hell of a time explaining to her why it felt like she just walked into an oven.

"I'm okay, thank you," I said. "I was just startled is all."

"All right, Dear. You two have a nice night, then."

"You too."

When I was sure she was gone, I rushed into the bathroom, pulled the robe off my shoulders, and took an apprehensive look at my arms.

A series of angry red marks remained where Callum's fingers had been a few minutes earlier. I would surely have bruises in the morning.

I knew I should be frightened of what I saw. Or at the very least, taken aback.

But instead, I smiled at the sight.

Tonight, Callum's dragon had tried to take him over.

But Callum had fought him back. He'd won the battle.

It gave me hope that he'd win the next one, too.

NIGHT

PULLING my robe tight around me, I called on my Shadow form again as I strode toward the French doors, slipped out onto the balcony, and proceeded down the stairs to the beach, one nebulous step at a time.

The night was clear and cloudless, and the almost full moon shed an impossible amount of light on the light-colored sand. I strolled down to the water's edge and sat down, too preoccupied to be fearful of Waergs.

I pulled my knees up under my chin and looked up at the sky, searching for the golden dragon.

It was several seconds before I found him, soaring low on the horizon, far out over the Atlantic. Occasionally his golden wings would glimmer in the moonlight like a dancing swarm of millions of distant fireflies.

It was beautiful.

What, I wondered, was in his mind right now? What was in Callum's? Which of them was in control?

Holding a hand out in front of me, I just barely made out the tendril-like wisps of swirling darkness I'd become. A mere fraction of myself, my body vanished like it was never there.

And yet I knew I was in control. I didn't have to worry that one day, the Shadow would destroy me from within.

I couldn't imagine how I'd feel if there was a chance it could.

Part of me longed for Callum's Naming Day to come, just so we could deal with it and move on with our lives.

But if tonight had provided any hints as to what might occur, I wasn't sure I would wish it upon my worst enemy, let alone the boy I loved.

The glow of his skin, the power that surged through his body as his hands grabbed me, the rage in his eyes…

All of it was horrifying.

Yet something told me Callum might come through this ordeal stronger than he'd ever been.

I was still pondering the thought when the dragon came in for a landing in the shallow water nearby, transforming into Callum's human form as he waded from the ocean toward the beach, still dressed in his pajama bottoms.

Silently, he made his way over and sat down next to me as I pulled myself out of Shadow form.

"You could see me sitting here?" I asked.

He shook his head. "No, but I could feel you. Vega, I'm…"

"You don't have to say it. Really. I'm fine."

He bit his lower lip and turned away, his shoulders rising before falling in a giant sigh.

"Can I ask you something?" I said.

"Anything."

"What was in your mind, when…"

"When I hurt you?"

"Yes."

He turned to look at me, and I saw pain. Pure, simple anguish. "It was like I'd fallen into a world of malice. An abyss. There was no way out. It was like I could see what he was seeing—I could see your face. The pain he—*I*—was inflicting. I could feel him experiencing pleasure, but I can't say if he was happy to be hurting you, or if it was something else. Either way, I hated him for it."

"But you pulled him back. You stopped him."

He shook his head. "I'm not so sure I did," he replied, clenching his jaw.

"What do you mean?"

"As I watched him, I begged him to stop. I pleaded with him not to hurt you. But when my hands released you…it wasn't me. It was *him*. I only managed to jump off the bed because he allowed me to. *He* was recoiling. *He* was retreating from what he'd done."

"But you said he felt pleasure. Why would he stop?"

"I…don't know." He balled his fingers into fists, squeezed, then released them again. "I wish I understood. I wish I could find a way to break through to him. I want to learn to understand him before it's too late."

He looked at me, lowered his chin, and frowned.

"Are you okay?" I asked.

He let out a bitter laugh. "It's funny, you know. No one ever asks me that. They assume that because I'm the mighty Callum Drake, I can take anything." He leaned back, pushing his hands into the sand, his arms tense with braided muscle. "No one ever asks if I'm scared. If I feel alone, terrified of what's happening to me. But the truth is, every night I go to bed terrified, and every day I wake up euphoric, relieved to discover I'm still me."

"I'm sorry," I said. "I should ask you more often. I'm as guilty as anyone else of thinking you can take anything the world throws at you."

"That's only because I don't want you to know how fragile I really am."

"You're not fragile, Callum. You're human."

He shot me a side-eyed glance and a smirk. "Barely," he said. "And I'm becoming less human by the day."

We sat in silence for a moment before I murmured, "Can I ask you something else?"

"Anything."

"The Naming—it's what it sounds like, right? The dragon is given a name."

"Yes, that's basically it. But the name—*his* name—is more than a simple group of letters. It defines him. It frees him in ways I don't yet understand."

"So, when the day comes, will you tell me his name?"

Callum shook his head.

"There is an unwritten law—a vow spoken silently between shifter and dragon." He looked away from me into the distance, and whispered, *"If his name is spoken, then shall he be cleft in two. A shadow will fall over the two worlds, and only his treasure will make him whole again."*

"Treasure," I repeated under my breath, remembering the treasure Merriwether had mentioned when he'd told me about the prophecy. I'd never forgotten his words:

"It is said that the heir will retake the throne...but also that he will unleash chaos and devastation on this land. Towns destroyed. Countless dead. The heir, the prophecy foretells, will become a tyrant worse than any we could possibly imagine. Worse, even, than the Usurper Queen. Unless he finds the Ulaidh—the Treasure."

"What does that mean, 'shall he be cleft in two.'" I asked. "He'll be killed?"

"I don't know, and I don't think I want to. It might just be a metaphor for suffering. Or it might be much, much worse."

He looked pained, distraught even, at the mere thought of it.

"I'll never ask you to say his name," I said. "I'm sorry—I didn't realize—"

"It's okay." He reached over and squeezed my hand. "There's no way you could have known." Taking in a deep breath, he added, "I think the dragon has settled down for the night. What say you and I get some sleep? Then maybe tomorrow, we can do something incredibly normal like go antiquing."

"You mean that thing where you look at old stuff nobody wants?"

"Hey, now. Some things get better with age. Dragon shifters, for instance."

I leaned over to kiss his lips and smiled. "How right you are, Callum Drake."

THE BOOK

IN THE MORNING, Callum and I each showered and dressed before heading down to breakfast.

Since waking up, I'd been dreading the thought of seeing Mrs. Robbins. Though she was a perfectly lovely hostess, I still couldn't shake the theory that she must think we were two overly hormonal teenagers, and I really wasn't in the mood to be judged.

As we headed down the creaking wooden staircase to the first floor, I resolved to grin and bear whatever dubious, scrutinizing looks she was about to throw our way.

To my relief, we found ourselves alone when we reached the foyer. There was a small, elegant sign on the front desk with an arrow pointing to the right:

Dining Room this way.
Help yourselves to breakfast!

"Thank God," I muttered under my breath, drawing an amused grin from Callum.

We ended up in a large, bright space halfway between a

library and a sunroom, with vast windows on one side, a wall covered in beautiful old books on the other.

A single round table at the room's center was laid out with a white cloth and a series of delicacies: fruit, fresh croissants, bacon, hard-boiled eggs, jams of various kinds. The scent alone was enough to remind me that I'd barely eaten anything since the previous day's lunch.

"This looks amazing," I said, euphoric to see the feast spread out before us.

"Agreed," Callum replied, grabbing a plate and proceeding to fill it up. "Don't know about you, but last night took a lot out of me. I'm famished."

Despite my hunger, I wandered over to the bookshelf and fingered the spines of a couple of the larger books. The sight of them reminded me of my grandfather's office in the Academy for the Blood-Born. Massive, hard-cover tomes about art, music, history, and anything else one could imagine.

I stopped as my eyes met a thick volume called *Historia Regum Britanniae.* I read its title out loud.

"The History of the Kings of Britain," Callum said as he took a bite of a croissant slathered in strawberry jam. "Quite a famous book, that. I heard about it many years ago."

I pulled it off the shelf and brought it over to the table, where I began to leaf through it.

The first thing I saw was a colorful, medieval-looking picture depicting a bunch of people standing just outside the gates of a castle. In the foreground, a comically small golden dragon—no bigger than a dog—was engaged in some kind of wrestling match with a white dragon of equal size.

I flipped through the book until I came to a chapter on King Arthur. Another picture jumped out at me, this time of a young man holding the sword known as Excalibur.

"The Sword of Viviane," I mouthed. So strange to find myself gawking at the weapon the other Seekers and I had recovered from its hiding place in the Otherwhere.

The sword was the sigil of the Academy. A legendary blade, with powers far greater than King Arthur ever knew.

As I stared at the picture, Mrs. Robbins wandered into the room and sang, "Good morning, dears!" I quickly closed the book and pushed it aside, unsure if I'd overstepped by pulling it off the shelf in the first place.

"I came in to see if you two would like some fresh coffee," she chirped, eyeing the book. "Ah, I see you've found a good one. Interesting stuff, that."

"I'm sorry," I replied. "I didn't mean to snoop."

"It's fine, dear. The books are for the guests. In fact, my husband and I have been saying for some time that we'd like to get rid of some of them. We have far too many in this house. More than we know what to do with, really."

I nodded, unsure of what to say. "Are you…selling them?"

"Oh, no. We have more money than we know what to do with, too." Nodding toward the thick book, she asked, "Would you like to keep that one?"

"I couldn't," I said. "It's yours."

She shrugged. "It's yours now. Something tells me you two were meant for one another."

"Really?"

"Of course," she said with a wave of her hand. "Now, about that coffee…"

Callum held up a cup, as did I, and thanked her for the fresh, hot liquid that was about to heat up our insides.

"You two were awfully quiet last night," our hostess said. "That is, after the toe-stubbing incident. Everything to your liking?"

"Um, yes," I replied, flushing. "This place is…lovely."

"It is, isn't it?" Mrs. Robbins set down the pot. "It's especially lovely just around dusk." With that, she pulled her eyes to

Callum. "When darkness hits, you can see all manner of creatures flying about the sky."

Without another word, she turned and left the room, whistling a happy-sounding tune.

"What the hell was that?" I whispered to Callum. "Do you think she knows about last night?"

His lips curled into a smile. "I think so," he said. "But it's fine."

"How can it possibly be fine?" I asked, agitated but trying not to raise my voice. "I was under the impression that Worlders—my people—weren't supposed to see the goings-on of magic users and shifters."

"Yeah, I'm not so sure she's really a Worlder," he said, gesturing toward the book on the table. "But if she is, she knows about the Otherwhere."

"What? Are you serious?"

He nodded again. "I think we were meant to be here. The way this place drew me in when I looked it up...the fact that no other guests are here, even though it's the weekend. And that book? She's right. You were meant to have it."

I laid a hand on the book and stroked its leather cover, thinking once again of my grandfather. Merriwether was a strong believer in fate.

And I was beginning to think I should be, as well.

Maybe Callum was right. Maybe there *was* a reason we'd found ourselves here. There was a feeling of the Otherwhere in this house, even though we hadn't ventured through a Breach or portal to get here. It was like the two worlds had collided and manifested themselves within the walls of this special place.

"If we *were* really meant to be here..." I murmured, "then..."

Excited, I opened the book and leafed through page after page, searching for something, though I had no idea what.

Finally, I closed it and let out a sigh.

"What were you looking for?" Callum asked.

"Not sure. A clue, I suppose."

"Ah. Well, here, have some food in the meantime," he said, handing me a plate. "No use searching on an empty stomach." I accepted it gratefully and proceeded to heap some much-needed breakfast onto the dish. When I'd finished, I set the plate down and picked up the book again, intending to move it to the empty chair next to mine.

But I ended up dropping it with a hard thud to the wooden floor. It landed open, its spine cracked.

"Damn it," I said, twisting around in my chair to survey the damage. "I'm such a clumsy oaf."

I reached down and picked it up, closing it and carefully setting it down on the table, this time with both hands.

"What's that?" Callum asked, pointing to the floor.

I looked down.

"Just a scrap of paper," I said, reaching for the object. "It must have fallen out."

The scrap was torn into a rough triangle, its paper yellowed with age. It didn't quite match the texture of the pages in the book. It was thicker, like parchment, and older-looking.

When I turned it over, I saw that instead of printed text, it was covered in someone's hand-written scrawl.

"Weird," I said. "It looks like a note. But I can't quite read it. The handwriting is ancient. It looks like calligraphy."

"May I?" Callum asked, and I laid it on the table for him to see.

"*The...something...of...something...*I think the first word starts with L, but I can't quite make it out...*Sings on the wind...In the chamber of something...On the day of Arthur's Feast...in...*"

"In what?" I asked, breathless.

"That's all there is," he said. "The rest is torn away."

I looked at the paper again, trying to make out the words in the first line, the ones Callum hadn't been able to read.

"That first one—looks like Lune? Like French for moon?"

"I don't think that's an N," Callum said. "An R, more likely."

"Lure. What's the next word…let's see. The Lure of…A-D-A-"

"Wait a minute," Callum said. "In that first word, I think that's a Y, not a U. It's not Lure. It's *Lyre*."

My eyes widened, and I sat back, my hands curling tight in my lap.

"The Lyre of Adair," I said. "I think it's one of the four Relics of Power."

"You're right," Callum said, eyeing it again. "That's *exactly* what it says. I can see it now."

"So, it *is* a clue. Not that it helps. All we know is that apparently it sings on the wind in some chamber…somewhere. It could be anywhere. In this world, in the Otherwhere…"

"True."

I picked up *Historia Regum Britanniae* once again and flipped my way through its pages but found no more scraps of paper, or anything else that could possibly help our cause.

I shut the book and let out a deep, frustrated breath.

The clue to the whereabouts of the next relic was finally coming to me.

But it was coming in pieces.

AFTER WE'D STASHED the book and the scrap of paper in our room behind locked doors, we spent the rest of the morning roaming through antique shops in town. It was like a window into the past lives of the people who had once lived in the region. An oil lamp here, a desk there. A hint as to strangers' pastimes, their loves, their quiet lives.

I spent the whole time searching for more clues. Pulling open this or that drawer, looking inside pockets of old army jackets…I even checked the soles of a pair of worn leather riding boots in hopes of finding a hint scratched into their surface.

But I found nothing.

The thought that the Relic was beginning to reveal itself both excited and saddened me. If I found it—if I brought it for safe-keeping to the Academy for the Blood-Born—then our side would be closer to defeating the Usurper Queen, and finding a foothold in the Otherwhere. We would stand a chance of keeping the current ruler from destroying the land—not to mention that Callum would be one step closer to ascending to the throne he deserved.

The Academy already had the Sword of Viviane in its possession. Finding the Lyre would mean we'd acquired half the Relics.

But it would also mean I'd be halfway to the end of my time as a Seeker. Halfway to saying good-bye to the Otherwhere forever, just as my grandmother had done.

After we'd returned to the Bed and Breakfast and checked out, we drove home to Fairhaven, enveloped in a sort of heavy silence. Callum asked once or twice if I was all right, and each time I told him I was fine.

A few times, I found myself asking him the same question.

Though neither of us wanted to admit it, we were both contemplating our uncertain futures, and the day we were both coming to dread.

I could only hope it wouldn't come too soon.

A GRISLY PROPOSAL

ON MONDAY MORNING, I headed to my first class, only to see Liv sitting at her usual desk, looking forlorn.

A sick feeling churned in my stomach when I realized Lachlan wasn't at his desk.

"What's wrong?" I asked when I'd sat down. "Where's Lachlan?"

"You remember how he said he couldn't get together on the weekend? Well, turns out it was a family emergency."

An emergency, yes, I thought. *But not a family one.*

"Oh...that sucks," I said, putting on my most convincing *I'm genuinely shocked by this news* face.

"It gets worse."

"Oh, Liv..."

She looked like she was on the verge of weeping. "This morning, he texted again to say he'll be gone for a few days. Possibly a few *weeks.*"

"What? Why?"

Even as I asked the question, I realized I knew the answer. The injury he'd sustained in the fight on the beach was serious. He'd told me he would heal fast, but even the strongest Waerg would struggle to recover from such a vicious wound without the help of a Healer.

He'd probably gone in search of medical care. Whether in my world or the Otherwhere, I couldn't guess.

"He said something about a sick family member in Europe," Liv replied. "I guess it doesn't matter anyhow. I'll be busy with rehearsals. It's just...I was really looking forward to seeing him."

"Wait—rehearsals?"

"Yeah. Drama Club, remember?"

"You're in the play? You got the role?"

"I did."

"How did I not know this?"

Liv lowered her chin and leveled me with a look of reprimand.

"You're in your own world these days, Vega. You could've just asked, you know. But you never ask me anything anymore."

I wanted to protest, but the fact was, she wasn't wrong.

"I'm sorry. You're right. Okay, so I'm asking now. You're playing Emily?"

A smile worked its way over Liv's lips as her irritation seemed to fade.

She nodded. "Isn't it exciting?"

"It's amazing! Congratulations!" I took a breath and added, "And don't worry about Lachlan. He'll be back soon, I'm sure."

"Thanks. It's just...he's fun to hang out with, you know? Even if we're not exactly dating. He's a good friend. I know you don't like him, but..."

"I like him just fine," I said. "He's sort of...growing on me."

Sort of.

"Good. I hope the four of us can hang out sometime. He's good for me, you know? He makes me laugh." She let out a little breath and added, "The truth is, you have Callum, and, well, I feel like I'm losing you. I'm just grateful to have someone in my life."

"You're not losing me, Liv. You'll never lose me." Even as I said the words, I knew I was making an impossible promise. Things changed. Lives altered. People moved away.

Sometimes to other worlds…

"I'm glad," Liv moaned, crossing her arms on her desk and dropping her head onto them. "Still, I guess while Lachlan's away, I'll just use my lonely-girl trauma as motivation for my acting."

"That's the spirit," I said, patting her shoulder.

It was horrible of me, but I wanted to laugh. Consoling Liv over the temporary loss of her Waerg love interest was one of the weirdest things I'd ever done.

As for Lachlan, he was turning into quite a mystery.

But I was more determined than ever to solve him.

ONE MORNING A FEW WEEKS LATER, Callum and I walked lazily to school, kicking up dry and decaying leaves as we went. The air was crisp, signaling the shift in seasons.

I finally felt like we'd settled properly into a routine at Plymouth High. I'd already written what felt like a hundred assignments for my various classes. As had Callum, who was, as it turned out, an infuriatingly brilliant student. Despite the fact that he had no vested interest in working his butt off, he managed to ace every one of his tests.

To be fair, I managed to do almost as well as he did. Which surprised me somewhat, given my preoccupation with Relics of Power, Waergs, and other life-or-death matters.

Not to mention that somewhere in the back of my mind, I was always thinking about the future that lay beyond my time as a Seeker. The uncertain years ahead, when Callum would probably cease to be part of my life.

I was *supposed* to follow in Will's footsteps and head off to college. Meet new people, go on dates, spend my time working at this job and that one while I decided how I wanted my life to go.

But it was impossible to look forward to a time when Callum would no longer be a part of my life. And even harder to motivate myself to succeed at school. As much as I prided myself on good grades, every A-plus on a test brought me one step closer to a scholarship to a prestigious university...which meant every A-plus pulled me further away from the boy I loved.

I was torn, to put it mildly.

In the meantime, I hadn't found any more clues that could help lead me to the Lyre. No word from the Academy's other Seekers. Nothing. Each morning when I woke up, I resolved to be patient, bide my time, and enjoy the calm before the inevitable storm to come.

Callum's dragon had been quiet since our mini-break. Apparently his escape over the Atlantic was enough to calm him for the time being.

But the truth was, I was a little reluctant to ask Callum if I was only imagining an improvement.

"It's always so pretty here in the fall," I said as we walked along, trying to steer my mind toward happy thoughts. "Tourists come from all over to stare at our leaves. It's kind of wild to think it'll be Halloween before we know it."

"Mmm," Callum replied absently.

"Kids running around dressed like horrifying little murderers," I added, trying to get his attention. "I wonder what they'd think if they found out who and what was walking among them. Maybe I should decorate the house to look like the Murder Shack."

At that, Callum seemed to perk up. "You really do need to show me this fabled place sometime. I'm curious to see it."

"Sure. Maybe we can take a creepy little hike through the woods some night. I'm sure Liv would love to join us."

"Which means bringing Lachlan, I suppose."

"Sure, I suppose. If he ever comes back."

"Oh, yeah, I meant to tell you," Callum lifted his chin and

sniffed at the air. "He's back. Expect to see him in class this morning."

"You and your nose really are impressive," I laughed. "Well, I have to admit that I'd like to talk to him. I need to figure out what his deal is. I still can't quite work out if he plans to kill me eventually, or…" I stopped talking and sucked in my cheeks, the memory of the assassin Waerg flashing through my mind. "I don't know."

Callum stopped walking and tightened, his hands curling into white-knuckled fists. "If he ever so much as hints at wanting to hurt you, or if that Sasser ever returns," he snarled, "I'll kill them both before either of them can blink."

His sudden change in tone chilled me to the bone.

I'd seldom heard that sort of quiet, raw anger in his voice, and there was zero doubt in my mind that he meant exactly what he said.

"I know you will," I replied. "Just…maybe do me a favor and let me get some answers before you turn Lachlan into a pile of smoking charcoal, okay?"

Callum seemed to snap out of whatever mood had possessed him, smiled, and said, "Fair enough."

WHEN CALLUM HAD HEADED off to his first class, I hunted down Liv, who was fetching something from her locker. When I filled her in on our plan to pay the Murder Shack a night-time visit, her face lit up.

"Oh my God, that would be amazing," she beamed. "Actually, the timing is perfect. Lachlan's back! I just saw him."

"Oh yeah?" I replied, trying my best to sound surprised. "How…is he?"

"Good, I think. You can ask him in class. Anyhow, we should *totally* go to the woods on the weekend for a creepy double-date."

"From Hell," I sang, my tone as ghoulish as I could muster.

"I haven't been to the Murder Shack in years. I'm not even sure I'll be able to find it anymore."

"Something tells me Lachlan will be able to help," I replied with a smile.

It was good to see Liv looking so happy. I'd been wracked with guilt since August, knowing I was constantly letting her down with my absence. There was a time not so long ago when we'd told each other everything—every crush, every thought about every class, regardless of how banal the information might be. Yet, since school had begun, we'd barely managed a complete conversation.

In my defense, it was hard to think of things to chat about when my mind was constantly clogged with thoughts of how best to take on my strange assortment of mortal enemies.

It was even harder to fathom explaining it to a lifelong friend who would never in a million years believe any of it, even if I could tell her.

"Okay, so Friday it is, then?" she asked.

"I'm in. Callum is, too."

"Great. In the meantime, we should arrange a girls' night out sometime. You know, when I'm less busy and you're less busy, and…"

"Sure. Maybe after everything is over," I said, my mind turning to other matters. "When I've found the—" I stopped and slammed my mouth shut, wishing I could slap myself across the face without Liv thinking I'd lost my mind.

Her brow furrowed. "After *what's* over? What do you need to find?"

Idiot.

"I…uh…I mean when I've found the secret formula for acing all my tests. And when you're done with rehearsals and all that."

"Great!" She gave me a quick hug, pulled away, and added, "I can't wait for the weekend. It'll be dark and sinister in the woods, and I'll have the perfect excuse to throw myself at Lachlan. I'm very good at playing the damsel in distress. Maybe if I cling to him in sheer terror, it'll be enough to get him to stop friend-zoning me to death."

I shrugged. "Don't underestimate the value of a good friend. Maybe he'll turn out to be the best one you've ever had, Liv."

"Second best," she said with a crooked smirk, reaching out to punch my arm.

"Second best, then."

The bell rang, and with unison sighs, we slung our bags over our shoulders and headed to class.

ANOTHER CLUE

LACHLAN and I didn't get a chance to speak privately over the next few days.

To be honest, I wasn't entirely sure I wanted to. I hadn't forgotten what he'd done for me on the beach. But nor had I forgotten Waergs were my sworn enemies for life.

To my surprise, Ms. Maddox, too, left me alone...though I often felt her eyes following me as I moved through Plymouth High's hallways. There was no doubt in my mind that she was waiting for something—a change in my demeanor, a hint that I'd uncovered an important clue.

I reveled in the knowledge that my silence on the matter caused her some level of discomfort.

As for the feral Waerg from the beach, the one Lachlan had called a Sasser—there had been no sign of him since our return to Fairhaven. I wondered occasionally what it was that kept him away, let alone what prevented others of his kind from breaking into my house while Callum and I slept.

All I could think was that he and others like him feared the golden dragon too much to come anywhere near the house—at least, when my protector was inside.

On the infrequent occasions when Callum headed out to allow his dragon the freedom of brief night-time flights over Fairhaven, I found myself awake, pacing my bedroom floor with my blade in hand as I listened intently for the sound of breaking glass or a lock being picked downstairs.

But no one ever came.

For the time being, at least, I seemed to be safe.

Of course, that would change soon enough.

AT LUNCH ON FRIDAY, I spotted Callum sitting at our usual corner table in the cafeteria. He looked up and smiled as I approached.

And as always, I found my heart skipping a beat when our eyes met.

Every now and then, the realization hit that it made no sense that he and I were a couple.

He was perfection: Gorgeous, intelligent, strong, even *regal.*

Whereas I was imperfect, to put it mildly.

Even though I wore a magical key around my neck and could turn myself into a gliding Shadow—even though I liked to tell myself I was unstoppable—the truth was that I was still awkward, unsure of myself, and uncomfortable in my own skin.

I was the epitome of a wallflower, and my boyfriend was literally the rightful heir to a throne.

Stop it, I told myself as I advanced through the maze of tables that littered the cafeteria. *Stop telling yourself why you suck, sucky girl.*

I was only a few feet away from Callum when I felt a set of eyes burning into me. I turned to my left to see Miranda glaring at me.

Surprise.

"Penny for your thoughts?" Callum asked when I'd sat down next to him and yanked my homemade lunch out of my bag.

"Right now, I'm thinking about how much Miranda still wants to kill me for having the audacity to be with you. That girl is like Old Faithful. Ready to explode and turn into a hot mess once every hour."

"Why do you let her get to you?" Callum asked as he turned to look at her, which was enough to convert her scowl into a coy smile.

I was about to tell him I didn't, in fact, let her get to me. But I couldn't. At least, not without lying. "Honest answer?" I asked.

"Of course."

"Because she spent years of her life trying to make me feel like a loser. I suppose it worked, and I resent her for it."

"You realize she's not worth worrying about, right? She's nothing compared to you."

I laughed. "Right. She's only tall and beautiful and ivory-skinned, and every guy's idea of the perfect woman."

"Not mine," Callum said, cupping my chin to trace the line of my cheekbone with his thumb. "Never mine. There's only one perfect woman in my world. And she's far more beautiful than any so-called 'Charmer' could ever be."

My face heated with a chemical cocktail of pleasure and shame.

"Sometimes I forget there are more important things in the world than worrying about people like Miranda," I said. "I just…I don't like that she uses my own insecurities against me. She's a reminder of everything I've ever done wrong. Every failure. Every time I've looked in the mirror and thought I was ugly. She's like the devil who lives on my shoulder, except instead of trying to tempt me, she's constantly whispering *You suuuck, Vega Sloane.*"

"She uses the strategies of bullies and narcissists, neither of whom deserve your time or energy. You have far more important things to focus on. If Miranda had the first clue how important you are—how strong you are—she would run away with her prehensile tail tucked between her legs."

I surprised myself by bursting into a hysterical fit of laughter, tears streaming down my cheeks at the thought of Miranda turning into some sort of screeching primate.

"Now," Callum said as I wiped the tears away and stopped shaking, "how about we finish eating, get to our afternoon classes, and meet later? I'm oddly excited about this weird horror-date you have planned for us tonight."

"*Double* date," I corrected.

"Right. Not so excited about that part, I'll admit."

I winked at him before taking a bite of my sandwich. "Something tells me it'll be interesting."

"Yeah. That's what I'm afraid of."

AT NINE P.M., long after the sun had set, I texted Liv to tell her we were on our way into the woods.

Callum and I, dressed in autumn jackets, jeans, and hiking boots, headed out in search of the Murder Shack.

But the second we took our first step into the darkness of the dense forest, I began to question my sanity for ever suggesting the outing.

Only a couple of weeks ago, a killer hired by some powerful entity in the Otherwhere had lunged at me on the beach in Mabel's Cove. A killer with eyes that could see through my Shadow form and fangs that looked like they could shear through metal.

A killer who'd incapacitated Lachlan for days.

Now we were about to walk into an isolated bit of forest where that very assassin could easily be waiting for us.

"I must be nuts," I said as we trudged along, the flashlight on my cell phone lighting our way. "I should have suggested we do this tomorrow morning instead." Every little sound around us was an alert, every snapping branch a warning of coming doom. "What if something happens to Liv?"

"She'll be fine," Callum said. "It's unlikely anyone would dare go near her. She's with Lachlan, remember?"

"Please, don't remind me about her ill-advised one-sided love affair," I muttered.

"I'm just saying she's probably quite safe. Besides, this shack of yours can't be too far into the woods, can it?"

"No, only a few minutes in," I replied, keeping my eyes peeled for the white marks painted on the tree bark that had always guided our route to the rickety old structure.

I finally found the first white streak, then another, and within a few minutes, we arrived at the small clearing I remembered so well from my youth.

As I turned to look for the Murder Shack, the light from my phone reflected off the small building's one window like a glowing eye peering out at us. I jumped and let out a shriek... then burst out laughing at my own expense.

"Freaked myself out," I said apologetically.

"I know. It was adorable."

I grabbed Callum's hand, leading him quietly forward.

"Hey...you're shaking," he said, pulling himself close.

"I can't explain it," I whispered. "I'm not scared, not exactly. It's just...I have that feeling I get sometimes. Like something is about to happen, but I can't quite figure out if it's good or bad."

"Or possibly both?"

I nodded as I reached for the shack's decrepit door. So strange to feel its handle under my fingers.

For months, the only mysterious doors I'd come across were the ones I'd summoned myself. But now, I was on the verge of opening a door that felt more terrifyingly arcane than any Breach ever could.

The door moved inward with a long, high-pitched creak that raised the hairs on the back of my neck.

A streak of pale light illuminated the floor where the moon shone through the small window. Callum and I stepped inside and proceeded to wander slowly around the small room, noting the old newspaper clippings that still clung to the walls like crude wallpaper, even after all these years.

Chains whose purpose was a mystery dangled from the ceiling, some with jagged hooks at their ends. It was like the place had been designed as a set for a horror movie.

At least there were no dead bodies or animal carcasses to be seen.

"Look at this," Callum said, staring at one of the news clippings. "A headline from 1937. *Body found in Lake Thatcher*. It says something about a serial killer in the area."

"I'm starting to remember why we call it the Murder Shack," I said with a nervous laugh.

As we made our way around the room, we perused bits of the various articles, most of which were from local New England newspapers. For whatever reason, the owner of the old shack really did seem to have a morbid fascination with strange and gruesome deaths, and had managed to compile a grisly assortment of headlines throughout the decades.

"What a twisted hobby," I said.

"Agreed."

I stopped when I got to an ancient-looking, yellowed article about a car accident. Tame, I thought, when compared to most of the headlines.

But it was the location of the accident that drew my eye and sent my heart rate into a sprint.

"Look. The newspaper is from St. Ives," I said. "Isn't that weird? It's near where my grandmother lives, in England."

"That *is* odd," Callum replied, staring at the headline and accompanying photo of a cliff leading down to the ocean far below. "Why would this even be here? I mean, who in this town would have access to an old newspaper from Cornwall?"

"I can't imagine."

I scanned the body of the article, which was standard fare: Details of the accident, the driver's age, family left behind.

But when my eyes hit the last paragraph, I let out a gasp.

"What is it?" Callum asked.

I read aloud:

 Rumors abound that the driver was searching for an artifact known as the Lyre of Adair. He had told his wife, Lucy, that he knew where it was. According to eye witness testimony, he'd been asking in the local shops where he could find a place called *Arthur's Lair*."

"What time of year was the accident?" Callum asked.

"Let's see…here it is. It says it was 'the day of *Arthur's Feast.*' The other note mentioned that."

I opened a search engine on my phone and typed the words in. Immediately, several websites popped up. "Here it is. They say it's supposed to replicate an event they used to hold each year centuries ago, at King Arthur's castle. 'Arthur's Feast takes place in a different location every…'"

"Every what?" asked Callum.

"Every fifty years," I breathed, my eyes meeting his. "Just like the appearance of the Relics of Power. It says it's happening in Cornwall this year."

"On what date?"

"October fifteenth," I said, pulling my head up to meet Callum's eyes. "Holy crap. That's next Sunday."

HOLY. CRAP.

"Boo!" a voice shouted from the shack's doorway, dashing any hopes of coming up with a plan.

I spun around to see Liv standing next to Lachlan, a phone lit up under her chin to give her face the menacing glow of someone who was about to tell a ghost story.

She let out a maniacal laugh. "Did we scare you?"

"Uh, yeah," I replied. "I nearly puked with terror."

"Success!" she shouted, thrusting her arms triumphantly in the air.

"Are you two having fun?" I asked, hoping to distract them both from any top secret information they might have overheard.

"Absolutely," Lachlan said. "Liv decided that in preparation for tonight, we should watch a movie about a child who's a little league player and also likes to take a chainsaw to people while they sleep. So *that* was awesome."

"Sounds very….romantic," I said, shifting my weight from one foot to the other and wishing I could head to Cornwall immediately.

Lachlan stepped forward, pulling Liv with him to look at the article we'd been reading. They eyed it casually, using Liv's phone for light, before turning to me.

"Lyre, huh?" Lachlan said. "Like a harp?" His tone was indifferent enough that I couldn't figure out if he knew the significance of what he was looking at. If he did, he was doing an excellent job of hiding it. "Seems like a silly thing to die over."

"Yeah, this place is full of articles about people who've died in weird and horrible ways," I replied with a shrug. "On the other wall, there's one about a guy who fell out of a barn onto a rusty pitchfork then somehow managed to catch fire. It's way more interesting. You should read it."

"Maybe," Lachlan said, scanning the articles and the shed's assortment of chains. "So, *this* is the famous Murder Shack."

"Infamous," Liv said, grabbing his hand. "Isn't it the best?"

I took advantage of Liv's momentary distraction to shoot Callum a look. He was tense, and I could tell without asking that he was on high alert. I could only assume he was troubled by what Lachlan might have overheard.

Damn it. Why had I said anything about Arthur's Feast? Why couldn't I just have stayed silent until we got home?

Stupid, stupid, stupid.

Meanwhile, Liv was leading Lachlan around the room as if they were in a museum, pointing out this and that photograph and date. The stains on the floor. The sagging roof above us.

"The shack hasn't aged a day. It's just like I remember. Right, Vega?" she asked with a grin, spinning around to look at me.

"Agreed," I said.

"It's something else," Lachlan interjected. "And you can't beat the location for bringing someone to the woods in secret and killing them."

Liv let out a high-pitched laugh.

But I could feel Callum growing more and more agitated next to me. He'd been silent ever since Liv and Lachlan had shown up, and I could only assume he wasn't happy to be in the presence of the Waerg.

I reached for his hand, which was burning hot.

"We...should maybe head back to town," I said, trying to muster a casual tone. "To be honest, I'm getting a little creeped out."

All I could think about was protecting Liv. If Lachlan tried something, I could transform into my Shadow form. Callum could transform into a dragon. But Liv had no natural defenses, and there was no guarantee that we could keep her from harm.

"We could head to the Crescent Diner and get some fries and shakes," I offered when no one replied.

"That sounds amazing!" Liv said, turning to Lachlan. "Can we? Please?"

He shook his head.

"No one's heading back into town just now," he said, his tone ominous.

"What?" Liv asked with a snicker. "Why not?"

Lachlan pulled his eyes to mine. "Because they're coming for Vega."

VISITORS

"Who's they?" Liv said with a hesitant chuckle. "What are you even talking about? Are you trying to freak us out?"

Lachlan had just threatened me, yet there was nothing we could do about it. It wasn't like Callum and I could take him on in front of Liv. Not without giving ourselves away.

Helpless, I threw Callum a stunned look.

To my surprise, he didn't look angry. He didn't make a move toward Lachlan or step between us in his usual protective manner.

Instead, he simply nodded.

"He's right," he said. "They're coming." He raised his chin, sniffing the air. "They're almost here."

"Who?" Liv asked. "What are you two talking about? I feel like I'm in a horror movie, all of a sudden."

"They're kidding around," I said, shooting a *Stop it* look at the boys. I still had no idea what they were talking about, but I couldn't imagine it was anything good. "Just trying to get under our skin."

"Well, it isn't funny," Liv said with a pout.

With fire dancing in his eyes, Callum nodded and smiled at

Liv. "Sorry. Vega's right—we were joking."

"Thank God," Liv laughed, crossing her arms as though she'd felt a sudden chill, and turning toward the door. "Come on, let's get out of here. I hear a shake and fries calling my name."

But before she made it one step, the door swung open. A brisk, chilly wind swept through the small shack, bringing a flurry of leaves with it.

And for the first time, I understood what Lachlan and Callum had been talking about.

I looked over at Liv, who suddenly stood frozen in time, a familiar, empty look in her eyes. One foot was in front of the other, her arms still crossed tight.

A scent wafted through the shack. A strange, awful musk that sent a chill of its own through my veins.

"Waergs?" I asked quietly.

The other two nodded before stepping outside to assume defensive positions.

Thinking fast, I leapt over and tore the article about the Lyre off the wall. I followed the two boys, closing the door and sealing Liv inside—not that the thin layer of rotting wood was about to offer her much protection from the approaching predators. As an extra precaution, I quickly closed my eyes and summoned a thick, transparent structure that surrounded the Murder Shack on all sides.

Liv wouldn't be able to get out.

But at least no one would be able to get to her, either.

"Are they your friends?" I hissed at Lachlan. "Did you tell them where to find us?"

"They have nothing to do with me," he snapped. "But something tells me they have a *great* deal to do with you."

"Nine o'clock," Callum whispered, grabbing my arm and nodding to his left. "And three o'clock. Look for the eyes between the trees."

I glanced to my left and right, squinting into the darkness

until I saw what he was talking about. At least four sets of glowing eyes stared out at me, none of them friendly.

I had to fight back the urge to hide behind Callum or morph into my Shadow form. I wasn't about to start this confrontation —however bloody it might end up being—with an act of cowardice.

Lachlan shifted into his wolf form and thrust himself between us and the figures who had now begun to emerge from the woods around the small clearing.

I counted five silhouettes in total. One human—tall and lean —the four others in wolf form, padding silently toward the shack.

I knew without seeing her face that the human was Ms. Maddox. And it came as no surprise that she'd chosen this moment to come after me.

Without thinking, I tore the article into small pieces, dropped it, and ground it into the damp earth with the sole of my shoe.

"You know why we've come," Ms. Maddox said, slipping toward us with her usual disquieting grace.

"I'm afraid I don't," I replied with a less than friendly smirk and a shrug. "You seem lost. If you like, I'm sure I could ask Callum to light you a path through the woods."

"Don't be insolent, girl." She stared at me, her strange eyes reflecting the moonlight like reflectors on a bicycle. "You know perfectly well why we're here. You also know that if you're not going to *tell* us what you've found, I have ways of extracting the information from you."

I concealed the shudder that overtook my body with the recollection of the one time she'd reached into my mind. She was what they called a Digger—a magic user who could get into the heads of others, extract information, and control them.

Desmond, a Seeker friend at the Academy, had the same ability. I'd once watched him take control of a Waerg's mind and force it to attack its ally.

"Don't even think about it, Waerg," Callum said, positioning himself in front of me. "You know full well that I could kill all five of you in a matter of seconds."

"There's no need for such talk, Mr. Drake. Besides, you wouldn't do such a thing. Not while that dragon of yours is so close to coming of age. You'd never risk satisfying the thirst for blood that keeps you awake at night with beads of sweat running down that handsome face of yours."

A low growl rose up in Callum's throat, but he stayed where he was.

"We simply want to know where the Relic of Power is," Maddox added. "I believe you've found enough clues by now to piece its location together."

"I'm not telling you anything," I snapped, stepping out from behind Callum.

"Vega—" he said. "I can take them down right now. Just say the word."

"It's fine," I replied. "I'm fine. Ms. Maddox, I have nothing to say to you."

"You don't need to *say* anything," she replied.

An instant later, I felt my head split open as she leapt inside my mind. Excavating, searching for the knowledge I'd just acquired about Arthur's Feast.

Instinctively, I pushed back, throwing a patchwork of banal thoughts in her way.

Visions of daily rituals. Brushing my teeth. Eating meals. Television shows. Books I'd read. The most boring, harmless series of mental barriers I could come up with. The color of my favorite shirt. My mother's old coffee mug. Ten times in a row, I repeated a mathematical formula I'd memorized the previous day.

But in my effort to think about anything other than the Lyre, brief flashes of information began to work their way in.

Nana.

A small cottage on the coast of Cornwall.

Quickly, I forced the image from my mind and thought of a playground where Will and I had spent many afternoons during our youth. Of my mother and my father, cooking and laughing in our kitchen. Of camping trips we'd taken in the White Mountains.

Vivid memories of my family, it seemed, were the most effective weapons against Maddox's cruelty, her malice, her greed.

And even as I stared into her eyes, I felt her recoil.

I loved my parents, I told her. *I loved them, and you took them from me.*

You murdered them.

I will not allow you to take anything else.

Do you hear me?

"You want to know what's inside my mind?" I said out loud, tears threatening to stream in rivers down my cheeks. "Go ahead. I want you to remember what you did to me. To my brother. I want you to know the pain you've brought us. I want you to *feel* it, you wretched bitch."

Wincing with pain, I felt myself pushing memories toward her as though I were flinging solid projectiles directly at her head. I stepped forward, watching her face wrinkle and distort itself into an agonized mess of emotion.

She doubled over in pain, crying out a scream that somehow encompassed every ounce of the torment I'd felt for years.

And in that moment, my mind cleared.

I was free of her.

She straightened herself, brushing her hair from her face as she erased all expression from her features.

She hadn't expected this. She had never guessed I would find the strength to keep her at bay, let alone to conceal the secrets I'd uncovered.

To be honest, I was surprised, myself.

"You thought you'd walk away with vital information," I said, scoffing. "But you can't have it. You're no Seeker, Maddox. You have no right to my knowledge. You're nothing more than a vicious sadist."

As I spoke, Lachlan's wolf skulked toward her, lowered his head, hackles up, and snarled.

I reached for Callum, squeezing his forearm in anticipation the inevitable bloody row. His skin was searing hot, the dragon inside him so close to the surface that I could feel him.

Instead of initiating a battle, Maddox simply lifted her chin and stared down at the dark gray wolf.

"I always suspected you were a traitor, boy," she said, "It's unfortunate. The warlock had such high hopes for you. He thought you'd gotten over your brief bout of humanity and come around to our side. He'll be disappointed to hear my report."

"The warlock..." I gasped, staring at Lachlan. "He knows Lumus?"

"Oh, yes," Maddox said with a grim smile. "Our pack is well acquainted with the Mistress's husband."

The Mistress. A title for the Usurper Queen I hadn't heard in some time.

Maddox's words were like a poisoned dagger in my heart. "You said *our* pack," I choked. "Lachlan...is one of you?"

"He used to be. Now, he's nothing and no one. He's an outcast, and he can rot, for all I care."

She shot me a final, enraged glare, and turned to lead her pack into the woods.

When they'd disappeared, Lachlan shifted back into human form and turned to face me.

"Vega...." His voice caught in his throat as he said the words. "I'm sorry."

I braced myself, and I felt Callum do the same next to me.

"Sorry...for what, exactly?" I asked, my voice trembling.

"For what my pack did to your family. For what happened the day they—*we*—killed your parents."

TRUTH

"You were there," I said, a swell of nausea throwing me off balance. "You were with her. You were part of Maddox's kill-squad."

"No, I wasn't part of it, not exactly." He hung his head, his shoulders slumping. "But I used to be in her pack, like she said. I *was* there that day. I was a kid. A mere boy. But I saw it. I watched what they did to your parents."

It horrified me to think of the accident. Waergs running out in front of my parents' car, forcing them at full speed off a country road outside of Fairhaven.

The hideous sound of the collision.

My parents' fractured bodies, motionless and pale.

"You watched it," I said. "You watched them die."

He nodded. "I was there after the other Waergs left. I…" He looked around, blinking back tears. "I was there when your mother died."

Feeling faint, I pressed myself against Callum, who reached an arm around me for support. I could feel him trembling, too.

Whether it was with sadness or rage, I wasn't sure.

Somewhere in the distance, I could hear knocking. No, pounding. And Liv's voice, crying out to let her out of the shack.

You can't come out, Liv. Not yet.

"My mother died instantly," I muttered. "That was what they told us. Just like my father."

Lachlan shook his head. "No. She was alive for a few minutes after the collision. I know, because I...I talked to her."

With a sob, my knees gave out, and I crumpled to the ground. Callum came with me, holding me so I wouldn't injure myself.

"This had better not be a sick joke of some sort, Waerg," he snarled, "or I swear to God..."

I could feel how hot he was. Like a fire raging next to me. His dragon was so close to manifesting itself.

So close to committing murder.

And I almost wished he would.

Lachlan shook his head. "I assure you, it's not a joke. I've tried to think of ways to tell you. Ways to explain. Vega, I know you must hate me, if only by association. And I can't possibly blame you for it. But you should know that she—your mother—spoke to me. It's only right that you know her final words."

I sneered at him. I didn't want to hear my mother's words. Not from him. Not from any member of the pack responsible for her death.

All I wanted to do was tear him to pieces.

"You knew it was wrong," I said, another sob chopping at my voice. "You could have stopped them from running out in front of my parents' car. So *what* if you were only a boy?"

"I didn't know what they were doing, not until it was too late. I didn't understand. Then it happened so fast...and I just...there was nothing I could do. You have to believe me."

I managed to push myself to my feet, with Callum rising next to me. "*Believe* you? I hate you, Lachlan," I hissed. "I despise you and your kind. I can only hope my mother told you the same. I hope she told you how awful you are and always will be."

With that, I turned and walked toward the path that led home, releasing Liv from my makeshift prison of glass.

Behind us, I heard the shack's door open, and Liv's voice asking Lachlan what had happened. "Why are you outside? Where are the other two?"

I couldn't let her see me like this. Not now—not while I wanted to murder the boy she liked so much.

With tears burning my eyes, I began to run. I could hear Callum behind me, asking me to wait. But I called on my Shadow form and disappeared, sweeping through the forest at lightning speed.

I wanted to sprint for days, until maybe I really *would* vanish. To flee the world and all its cruelty, never to be heard from again.

When I got to my house, I called on my physical form again, opened the front door, and raced upstairs, throwing myself on my bed to weep.

Lachlan had been a part of the pack that had killed my parents.

But that wasn't why I hated him.

I hated him because he was the last person ever to spend time with my mother while she was alive.

And that person *should have been me.*

HOME

AFTER A FEW SECONDS, I heard Callum close the front door, then came the soft padding of his feet as he jogged up the stairs.

"Are you all right?" his deep voice asked from the doorway.

I wanted to scream.

Of course I'm not! How could I possibly be all right?

But I didn't say a word.

I could taste my tears. Grim, salty reminders of every time I'd cried in this bed over the course of my young life. All the tears that had tried and failed to fill the void left when my parents died.

Some part of me had been sliced away that day, never to return.

I'll never be all right again.

I managed to roll onto my back, wipe my eyes, and lie through my teeth.

"I'll be fine."

"Do you want to talk about what happened back there?"

"I can't," I muttered. "Not right now."

"Okay."

But he didn't move, didn't leave me alone.

Half of me wished he would. The other half wanted him to come over, kneel down next to me and cradle my head against his chest.

Which was exactly what he did.

Feeling the pressure of his arms around me, the gentle grip of his fingers, was enough. I let the tears flow, sobs heaving my shoulders in uncontrolled bursts.

"It's wrong," I managed to moan when I could catch my breath. "It's not fair. I should have been there. Not him."

"I know," he replied. "I know. It should never have happened to you, to Will. It was cruel." He stopped for a second, seeming to hesitate, then added, "But…it also wasn't Lachlan's fault."

I jerked myself away and glared at him, incensed. "How can you say that? He's one of them! I could have told myself he wasn't part of it, but he literally was. He was there. He watched."

"He was as young as you were at the time, Vega. He was a child. It was a trauma for him. You can see that, just by looking at him."

I let out a cynical snicker. "Oh, come on. Killing is no trauma to a Waerg. They're sadists. They thrive on it."

But Callum shook his head. "He's not a sadist. Even so, he would have killed tonight, to protect you. He would probably have given his life to save yours. You realize that, don't you?"

I pushed my head and shoulders back against the headboard, wiping my tears away. My sadness was being replaced by a crawling, insidious rage, and I could feel myself about to burst.

"He's not our friend, Callum," I said, my voice trembling. "He's not our ally. He's the enemy. And I want to kill him."

"You don't mean that."

"Yes, I do."

I pushed myself off the bed. "I need some time," I said, heading for the door and grabbing hold of its edge to keep myself balanced. "Please—just leave me alone for a few minutes."

"Vega—"

"What?" I snarled.

I regretted my tone as I spun to face him and saw his eyes. The sadness, the pain—pain that I was inflicting, that was weighing him down on top of everything else he was facing.

"The Lyre will show itself soon," he said, rising to his feet and stepping toward me. "You need to find it. Whatever rage you're feeling about Lachlan—whatever hurt you're suffering—this will be your only chance. Don't forget who you are. Don't forget how good you are."

The Lyre of Adair was the furthest thing from my mind. But he was right. Finding it was the only thing I could control.

I couldn't bring my parents back.

I couldn't kill Lachlan.

But I could find that damned Lyre and bring it to the Academy for safe-keeping. I could fulfill part of my destiny as a Seeker.

I still had a family out there. I still had Will. I could still make my grandfather—and grandmother—proud.

"You're right," I said. "You're right. I'm sorry."

"I'll be downstairs," he said. Something in his voice shook, as if he was fighting back an emotion he didn't dare share.

"I'll be right there, Callum. I just need a few minutes."

"Uh-huh."

When he'd left the room, I closed the door, sealing myself in, and, closing my eyes, summoned a Breach.

When the conjured door appeared, I pulled my dragon key from its faithful chain around my neck, pushed it into the lock, and turned.

There was someone I needed to see.

A VISIT

MERRIWETHER WAS SITTING at his desk, hands folded in front of him, his gaze fixed on a point straight ahead. When I stepped through the door, his eyes flicked my way, a smile curling his lips.

It was as though he'd been waiting for me to show up. *Expecting* me.

As the conjured door disappeared, I stared down at my grandfather. He looked the same as always, dressed in a purple velvet waistcoat and a white shirt with its sleeves rolled up to the elbows.

His intricate topography of wrinkles deepened with a broad grin as he rose to his feet.

"It's good to see you, Vega."

I fought back the urge to race around his desk and throw my arms around him. It felt like years since I'd been in the presence of family. My flesh and blood. The grandfather who was always so calm, so in control of his emotions, his actions.

"Headmaster. I…"

Those few syllables were all my mouth managed to form before the tears began to flow again.

"What's happened?" he asked.

I had to wonder if he already knew. Merriwether was always three steps ahead of me, as if his mind was a crystal ball attuned to the futures of everyone around him.

"There's a Waerg in Fairhaven. One who's been watching me for a while now."

"Ah. The boy, Lachlan," he said with a nod.

"You know about him?"

"I do."

"It was his pack who killed my parents. He told me he was there when it happened."

My grandfather didn't look remotely surprised to hear the news.

"It's true," he said. "He was there when my son and his wife— your mother—died."

I wanted to yell at him—to ask why he'd never warned me about Lachlan.

But hearing the words *my son* from Merriwether's lips, uttered with so much affection for the child he'd never known, nearly destroyed me.

Looking for support, I reached out and clenched my fingers around the back of the chair in front of me.

"How do you do it?" I asked, my voice quivering. "How do you talk about that day like you're not livid? How are you able to sound so calm?"

"Because death comes with war, Vega. And I have been at war my entire life, my dearest girl." He slipped around the desk to half-sit on its edge in front of me and extended a hand. I moved around the chair and took it.

"You are young, and the grief that came with the loss of your parents is still with you. It always will be, of course. But it will alter and reshape itself, like the wax on a melting candle. It will change, and it will change you."

I pulled my chin down and let the tears come, my shoulders shaking.

161

"You are young," my grandfather repeated, "but so is Lachlan. The day of the incident that killed your parents, he didn't yet know how cruel the world could be. He simply didn't know. He learned the hard way, just as you did."

"But he didn't do anything to stop them…he didn't do anything to help my parents."

"Didn't he?" Merriwether asked.

"What do you mean?"

"He spoke to your mother, did he not?"

"How—how do you know that?"

Merriwether let go of my hand and walked over to the book-shelf on the far wall.

"Lachlan spent part of his youth here, in the Otherwhere," he said, turning to face me. "The Waergs in Fairhaven were concerned that he didn't have it in him to be a subordinate to their leader—the woman you know as Maddox. So she sent him here, to work under the warlock Lumus."

"*Maddox*," I said, her name like venom on my lips.

Merriwether nodded. "Lachlan was here for a time, training. Learning. Maddox had hoped he'd have some sense beaten into him, if you will. Only, it didn't exactly work. Every time they tried to turn him against our side, he only became more stubborn. Lumus sent him back to Fairhaven in hopes that he was reformed—but as you and I both know, he was not. It was as if something had changed in him the day your parents died…something that couldn't be undone."

"You think it's what my mother said to him?"

"Perhaps," Merriwether replied. "He came to see me once, but he never told me what she said. It's possible that he simply didn't like knowing he was witness to the deaths of two innocent people."

"Why did he come see you? Did he know…"

No. There was no way Lachlan could know Merriwether was my grandfather.

As if to confirm, my grandfather shook his head. "He simply wanted advice from someone on our side. He wanted help. So I chose to help him."

"What did you say?"

"I told him there would, one day, be a time when a Seeker needed his aid. That perhaps he could atone for the sin of living among Waergs by using his talents to protect, rather than to hurt. I asked him specifically to keep an eye on a girl and a boy who lived in a house on Cardyn Lane. And the funny this is, it turns out he was already doing exactly that."

"What?" I asked. "Are you serious?"

"Dead serious. He hasn't been watching you for mere months, Vega. Lachlan has had an eye on you for years now. You weren't aware of it because he kept a low profile. He didn't attend school, even. He simply watched over you from a distance."

I stared at him, mute.

"He's always wanted to do the right thing, Vega. So I hope you'll let him."

"I hate him," I finally murmured. "I don't want him anywhere near me."

When Merriwether frowned, I added, "Okay, maybe *hate* is too strong a word. But I'm not sure I can be around him, knowing what I know."

"What you know is that he, like Callum, was born into a cruel, power-hungry family. When you're raised as a part of a pack like Lachlan's, your loyalty is to those around you—it's in a Waerg's blood to bond with his pack. That he has gone against them and sought a better—a kinder—life…well, it shows great strength of character. He has found himself expelled from their society. That should be enough to prove which side he's on. You lost your parents. *He* lost his entire pack, and they probably loathe him even more than you do."

"It was his choice," I muttered. "He *chose* to leave them. I wasn't given a choice."

163

"Vega, he did not kill your parents. He witnessed their death. There is a difference, and believe me when I tell you that what he saw will haunt him as long as it haunts you. He did not need to stay with your mother, to hold her hand as she died. He could have run off with the others. He could have kept his face from her, but he showed it instead. So that she could look into his eyes —his frightened, distraught eyes—as she died. He stayed with her until the end. Believe it or not, what he did was a kindness. I, for one, am grateful to him. I'm not sure I would have had the strength to behave as he did. At least, not at that age."

"He's still a Waerg," I protested, though my voice had lost all conviction. Merriwether was right—Lachlan had rendered my mother a kindness in her last moments.

"Do not hate someone for their species," Merriwether chastised. "Hate them for their character, if you must hate at all. But don't let prejudice be your guide. Just as Callum is not the monster that some dragon shifters have been, Lachlan may not be the beast you think he is. He may, in fact, turn out to be the ally you need most in the days to come."

I let out a sigh, finally expelling all the toxins I'd been holding in alongside my anger and hatred.

He was right, of course. I wasn't willing to give Lachlan a chance—not because of what he'd witnessed, but because of what he was.

It was wrong of me. It was shameful.

"Now," Merriwether said, apparently satisfied that our conversation had come to an end, "I have somewhere to go. Somewhere quite far from here."

"Oh?" I asked. "Where?"

"There is a meeting of the Twelve—my Order of Wizards. It is to take place in Anara in two days' time, so I need to find my way there."

"A meeting? Does this happen often?"

"Not at all. The Twelve only congregate when something

momentous has occurred. It seems that one of ours has turned against us. So those in my Order intend to discuss the matter along with the Witches of the Mountains."

"Witches? Wait—the Otherwhere has *Witches?*" I asked, unsure whether to be excited or terrified.

Merriwether smiled. "There's so much you still don't know about this land. And I hope to show you one day. But for now, my dear, I must head off."

"I wish you didn't have to leave. Or at least, I wish I could stay for a while. I miss our talks."

He smiled at me, winked, and said, "As do I, Granddaughter." He slipped to the far corner of his office and grabbed a jacket that was hanging from a hook. "We will see one another soon. I believe you have a Relic of Power to find, and when you do, I expect you to bring it to me for safe-keeping."

"The Lyre of Adair," I said. "Yes. In a few days, I'm going to Cornwall."

"Excellent."

I tilted my head curiously.

"Do you have any advice for me?"

"I'd suggest you pay your grandmother a visit, of course. She will be better able to advise you than I am. The Lyre is an unusual relic. It has strange ways of playing with one's mind. Also, keep your numbers small, but don't go alone. There are a few Seekers in your world who would be only too happy to help."

"Right. Misery does love company," I moaned. "I'll ask Meg, of course. And Desmond, and Oleana."

"Sounds like a brilliant group."

"What about the Zerkers or Casters from the Academy? Or the other Seekers?"

Merriwether shook his head. "You don't want to draw attention to yourselves. The residents of small-town Cornwall might be a little confused otherwise. The others will have their turn in the spotlight soon enough. But until then, I need them to occupy themselves—at least for now—with other affairs. You may find, however, that Niala and Rourke come to you when the need arises."

On hearing that, my spirits immediately improved. "There will come a time when we're all together again, won't there?" I asked. "All of us, back here at the Academy."

"Oh, yes," said Merriwether, grabbing a silver-handled walking stick and making his way to the door. "You will certainly be together again soon enough."

He pulled the door open, smiled at me with a warmth I'd craved for months, and said, "Good luck, Vega dear. I'll be thinking of you."

"Merriwether—"

"Yes?"

"Thank you for the money you deposited into my account."

"It was nothing," he replied, flicking a hand in the air. "Just a simple transaction across worlds."

And then he was gone.

GONE BOY

WHEN I RETURNED from the Otherwhere, I found Callum downstairs.

"You must be tired," I said.

"I am," he replied wearily. "But I'm glad you seem to be feeling better."

"Much better."

I told him about my visit with Merriwether. About what he'd said about Lachlan's role the day of my parents' death, and about the wizard in his Order who'd allegedly strayed.

Even as we crawled into bed after we'd both changed into our pajamas, the conversation continued.

"In all the time I've known him," I said, "Merriwether has never once steered me wrong. He's protective and kind, and he knows more about the world than anyone I've ever met. He also knows Lachlan better than I do. After talking to him—and to you—I have to admit, I feel like an ass for the way I acted."

"You were perfectly justified," Callum told me, stroking my arm with his fingertips as he lay on his side next to me. "Anyone would have reacted the same way."

"Lachlan is alone. No family, no pack, nothing. Because he

hated what they did to my parents. He wants to help me, and I owe him an apology."

"So apologize on Monday, when you see him at school. Or whenever you get a chance." Callum wrapped his arm around me and pulled me close. "Everything will be okay."

"I'm starting to believe you," I replied. "And it scares me a little."

With that, I closed my eyes, savoring the warmth of his body as I drifted into a deep, restful sleep.

SATURDAY PASSED QUIETLY. Callum and I each busied ourselves around the house, tidying, cooking, and generally distracting ourselves from thoughts of what might happen in a week, when the Lyre revealed itself.

On Sunday afternoon, I went grocery shopping alone after Callum told me he was feeling in need of a nap. I took the opportunity to buy enough food to last until our departure for Cornwall the following week.

Despite my fears, I was looking forward to beginning the search. Friday's heaviness had slipped off my shoulders, and I was ready to start a new adventure.

And with Callum by my side, I could accomplish anything.

When I finished running errands, I headed home, feeling newly invigorated and hopeful.

"Callum?" I called out when I'd stepped through the front door.

Nothing.

I headed to the kitchen to look for him, calling his name again. When no reply came, I bounded back to the front hall and started up the stairs.

"Up here," he said.

His voice sounded weak.

168

I leapt up the stairs, breathing heavily by the time I laid my eyes on him.

A smile formed on my lips, and I was about to blurt out something about how grateful I was to him for being so understanding about my emotional state, for supporting me through my pain… But my smile vanished when he turned to meet my eyes.

He was as pale as an eggshell, his skin beaded with perspiration. His irises, usually a bright shimmering blue, had turned gray and empty.

His hands, which were gripping the edge of the bed, were trembling.

"Callum," I said again, this time in a thin, meek voice. I raced over and knelt in front of him, reaching for him. But he pulled back, shaking his head.

"Don't touch me," he said, a distinct, horrifying growl lacing his tone. Shuddering with a strange convulsion, he added, "I'm sorry. It's for your own good."

"What is it?" I asked.

"It started Friday," he said, his voice hoarse. "I didn't want to say anything because of what you were going through. I didn't want to worry you."

"Tell me," I said. "*What* started? What's happening?"

"When we were in the woods—with Lachlan and that Maddox woman…when they she was talking about the day your parents died…"

"Yes?"

He looked away, but I could see the fire rimming his pupils. His dragon was coming to life.

"I wanted to kill them both, Vega," he snarled. "I wanted to tear their heads from their bodies, because I could feel your pain. I could feel what that woman did to you that day. *He* could feel it, too. The dragon. His anger, inside me—his pure rage—it nearly tore me apart. I couldn't speak. I couldn't move. Because if I had, he would have come. And Maddox was right. He would have taken me over, and I probably would have burned the woods and all of Fairhaven to the ground."

He fixed me in his gaze again, his eyes bloodshot. "It took every ounce of my strength to hold him inside me. I truly thought I was going to explode. The pain of it—the battle being fought inside my mind—it was too much. He's too strong now. It's time to set him free."

"The Naming," I whispered. "It's time?"

He nodded. "I'm so sorry." His voice had lost its threat now.

And for the first time that I could remember, he sounded genuinely scared.

"It'll be all right, you know," he told me. "You will find the Lyre. With or without me."

Now it was my turn to be scared.

I slammed my eyes shut, wincing away the thought of the days to come. "I don't want to do it without you. I can't…"

"You know that's not true."

I pulled away and looked at him, shaking my head. "You have to fight him off," I said, even though I knew it was an absurd request.

"You know I can't control this. It's not up to me, not anymore." He pulled his eyes to the window and stared out. Fire flickered along his skin, a terrifying, hot glow, licking its way through his veins.

He snickered. "All this time, I've told myself I'm keeping him at bay. Contained, controlled, like a campfire. But I've come to realize it's actually the other way around."

"What do you mean?"

"He's been playing with me. Toying. Allowing me to think I have the upper hand, when really, it's him. He's known all along that he had the power in this relationship of ours. I…I'm not as strong as he is, Vega. No matter what I tell myself. That night in the Bed and Breakfast, I nearly killed you. *We* nearly killed you."

"No, you didn't." I sucked in a breath. "He's part of you," I insisted. "You—*he*—would never hurt me. I know it."

"Don't. Don't try to make this into something simplistic. A dragon is not a simple creature. He's a monster of fire, ice, cruelty, violence. I nearly failed you. I can't fail you again. I need to let the Naming come. I need to understand what I'm dealing with, or I'll hurt us both. You need to let me go."

I wanted to ask him to do everything in his power to stay with me. To remain my Callum for every second he could possibly stand it.

But it would have been the most selfish thing I'd ever done. I may as well have demanded that he not breathe air.

His dragon was maturing, just as every human being did. There was no stopping the passage of time.

There was nothing to be done.

"I'm scared," I finally confessed, dropping my head. "I'm so scared of losing you. I'm sorry. I don't mean to be selfish. Of course you need to go. And of course I won't stop you."

"I'm scared, too. But all the fear in the world won't be enough to prevent the inevitable from happening." He reached out and pulled my chin up as he'd done so many times, stroking his thumb over my cheek. His hand was hot, but I refused to pull back. I wanted to feel the pain of it, if it was the last time he was to touch me.

For a moment he smiled, and it was like the sun emerging from behind a thick layer of dark clouds.

"I will fight with everything I have," he said. "I will not let him destroy me. I'll make sure we both come out of this alive and intact."

I nodded. "I know you will."

It took me a moment to summon the courage to ask the next question.

"Will you leave now?"

"Do you want me to stay with you?"

I reached out and tangled my fingers with his. "Of course I do," I replied softly. "But I understand if you can't."

He ground his jaw. "Lachlan will help you," he said.

"I know."

"I want you to watch for him. Talk to him when you get the chance. Will you do that for me?"

I nodded.

"I love you," he said.

"I love you, too. But I don't want to lose us."

"You aren't losing me. The me that exists now—the me that you see in front of you right at this moment—he loves you, and always will. If anything, I'm losing my*self*."

"Callum…" I slouched down, pressing my face into his lap. "What's going to happen? How do we know we can survive this?"

"We don't. Nothing is certain, except for how you and I feel about one another." He caressed my neck with trembling finger-tips. "Have faith in that much. Because it's all we have. In seventy years, wherever you or I may be, whether we're together or apart, we will always have this moment—how we feel about each other right now—tucked into our minds, our memories. Nothing will ever match it. Because there will never be another now."

My eyes grew hot with tears.

The thought of waking up somewhere in seventy years and finding myself without Callum Drake broke my heart.

I'd tried to learn to live in the present. To embrace my always tenuous relationship with him from moment to moment, while balancing my life at school and an eternal, inner struggle to keep my other life a secret from my best friend and brother.

I'd tried to find a quiet sort of happiness amid the mayhem.

But the truth was, that kind of happiness was impossible for me, at least for more than a few minutes at a time.

I was a Seeker who hadn't yet accomplished her goals. There would always be a hole in my heart. And part of me would always feel empty until my fate had been fulfilled.

I told myself that my fate included a dragon.

One who would either turn out to be a benevolent ally, or a vicious enemy.

With a kiss to the top of my head, Callum gently urged me to get up. I did so, barely strong enough to stand facing him.

He tangled his arms around me. His body was scalding hot, and I could feel his blood pulsing through his veins like roiling lava.

Still, I never wanted him to let me go.

But a moment later, he did.

"It'll be okay," he said as he backed toward the door. "Watch for Lachlan. Do what you need to do. Find the Lyre. I promise I'll find you, the first chance I get. No matter where you are."

"Where will you go?" I asked.

"Wherever he takes me."

"But what if—" I began, but he cut me off with a hand in the air.

I bit my cheek, stopping my lips from forming the next words. *What if he kills you?*

"Don't you dare," he said. "You, Vega Sloane, are the strongest person I know. I need your strength. I need you to believe in me. Don't you dare lose faith in me."

"I won't," I mouthed, the words coming out in a strained whisper.

"Good."

With one final glance, he left my room and headed down the stairs to the front door.

"I have faith in you," I murmured as I watched him go.

I'm just not sure I have faith in myself.

I wasn't sure how long I stood at the top of the stairs, staring at the door. Hoping he'd come back to me.

But he didn't come.

For the first time since our return to Fairhaven, I was truly alone.

My world had gone silent, its light fading. My heart was weighed down with a brutal, aching sadness.

I felt helpless.

"No," I said, curling my hands into tight fists at my sides. "I'm not even *remotely* helpless."

I pulled my eyes to the calendar hanging on my wall. In five days, no matter where Callum was, I would find my way to Cornwall. I would to find the Lyre of Adair and claim it for the Academy for the Blood-Born.

And nothing would stop me.

CONFRONTATION

THE FOLLOWING WEEK, I wandered Plymouth High's halls like a soulless zombie, willing the days to accelerate to a blinding pace so that Friday could come as soon as possible.

I needed to find my way to Cornwall. I needed to fulfill my promise as a Seeker.

I needed to get away from Fairhaven.

At noon each day, I scarfed my lunch down in one of the school's quieter stairwells, rather than risk having to be sociable. I didn't want to be around Liv or field her myriad questions about Callum's whereabouts. She'd already asked on Monday morning where he was, and I'd only partly satisfied her curiosity by coming up with a brief, detail-free story about a bad cold.

Meanwhile, Liv was her usual perky self, flirting with Lachlan in class every chance she got, even as he threw me quick, quiet looks that said, "Do you still hate me?" or "Don't worry, I'm sure Callum is fine."

I didn't get a chance to talk to him alone. Every time I saw him, he was with Liv, who was still trying with all her might to convert him into a full-on boyfriend.

She still touched him frequently, laying her fingers on his arm as she talked to him, or setting her hand on top of his. But I couldn't help noticing that he never touched her. He was friendly, but not overly flirtatious. I never heard him say a word to lead her on.

It was like he was working overtime to maintain a barrier between them—a protective measure, I supposed, to see that she didn't get hurt.

It was noble of him. But it was also becoming painful to watch.

Meanwhile, I spent every waking moment thinking about Callum. I missed his companionship, his confidence. His ability to calm me down, no matter what mayhem the world threw his— or my—way.

I missed his face, his voice, his eyes.

Since he'd left, I'd reached out to him what felt like a thousand times with my mind. But all I'd received in return was mental static, as if there was something large and obtrusive blocking our connection to one another.

The only thing I knew for sure was that he was still alive.

For now, that would have to be enough.

ON WEDNESDAY NIGHT, I found myself going stir-crazy at home. I couldn't stop thinking about the Naming—about what Callum must be enduring, the risks he was taking. I wanted so badly to find him, to offer him the support he'd so often given me over the months while I'd struggled with my powers and a mountain of cruel self-doubt.

"What can I do?" I asked the empty space around me as I slumped down onto my bed at eleven P.M. "How do I stop freaking out?"

In response, a memory flashed through my mind of the words Callum had said before he'd left.

"Lachlan will help you...I want you to watch for him. Talk to him when you get the chance."

On a whim, I darted to my window and looked out, hopeful.

At first, the street was empty and quiet. A few fallen leaves tumbled along the sidewalk in the breeze, curling in on themselves as they went.

But after a few seconds, a silhouette emerged from the woods, padding toward the middle of the street. A large wolf, its tongue lolling out as its eyes fixed themselves on my bedroom window.

I wasn't sure if I'd summoned him or if he'd just shown up.

But either way, I was grateful.

In a state of near-oblivion, I raced downstairs, opened the front door, and ran outside, looking out to meet the wolf's eyes. He moved toward me, shifting into human form as he walked. Hesitant, he climbed the stairs up to the porch to stand a few feet from me.

"Lachlan," I said. "I've been wanting to talk to you—"

"Me too," he said, his strange green eyes glowing bright despite the darkness. "I need you to understand that I can't help what I am. I can't help my bloodline. But I can fight for you and your allies. I will help keep you safe from your enemies, whatever it takes." He lowered himself slowly to one knee and looked up at me. "I pledge my loyalty to you, Vega Sloane, Chosen Seeker of the Academy for the Blood-Born."

My cheeks went hot with embarrassment.

I wasn't sure whether I should pull him up, slap him, or slap myself.

"I'm *not* the Chosen Seeker," I said. "I keep telling people that. There is no single—"

"You are the one who found the clue inside the shack," he replied. "There may be other Seekers, but you know as well as I do that you *will* find the Lyre. It's your fate. And I want to help you."

177

"But I...*we*...will have to go to Cornwall to find it. What about Liv? What would you even tell her if I took you with me?"

I stumbled over the words as I spoke. I was stupid to protest. He was talking about eternal fealty and I was doing everything I could to point out why it was a bad idea.

The truth was, I needed him. I needed to know I wasn't alone in this quest.

And whether I trusted Lachlan entirely or not—whether I even *liked* him or not—he was the closest thing I had right now to an ally.

"I'll figure out what to tell Liv," he said. "All I care about right now is ensuring that our side—the *right* side—wins this war. I'm here to help you. That's the only thing that matters to me. The only thing I've thought about for years—after...after what happened to your parents. I'll do everything for you that I can. Please believe that."

"Thanks?" I said, too confused to come up with a more appropriate response. "It's just...I'm confused. I wanted to eviscerate you with Murphy, and now it's like we're a two-person Fellowship of the Ring or something." I realized I was looking down into his eyes, and it was freaking me out. "Get up, would you? This is weird, and mildly embarrassing, and I'm really not in the mood to have anyone swear their fealty to me. Let's just be normal for a minute."

He did as I asked and I led him into the house, locking the door behind us.

"Do you want a drink?" I asked. "Water? Juice?"

"Water," he replied as we made our way toward the kitchen.

I poured him a glass and we sat opposite one another at the island. I stared at him for a long moment, mulling over whether I felt I could really trust him after everything I'd learned. He was so strange, so un-Waerg-like. His green eyes were kind, like Callum's.

Why had I never noticed how kind they were?

"I'm sorry," he said.

"About what?"

"About your mother and father. About being there when your mother...well, you know."

"It's all right," I replied, pulling my eyes down to my hands, which were sitting on the countertop. "I overreacted when you told me. The truth is, I was jealous of you. You have no idea what I would have given to have spent one extra minute with her...let alone hear her last words." I sucked in my cheeks before letting out a sigh. "What were they?"

"You...you really want to know?"

I nodded. "I do. I think I need to hear them from you."

He took a swig of water, then said, "She told me to watch over her children. Her Will, she said, and her Vega. She said to tell them both how loved they were, and always would be. That she was sorry to leave them in this way. That she and your father were both sorry, even though your father was already..."

"Dead."

"Yes." Lachlan blew out a hard breath. "She said something strange toward the end. Something that has always stuck with me."

"What was it?"

"She asked me to make sure that when the time came, I helped you. Not your brother. Just you."

"When the time came?" I asked. "What did she mean?"

"I think...I think she meant this, right now. The Lyre. The quest."

"No. That doesn't make any sense. My mother didn't know about any of this. My father didn't even know he was from a long line of Seekers, let alone what a Seeker even was."

"I'm not so sure about that. Somehow, your mother knew how important you were, Vega. Beyond simply being her child. She knew you would do great things."

I took in the words, eating them up with my heart and soul,

repeating them inside my head in her familiar voice. They were music. Rhythmic, warm, soothing.

But they stung, too.

"She knew she was dying," I said. "She knew she'd never see Will or me again. She knew your face was the last one she'd ever see."

"Yes. She did."

"I'm…glad you were there, Lachlan," I murmured. He reached out and took hold of my hand, squeezing for a second before letting go. "Thank you for telling me."

"I'm sorry I didn't stop the others," he said. "I'm sorry I was too weak."

"I can't exactly hold that against you. Being too weak is a feeling I'm very familiar with," I replied, recalling the moment when I'd watched Lumus kill a fellow Seeker. The pain of it. The helplessness I'd felt, knowing I could do nothing to prevent it. "There was nothing you could have done. I know that now."

He leaned back and exhaled, and for a few minutes, neither of us spoke.

"You know Lumus," I finally said.

He nodded, frowning. "Oh, yeah. I know him. When I was younger, Maddox sent me to the Otherwhere to train with the queen's Waerg army. I was supposed to return here as a spy of sorts. A sentinel trained in stealth reconnaissance and, if necessary, murder."

"But you never followed through?"

"Oh, I did. Just not in the way they wanted me to. I used the knowledge and skills I'd acquired to keep an eye on you. I kept a low profile for a long time. It was lonely work, if I'm being honest. I was supposed to keep an eye on you and report back to Maddox if I learned anything important."

"But you didn't," I said.

"I only ever told her enough to keep her satisfied. She didn't know I followed you and Callum to Mabel's Cove. Or about the

Sasser on the beach." He let out an exhalation. "She suspected that I was a traitor, but because she never had evidence of it, she couldn't act on it. Now there's no doubt in her mind."

"Thank you," I said. "For coming to our side. For defending me on the beach, and for the other night. I do know what you've sacrificed."

"It's nothing," he said. "What they did to you and your brother…" Instead of finishing the thought, he shook his head.

"Where's Callum?" he finally asked.

"He…um…"

I'd been perilously close to tears ever since we'd started talking. But that question sent me over the edge.

I looked down again, twisting my fingers together in my lap, my lower lip trembling.

"He's gone," I said. "He had no choice but to leave. I don't know when I'll see him again."

"The Naming. I've heard dragons come of age in a brutal way. I'm sorry."

I nodded, miserable.

"He's strong, Vega. So strong. He'll survive this. Don't worry."

"I know he'll survive. I know how strong he is. But I also know he'll change, and I don't know what that means for him or us."

"Everyone grows. Everyone changes. It's part of life."

"It's not that," I muttered. "I can handle a little evolution just fine."

"So what is it?"

"Nothing. Forget it." I shook my head, wiped a tear from my eye, and looked at him. "Look—on Friday, I have to leave town. I need to find the Lyre of Adair, whether Callum is back or not. You'll really help me?"

"Of course I will. It would be my honor."

DEPARTURE DAY

ON FRIDAY AFTERNOON, I breathed a detoxifying sigh of relief to realize I'd made it through the week without bursting into hysterical tears in the middle of one of my classes.

Well done, Sloane, I muttered to myself as I left Plymouth High at the end of the day. *You made it.*

As I marched down the maze of streets toward my house on Cardyn Lane, I cursed myself for having chosen to walk that morning instead of driving the Rust-Mobile. With Callum gone, I wanted more than ever to begin the search for the Lyre. To leave Fairhaven and gather my Academy friends to my side, if only to fight off my loneliness.

When I got home, I threw some things in a small duffel bag and paced my room, waiting.

I'd never chewed my nails in my life. Not once. But I was doing it now.

At precisely four o'clock, a knock sounded at the front door. I raced down the stairs with my duffel in hand, halted in my tracks, and called out, "Who is it?"

A muffled, deep voice answered.

"It's Lachlan. I'm ready to go."

He and I hadn't spoken much since Wednesday, despite our proximity in English class. We seemed to have come to a silent, devious agreement not to let Liv in on our little—but not so little—secret.

When I opened the front door, I looked up at him, managing a weak smile. "I'm glad you're ready. I just hope I am, too."

"Come on!" he replied cheerfully as he stepped inside. "Aren't you excited? This is what you trained for. I thought it was every Seeker's dream to recover the Relics of Power."

"You're right, it is. But I was hoping to have Callum by my side when I set out to find the Lyre. Not to mention Niala, and Rourke…and maybe Crow…"

"Niala? Rourke? Crow…?"

"Friends," I said. "From the Otherwhere. *Good* friends. Loyal, strong, helpful. They'd know what to do."

"I get it. You don't like being in charge," Lachlan said with a wry grin.

"I didn't say that."

"You didn't have to. It's written all over your face. You got used to having someone else barking orders when you were at the Academy, and you liked it. And now, you have to make decisions, and it bothers you."

"Of course it bothers me!" I snapped. "I don't know what I'm doing. I may have found a couple of clues, but I don't *know* where the Lyre is. I don't even know where to begin."

"You know to begin in Cornwall. And I'd venture to guess you're the *only* Seeker who knows that."

"Maybe," I muttered. "Ugh. I guess there's one good thing about all this."

"What's that?"

"My grandmother. I'll get to see her."

"Great. So what are we waiting for?" Lachlan asked, rubbing his hands together in a conniving, conspiratorial way that actually managed to crack me up. "Let's go find your friends and head to Cornwall."

"Fine, keener." Nervous and excited, I led him to the kitchen, pulled my laptop out of my school bag, opened it, and dug up a series of photos I had stored in a secure folder.

"What are you looking at?" Lachlan asked. "Directions?"

"Photos of the other Seekers' houses," I told him. "We'll go get Meg first."

"Wait. Photos?" Lachlan asked, pressing his hands to the counter. "Why? Wouldn't an address be better?"

"I don't need an address. I just have to be able to picture the location before I can get us there. The street number doesn't matter as much as the mental image. As soon as I can feel our destination in my mind, I can summon a Breach to take us directly there."

Lachlan grinned. "You're more talented than I knew, Vega. I'm impressed."

"Don't be. At least, not yet. I've only opened two Breaches in the last few months, and both were to the Academy. I'm not sure I even remember how to open one to a new location."

"Pfft. I'm sure it's just like riding a bicycle. With your brain."

"That sounds incredibly painful," I chuckled. "Okay, be quiet. I need to focus for a second."

"Oh. So I shouldn't scream at the top of my lungs, then? Or belt out an opera aria?"

"I'd appreciate it if you didn't."

"You're no fun."

As I went back to staring at my computer screen, a shocking realization hit me.

I was actually beginning to enjoy Lachlan's company.

Which was…crazy.

But it was impossible *not* to enjoy him. He was cheeky, goofy, and serious, all at the same time. Exactly what I needed to distract me from Callum's absence and keep me from languishing in self-pity or fear.

When I'd gotten a good look at Meg's house, I closed my eyes and pictured it in my mind's eye—every detail of the trim around the porch, every window, every flower box.

"Take us there," I said softly as I opened my eyes to see that my summoned door had appeared in the middle of the kitchen. It was pure, glossy white, with the cheerful outline of Meg's family home carved into its center.

It was more welcoming than any Breach I'd ever walked through, and for the first time, I was beginning to feel confident in our mission.

I glanced over at Lachlan, who was staring at the door like a bewildered child. He stepped over and traced his finger over the design on its surface, then turned to look at me.

"I've been through portals," he said. "Between here and the Otherwhere, I mean. I've gone back and forth more times than I can count. But I've never seen a Summoner do something like this before. It's...incredible."

"Thanks, I guess," I said, my cheeks heating as they always did when someone said something flattering to me. "It's really nothing."

"Something tells me that *nothing* you do is nothing," he said, his tone earnest. "You're amazing. I mean, you could probably summon all the money in the world and buy a yacht, or a mansion. It would be easy for you to..."

I threw him a semi-glare, and said, "I would never do that. I'm not a thief."

"Of course not. But you could be, if you wanted to. The fact that you don't use your power for selfish means only makes you more impressive. Someone who can vanish into thin air and summon doors and other objects? It seems to me you're cut out for thievery."

"I may be cut out for it, but I choose to use my talents for good. I intend to find the Lyre and bring it to the Academy. No stealing, no foul play. Just an honest day's work. And no—taking the Relics of Power isn't the same thing as stealing, in case that's what you're thinking." I grabbed the duffel bag off the counter and added, "You ready to go?"

"I've never been more ready than anything in my life," he replied with a bow.

"Well, then, let's get on with it."

IT BEGINS

THE WHITE DOOR opened to reveal a tidy stone walkway leading up to Meg's family home.

The lawn was impeccably groomed, and a bed of pretty, late-season mums sat on full display in ceramic planters on either side of the small porch. A series of small, colorful gourds led the way up the steps to the door.

"It looks like everyone's dream house," I said as we proceeded up to the porch. "There's even a white picket fence. It's so...*Meg*."

I rang the doorbell, took a breath, and turned to Lachlan. "I should probably have warned you—I have no idea how any of the other Seekers will react to you. But it probably won't be super-positive. We haven't had the greatest experiences with Waergs."

"Not a big surprise. But maybe I can convince them that we're not all blood-thirsty killing machines."

"You can try. But I can't promise anything."

A second later, the front door swung open, and Meg flew at me, embracing me with a huge bear hug.

"Vega! I wasn't sure you'd come!"

"Wait—you were expecting me?"

She nodded, pulling back and smiling so wide I thought her

face might break. "There was a strange note in one of my text-books. Handwritten by I have no idea who. It just said "*V will come to you Friday. Watch for her.*" It was totally mysterious, but I knew exactly what it meant. I'm just so happy to see you. Come in, come in!"

I followed her inside, with Lachlan right behind me.

The interior of the large suburban home was as welcoming as its exterior, with mounds of comfortable-looking furniture and a massive flat-screen TV hanging over an inviting fireplace.

"My parents have gone away for a few days," Meg told us.

"Well, that's convenient."

"I may have encouraged them to spend a romantic weekend in the countryside." With that, she shot an inquisitive glance at Lachlan. "Sorry, we haven't met. You're not from the Academy."

"No," he replied, extending a hand to shake. "I'm not. My name is Lachlan Sinclair. I…live in Fairhaven. I go to school with Vega."

"Wait—Vega, you're bringing some random high school student along?" Meg asked. "That seems like a really bad idea." She threw Lachlan a smile and added, "No offense."

"None taken."

"Lachlan's not exactly a random a high school student," I replied, choosing my next words carefully. "He's…a friend. He knows the Otherwhere—and Merriwether."

"Oh." With that, she seemed to relax. "You've lived there?" she asked.

He nodded. "Off and on." Turning to me, he added, "We have to tell her, you know. There's no point in hiding it."

"Tell me what?" Meg asked.

"Lachlan is a…Waerg," I said, wincing as I uttered the last word.

Meg recoiled in fear, backing away with a look in her eyes I hadn't seen since we'd been in Lumus's presence. I couldn't say I blamed her for it; if someone had brought a Waerg into my house uninvited, my first instinct would have been to run screaming to the kitchen and grab the sharpest knife I could find.

"I know it comes as a shock," I said softly, positioning myself between them in hopes of reassuring her. "But he's an ally, I promise. He saved my life a few weeks back. It's complicated, but I swear to you, he's not on their side."

"Vega, how can you be sure of that?" Meg asked, her eyes fixed on mine in a moment of desperation. "You know this is exactly the kind of thing they'd do—send a spy to follow us on the hunt…"

I held a hand up to stop her from saying anything more. "You know me better than that. Look into my eyes and ask yourself if I'd bring Lachlan with me through a Breach if I wasn't absolutely sure of what kind of person he was."

She still looked skeptical, so I sighed before adding, "Would it help if I said Merriwether *told* me to bring him?"

"Merriwether did what now? When did you talk to him?"

"I went to see him a few days ago, at the Academy. I was kind of desperate for guidance. Look—can we sit down?"

"I guess so. But one move from the Waerg, and I'm out the door."

"Fair enough."

When Lachlan and I had plopped down on the couch, with Meg across the room, perched on the edge of an armchair, I filled her in on Callum's disappearance. My visit to the Headmaster. What he'd said about Lachlan's pack's role in my parents' deaths.

"Wow," she exhaled when I'd finished. "I'll admit, it sort of makes sense, in a weird, twisty kind of way."

"I know."

Finally, she turned to Lachlan and issued him a friendly smile. "Well, I can't believe I'm saying this, but welcome to our little group. I'm sorry about how I reacted earlier."

"I'm used to it," he replied with a disarming grin. "To be

honest, it's amazing that Vega hasn't murdered me by now. She would have had every right to."

"She's not exactly the murdering type. So, Vega, I take it you've found a clue? That *is* why you're here, right?"

I nodded. "I have—more than one. But before I say anything more, let's grab Olly and Desmond. When we get to Cornwall, I'll explain everything."

"Wait—we're going to *Cornwall*? Like as in England?"

"Yeah. Are you okay with that?"

"Are you kidding? I couldn't be more excited."

"Good. Grab your bag. We're heading out."

WE WENT to Oleana's house just outside New York City next—a beautiful villa-style property that looked like it belonged to a movie star.

As with Meg's house, the place suited Olly perfectly. She was one of the most elegantly beautiful girls I'd ever seen. Not to mention that she was a talented Seeker with the ability to fling ice projectiles at her enemies.

"I've been waiting for you," she told us when she opened the door. She hugged Meg and me before greeting Lachlan with a curious look.

"You're a Waerg," she said calmly after a second.

"You don't seem surprised," he replied.

"I think I lost my capacity to be surprised back at the Academy," she said with a shrug. "Besides, if you're here, Vega must've had a good reason to bring you."

"*Thank* you," I said, shooting Meg a playful glance.

"I feel like I should warn you, though," Olly added, "I'm not sure how Desmond will feel about having you along for the ride. He tends to panic in the presence of Waergs."

"Well," Lachlan said, "I suppose there's only one way to find out."

Once Olly had grabbed the overnight bag she'd already packed, she phoned her father to explain our plan. Meg and I shot each other looks of horror when we overheard her telling him we were going to Cornwall to find a Relic of Power.

"I never told you? My paternal grandfather was a Seeker," she explained when she was off the phone. "So my dad knows what's happening. He says to tell you all *good luck*."

"You don't know how glad I am to hear it," I replied. "Now, let's go get Desmond...then on to our destination."

TO CORNWALL

WHEN WE ARRIVED at Desmond's house in England, we found ourselves surrounded by darkness, except for the pale glow of a flickering streetlight.

"I'd forgotten about the time change," I said as we stepped through the Breach. "It's got to be ten o'clock here by now."

As with the other Seekers, Desmond lived in a very Desmond-like house: a small country cottage with a thatched roof just outside of a small town called Langbourne, which was artfully nestled among rolling green hills.

Desmond was already outside waiting for us as if he, too, had known we were coming. Standing with him were two people I assumed were his parents: a tall, balding man with a well-groomed moustache, and a short, round, red-cheeked woman dressed in a pink sweater, cotton pants, and warm-looking slippers.

"Don't worry—they know," Desmond said when I shot him a confused look. "Mum's mum was a Seeker back in the day—actually, she knew your grandmother at the Academy, Vega."

"Small world," I said, smirking awkwardly at his parents.

"Oh yes it is. Tiny, really. Or rather, a small *two* worlds," his mother said with a smile. "So, you five are off on a new set of adventures, are you?"

"Yes," I replied. "Hopefully they won't be too exciting."

"Come now, I thought a Seeker's job was to look death in the face," she replied with a belly laugh, as if we were talking about nothing more than a quick trip to the county fair to go on some rickety-looking roller coaster or other. "I'm sure you'll meet your share of enemies. These things always go sideways, don't they?" She tousled Desmond's brown hair and added, "See that this one doesn't get into too much mischief. He's been stir-crazy these last few months. I think he's itching to put a sword in someone's neck."

"Mum!" Desmond hissed. "I'm not going to stab anyone."

"Oh, you never know. You may yet, Mr. Stabbykins."

"You're *so* embarrassing. Look—we need to go."

When he'd said good-bye to his parents and sent them back inside, Desmond turned back to us.

"Now, who's this, then?" he asked, gawking at Lachlan. "I didn't want to ask until we were alone, in case my parents got extra-nosy. But you're new, aren't you?"

"He's a Waerg," I replied. *May as well cut to the chase.*

As if living out the future his mother had just described, Desmond reached for the hilt of a sheathed short sword that was attached to his backpack.

I held up my hand. "It's okay, Des. He's a friend. A loyal one."

"Tell that to my nausea," Desmond retorted.

I couldn't exactly blame him for his hostility. I had no doubt that he was currently reliving the memory of the small army of Waergs who'd wanted to tear us to pieces the night we went looking for the Sword of Viviane.

"Fine," he finally huffed, relaxing a little as he removed the sheathed weapon from his pack and fastened it to his waist. "But you're going to have to fill me in on why on earth you've brought the enemy with you."

"As I said, he's not the enemy. But don't worry. I'll tell you everything."

With a nod of acceptance, Desmond reached a hand out, and Lachlan took it.

"Lachlan," he said. "Nice to meet you, Desmond."

"I'd like to say the same, but the last time I met one of you, it didn't go so well for either of us. The good news is, I know how to take over your mind if you try anything. Don't think I'll hesitate to make you punch yourself in the face."

"Looking forward to it."

When everyone was ready, I summoned a final door. This one was decorated with an embossed pattern of rocky shores and white-capped waves. Pulling the dragon key from its chain around my neck, I unlocked it.

Seconds later, we were all standing outside my Nana's small cottage on the coast of Cornwall, with the door fizzling away behind us like mist. Wind whipped around us, bringing with it the unmistakable scent of the ocean.

"Oh my gosh, I'll bet it's so beautiful here in daylight," Olly said, inhaling the air as she turned to look out toward the horizon silhouetted against the purplish night sky. "I can see why she chose to live here. It feels like another world."

"I'm sure she'd rather live in the Otherwhere," I said quietly before wandering over to knock on the door. I knew how much my Nana had loved Merriwether, and how painful it had been for both of them to have to go their separate ways when they were young.

I could only imagine that some part of her hoped one day to be reunited with him...though I couldn't imagine how it could ever happen.

After a few seconds, my grandmother opened the door, and immediately the aroma of fresh baking wafted out from her kitchen in welcoming waves, as if she'd known we were coming.

"Vega dear!" she exclaimed, pulling me in for a giant hug. "So glad to see you got here before the Revelation Ball. I see you've brought the whole gang with you. Well, most of it, anyway."

"Revelation Ball?" I asked.

"Come in, and I'll tell you all about it. Come, come, all of you. We'll have some tea and scones."

We followed her inside and seated ourselves at her large kitchen table, where teacups and saucers were already laid out for each of us, including Lachlan.

"Four Seekers and a Waerg," Nana said. "What an odd party you are."

"So you know," I said. "About Lachlan, I mean."

"I've had my share of encounters with Waergs," she said. "I'm sure you haven't forgotten that there was a time when those at the Academy thought I'd run off with one." With that, she winked at Lachlan. "Some of them are very handsome creatures, after all."

I felt my cheeks heat up when Lachlan grinned in response. He *was* handsome; there was no denying that.

But for some reason, I didn't like being reminded of the fact.

"Now," Nana said when we were all seated, "You say you haven't heard of the Revelation Ball."

"No," Desmond replied, stuffing a scone into his mouth, "never."

"I read about something called 'Arthur's Feast' when I found the clues," I said. "Is that what you're talking about?"

"The feast itself is a huge party, attended by hundreds. But on the same day, the Revelation Ball opens its doors to a very exclusive crowd called the *Selected*."

"Selected?" asked Meg. "That sounds ominous."

"How does it work?" I asked. "Are invitations sent out or something?"

"No. Quite the opposite. Those who find themselves at the

ball very often do so by accident. Some say they're lured, as if they have little to no choice. Of course, the very powerful—wizards and the like—sometimes find their way there of their own volition."

"You said lured?"

"When the time comes, you'll understand," Nana assured me. "I can't say how you'll get there—only that I can guarantee you will. When I was a Seeker, I was brought to Barcelona to attend. Only the ball didn't exactly take place in the city itself." She smiled then, and her eyes seemed to glaze over as she relived a distant memory. "It was so, so beautiful."

After taking a sip of her tea, she continued.

"There's lovely music, dancing. Unrecognizable faces—that's by design, of course. No one wants anyone to know who they are. It's one of the few events that is attended both by the Other-where's residents and our own."

"But you say it takes place here? In our world?" I asked.

"No, I didn't say that. Not exactly. Only that the entrance sometimes is."

"Excuse me, Miss...Missus...*Nana*," Desmond said, shifting uneasily in his chair. "Do you know where, exactly, the entrance will be?"

"I'm so sorry, Desmond. I don't. I can only tell you that it will show itself when the time comes."

I buried my face in my hands and groaned. "Why is it that I have no control over anything that happens in my life?" I asked. "My entire existence involves waiting for things to happen. I'm so tired of it."

I felt a hand on my back, gentle, yet firm. For a second, I forgot that Callum wasn't with me. I twisted around to see Lachlan's eyes fixed on my own.

"It's all right. We'll find it...together. We've come this far, haven't we?"

"I can't believe I'm saying this, but I like the Waerg's attitude," Desmond said.

"Nana," I blurted out, "the clues I found mentioned something about a place called Arthur's Lair. Do you have any idea where that could be?"

She contemplated the question for a moment. "Now, that's interesting. It could be any number of locations, I suppose. There's all manner of ruins and caves around these parts. Places they say he used to inhabit. Secret caverns and underground labyrinths and the like. But you might want to start by heading to Pevethy. It's a small town, not too far from here. Pretty little place, even if its residents are a little odd. There's an inn there where you should spend the night. Of course I'd invite you all to stay here, but as you can see, this cottage is barely big enough for one aging woman."

"It's fine," I said with a smile. "We can go to Pevethy."

"While you're there, ask about the sights nearby. Ask about that accident that happened some years ago—when that poor man did himself in looking for the Lyre."

"Why do you suppose that man was looking in Cornwall?" I asked. "Did *you* find the Lyre here?"

My grandmother's eyes took on a strange glow for a second as she looked my way.

It's just a flash of light, a reflection, I thought.

Though it felt like more than that.

"I am no longer a Seeker," she said, "at least, not an active one. When I found the Lyre, it was very, very far from here. So I can't possibly tell you why the man was hunting in Cornwall. This is your quest, Vega—yours and your friends'. There will be more clues coming your way, of course. But you need to let them find you. I can't help you, I'm afraid."

I bit my lip and nodded.

"You wish it could be easier," Nana said, taking my hand across the table. "That the Relics would simply *reveal* themselves to you, instead of making life so difficult. I know the feeling all too well."

"Well, yeah," Meg said. "That would be nice."

"You lot know better than anyone that Relics of Power are difficult to come by. Even if you know their precise location, their recovery is a battle. You will find that your enemies are on the hunt as well—no matter how careful you've been to stay quiet. I'm afraid the next few days will prove difficult beyond your imagining—but be warned: the enemies you encounter may not be the ones you're expecting."

She sounded tired, as though the very thought of what we were about to go through was enough to sap her of half her energy.

"We'll find a way," I said, trying to sound encouraging. "You managed on your own. I'm sure the five of us together can find it. Plus, there's Callum…"

I blurted out his name before I could stop myself. Everyone turned to me, waiting to hear the next words out of my mouth.

"I mean, it's possible that he'll show up. If he's able."

"Where *is* he?" Oleana asked. "I wasn't sure if I should ask. Are you two…"

I bit my cheek and looked at Lachlan, who frowned and lowered his head.

"He's going through something difficult," I replied. "But it will end soon, and I'm hoping he'll find us. He knows I—*we*—need him."

"I'm sure he'll find his way, my dear," Nana said. "I'm sorry to say it, but this search will be more dangerous by far than mine was. There are powerful agents—other than the queen—at work in the Otherwhere. I will give you one piece of advice, however."

"What's that?"

"Don't be afraid to split up, when the time comes. You may find it's the only way."

A sudden wind whipped around the cottage, screaming through the eaves, and Desmond jumped.

"Bloody hell!" he shouted with a laugh. "Sounded like an army of ghosts was attacking."

"Not ghosts," Nana replied, turning toward the window. "Trust me, love—what's out there is far worse than ghosts."

THE INN AT PEVETHY

WHEN WE'D HEADED BACK OUTSIDE to make our way to Pevethy, Nana pulled me aside while the others looked out at the sea and chatted about the coming weekend.

"Vega dear," she said under her breath, "I need to warn you about something."

"Something other than the fact that the enemy is everywhere and we're probably all going to die, you mean?"

"I'm afraid so."

"Well, crap."

Nana half-smiled, but it faded quickly.

"When I had to choose to leave your grandfather—Merri-wether—behind in the Otherwhere, it was the hardest choice I ever had to make. But I did it because he was a wizard, and I was a Seeker, and that's what we do. We devote ourselves to a cause that's bigger than ourselves. We do it with honor. Because we know our actions will save lives—even if they destroy our own."

"It seems so wrong to have to give up the love of your life like that."

"I suppose I always knew I would lose him. I just didn't know how it would happen…until it happened."

I swallowed hard, pushing down the feeling of nausea that had begun to creep in. I'd always known I'd lose Callum, too. We'd fought it, pushed it back, even defeated our dubiously intertwined fate once or twice—but there were only so many times we could win.

"Why are you telling me this, Nana?"

"If you find your way to the Lyre," she said, "you, too, may be offered a choice—or someone close to you will be. I can only hope the pain you'll suffer won't be as acute as it was for me. Now go. Find the Lyre, as I know you will. And watch your back. The world can be a cruel, merciless place."

I nodded, gave her a squeeze, and turned to the others.

"Let's go," I said. "The sooner we start, the sooner we'll be finished."

ON NANA'S ADVICE, I opened a Breach to Pevethy, a tiny town made up of about twelve houses, two of which surrounded a two-story white stone inn with a black slate roof.

The door I summoned brought us to the edge of a large field just outside the town, and we hiked through the darkness toward the inn, excited and nervous.

I found my eyes darting around as we advanced, searching for any sign of enemies. But aside from the occasional car rattling down the road, throwing up dust and stones in its wake, everything was silent.

I was relieved when the inn's front door shut behind us. The building's main floor, it seemed, was mostly taken up with the local pub—a wood-paneled, warm and welcoming space that looked like something out of an artist's rendering of what a typical English pub *should* look like.

The smell of fish and chips met our noses as we walked into

the foyer, and I quickly realized I hadn't had a single bite of my Nana's baking.

"I'm starving," Desmond said. "Let's come down and get some food when we've had a look at our rooms."

"Totally," Meg replied. "I can't possibly resist whatever it is that I'm smelling."

A short woman with a friendly demeanor slipped out of a side room to make her way to the front desk. "You lot checking in, then?" she asked with a smile. "All of ya?"

"Yes. Three rooms, please," I replied.

"Three?" Desmond asked. "You three girls must be sharing, because there's no way I'm staying in a room with the Wae—I mean Lachlan."

"I'm getting my own room," I said. "You and Lachlan can share. Olly and Meg will share. I'm paying for everything, so I get to be alone. Those are the rules."

Desmond said, "You're joking, right? For a laugh?"

I shook my head.

"Well, if I you find me tucked into my bed with no head in the morning," he muttered, "avenge my death, would you?"

"I'll certainly do that for you, Des," I said with a chuckle, turning back to our hostess. "Can you tell me if the pub will still be open for a little while? We're sort of famished."

"Oh, yes. Until two A.M. Lots of late eaters around here."

"Great, thanks."

When she'd handed me three keys, we headed up to the second floor to check out our temporary living quarters.

Meg and Olly were in a corner room that overlooked distant rolling fields, as well as what looked like the outline of an old barn. Lachlan and Desmond's room looked out onto the road, and mine was next to theirs, with a door in between.

"See, Des?" I asked from the doorway, my arms crossed. "I can get to you in mere seconds if I hear you screaming while Lachlan tears your spleen out."

"Reassuring."

Lachlan shot me a sideways glance, and I couldn't tell if he was amused or irritated at the ongoing joke at his expense.

"I'll meet you downstairs in a minute," I told them. "Just need to get settled in."

When I was alone, I sat down on the edge of the bed and pressed my face into my hands.

I was meant to be a talented Seeker. A strong, independent young woman who was setting out on a journey that could help save not one, but two worlds. I should have been proud, not to mention thrilled, to be on this particular adventure.

But instead, I felt alone and miserable, and I missed Callum more with every second that passed.

"Pathetic," I muttered as I rose to my feet and stared out the window at the road below. "I'm absolutely pathetic."

A knock sounded at the door, and I trudged over to open it.

"May I come in?" Lachlan asked, his tone exceedingly polite.

I nodded and stepped back. He slipped into my room, closing the door behind him.

"Just wanted to make sure you're all right. You looked a little…I don't know, distraught."

"I'll be better in the morning. But thanks for asking. I'm just feeling a little homesick or something."

"Or something," he repeated, sitting down on the edge of my bed. "You miss him, huh?"

"I do. Are you missing Liv?"

He looked at me, then down at his hands, which were tangled in his lap. "No, I don't," he replied, pulling his face up again. "I hope that doesn't sound awful. It's not that I don't care about her. It's just that this—what we're doing here and now—is the important thing, you know? I can't think about Liv or anyone back in Fairhaven until we've finished what we started."

"Wow," I said, half admiringly and half accusatory. "I wish I could compartmentalize like that."

"Truth be told, it's easier for me because I'm not in love with Liv," Lachlan said. "It's different."

I slid over to sit down next to him. "What exactly *are* you two, anyway? I mean, are you dating? Just friends? Taking it slow?"

"We're…good friends," he said. "She wants more. I know that. The truth is…" He looked away, his bright green eyes moving to the window for a moment. "The truth is, I first introduced myself to her to get close to you. I'm sure that comes as no surprise."

"No. I suspected as much. So did Callum."

"In the end, though, she turned out to be pretty great. She's nice to be around. The truth is, even if girls don't entirely know what I am—even if they think they want me—they usually push me away in the end. It's like an instinct. But Liv doesn't judge me. She doesn't recoil in terror when she sees me."

"Oh, I don't know," I replied with a snicker. "I'd say Liv judges you. I mean positively. You know, for being gorgeous."

I bit my lip then, kicking myself for offering up the compliment.

Stupid. Stupid. Stupid. You're not supposed to tell your best friend's love interest he's good-looking, idiot.

"I mean, *she* thinks you are," I added quickly.

I could feel Lachlan's gaze burning into me, but I avoided his eyes. So strange that I'd gone from despising him a few days ago to regarding him as a friend, let alone that I found myself tossing him uncharacteristic compliments.

The world had turned upside down.

"Anyhow, we should head downstairs to eat," I said. "I have no doubt Desmond is shoving an entire beer-battered fish down his throat right about now."

"Yes, of course," Lachlan said, rising to his feet. I finally summoned the courage to look up at him, only to see that he was still staring at me.

"What?" I said.

"You need to make sure you get some sleep tonight."

"Why do you say that?"

"Just a feeling. An instinct, rather. Come on." He held out his hand, and to my own surprise, I took it and let him pull me to my feet.

"We need to get downstairs," I said, yanking my hand free and heading for the door. "The others will be waiting."

THE PUB

WHEN WE GOT down to the pub, the others were sitting around a corner table. As predicted, Desmond had already gotten his hands on a serving of extremely tasty-looking fish and chips.

"How are things going down here?" I asked.

Meg and Olly looked at one another, then started laughing hysterically.

"What?" I asked with an awkward smile.

"Des is being a drama llama," Meg said, rolling her eyes and wiping away a tear.

"Am not," Desmond retorted with a scowl. "I just don't want to die. Is that really asking so much?"

"As if you're going to die."

I rolled my eyes and said, "Enough. He's not going to hurt you, Desmond. You know I wouldn't bring someone with us if I thought for a second that he might sink his giant wolf-teeth into your face."

"But you can't know for sure," he muttered. "What if he tries to eat me in my sleep?"

"Well, *I'm* not sleeping with you, so you don't have much of a choice, unless you want to pay for your own room."

"Don't worry," Lachlan told him. "I *probably* won't devour you. Unless I'm hungry, that is. So you'd be wise to share your food with me."

Desmond pushed his plate over, reluctantly offering it up. "Fine," he said. "But if I die, I'm going to lord it over all of you forever."

"Looking forward to meeting your bitter, petty ghost," Olly said before cracking up again.

I chuckled. "How about this, Des—if you're even close to worried, just call me. You have a cell phone, yeah? I'll be right next door."

He pulled out his phone and handed it over, and I typed my number in. "No matter what, I'll be close. And remember, I can get to you in seconds. I can help you fight off the murderous old Waerg. Then again, you can mind-control him, which is probably way more effective than anything I could possibly do."

"Mind-control only works if one's victim has a mind," Desmond scowled.

"Hey!" Lachlan said.

"I'm joking," Desmond replied with a proud grin. "Still, I might have to try it out on you. I haven't exactly had a lot of chances to use my talents at home. Except on my younger brother. Made him tidy my room four times so far, and once, I even managed to get him to do my homework—badly. Still, it was very satisfying."

"That's pure evil!" I laughed.

"I suppose it is. But so is he."

WHEN THE OTHERS were ready to head up to bed, I told them to go on without me.

"I—uh—I'm going to ask the bartender if he knows anything about Arthur's Lair."

"Good luck," Desmond said, throwing Lachlan a quick, hostile look. "I'm going to bed."

I said good-night to the others and had just begun to head toward the bar when a voice behind me said, "I'll stay with you."

I turned around to protest, but Lachlan was already approaching, a determined look on his face. "Desmond doesn't want me up there anyhow. Something tells me he'll be sleeping with the hilt of his sword clenched in his hand."

"Great. He'll probably slice his nose off in the night. Don't mind him. He's just...I don't know...paranoid. It's not like he doesn't have good reason to be."

We sat down at the bar, elbows resting on its polished wood surface. "Tell me something—have you ever met a Grell?" Lachlan asked.

"A Grell? Why?"

"Just answer the question. Please."

I looked over at the bartender, who was in the midst of chatting with a half-drunk customer.

"Yeah," I said quietly. "In the Otherwhere. His name was Kohrin. I liked him a lot. He was...special."

"So your assumption, after meeting him, is probably that Grells are kind, friendly souls. Helpful, protective. All the good things. Right?"

"Judging from him, I suppose that's right. But I don't know any others."

"And until me, you've only met a few nasty Waergs who wanted to hurt you."

"I...well, yes."

"So it never occurred to you that there could be one or more out there who aren't in the employ of the Usurper Queen, or influenced by some other horrible person."

"I suppose not."

Lachlan sat back. "Point made," he said.

"I get it. You're telling me I'm prejudiced. I'm racist against wolf-people, and so are my friends."

"Of course you are. We all are. We're fed messages all our lives about how this or that group of people—or animals—is vicious and will probably hurt us. We're taught to live in constant fear of others. I suppose that's what's called human nature: an instinct to protect one's self from those we don't understand. It's what's driving Desmond to despise me, without ever having so much as had a conversation with me."

I was about to reply when the bartender took a few steps in our direction.

"Can I get you two anything?" he asked.

"A diet cola for me," I replied.

"Water, please," Lachlan said.

"Wait—actually," I added before the man had a chance to leave, "I have a question for you."

"Ah," he breathed, leaning forward and pressing his elbows against the bar. "I love questions."

I grinned apologetically and said, "I'm wondering if you know the area around here well?"

"I've lived here all my life, so I'd say yeah," he laughed as he reached for a glass and cracked a bottle of soda open. "I take it you have some questions about the local sights?"

"I'm—I mean *we're*—just wondering if you know where a place called Arthur's Lair might be."

The man stopped pouring my drink for a moment and froze. A second later, he finished and set the glass down in front of me.

"Arthur's Lair," he said. "There's a name I haven't heard in some time."

"So you do know it."

He shook his head. "Nah. Only the name. It's a mystery, to be honest. There was a man...quite a few years ago now...drove off a cliff near here, looking for the same. No one is quite sure why he was looking around here. King Arthur does have his share of history around these lands, of course, but Arthur's Lair? Not a place that actually exists, at least, not that anyone knows of. Most of the remnants from his days are long gone."

"But there is some Arthurian stuff around here, right?" asked Lachlan.

"Sure. There are the standing stones at Terrach, and the cave near Land's End. And of course there's Tintagel."

"That's Arthur's castle, right?" I asked.

"What's left of it, yeah. It's really just a pile of rubble at this point. Nothing much to look at. Certainly nothing I would call a Lair."

I took a sip of my drink.

"May I ask what exactly you're hoping to find?" the man asked.

It was a perfectly innocent question, but I had no answer to give him. Nothing that wouldn't give us away, anyhow.

I shrugged. "It's just….something my grandmother mentioned once. She lives here in Cornwall. I was kind of interested in the mythology and such, and I was curious to know if Arthur's Lair is a real place."

"Ah, I see." The bartender leaned forward again, pressing his forearms against the bar and looking me in the eye. I could see now that his eyes were the oddest color—a sort of gun-metal gray, surrounded by thick black lashes to match his black hair. His skin was olive-toned, and he looked a little like the pirates I'd pictured when I was a child listening to stories and legends. "You know, there are many people around these parts who say we're all of us descended from Arthur and them. His knights, his servants. Even the magic users."

"Magic users?"

"You know. Wizards and such."

"Like Merlin the Magician, you mean?" I asked, trying my best to sound incredulous.

The man nodded. "Merlin, yes. They say he used to keep birds

—birds with keen eyes, who would fly over the land and spy on his enemies."

"Spy-birds," Lachlan replied with a laugh. "That's quite a stretch, isn't it?"

I looked over at him and smiled. For someone who wasn't keen on taking part in Plymouth High's school play, he was actually quite gifted at acting.

"True. It's a little ridiculous," I said, trying to muster a skeptical look, but all too aware that there were many in the Otherwhere, including the Usurper Queen and our allies the Grells, who used birds and other creatures for the purposes of espionage.

"You don't believe me," the bartender replied.

"I don't know what to believe right now," I said. "I just wish I knew where this place was that we're trying to find."

"You should start with Penzance. It's where the man—the one who had the accident—was said to be from. Who knows? Maybe someone there will know what you need to look for. Besides, they have some great restaurants. You'll want breakfast in the morning, and we don't serve it here. I'm assuming you have a car to get you there?"

"I...we...we'll manage. Thank you."

"You're welcome."

With one final, appraising glance, the bartender made his way back to his drunken customer and struck up a new conversation.

"Something's a little off about that guy," Lachlan said, leaning in close. "I'm not sure I trust him."

I shrugged. "Sounds to me like you're prejudiced."

"Ha. Touché."

When we'd both finished our drinks, I left a couple of pounds on the counter and headed toward the foyer, turning to look back when I got to the base of the stairs.

The bartender was watching me, his strange eyes intent on my own.

TO PENZANCE

WHEN WE GOT to my door, I turned to Lachlan.

"Well," I said, grasping my room key in my hand, "thanks for keeping me company."

"No problem," he replied. "I guess it's time for me to go torment Desmond with my presence, huh?"

"Guess so," I said with a smile. "Good night."

"Night, Vega."

I opened my door and stepped inside, pushing out a long breath as I closed it behind me.

Without turning the light on, I headed for the window and peered out into the darkness. All I could see was the vague outline of the asphalt road outside. Not a headlight in sight.

I changed into an old t-shirt and a pair of shorts, headed into the bathroom with my toiletries bag, and brushed my teeth, surprised at how tired I was. It was still early, at least according to Fairhaven time. But it seemed the day's events and my summoning of a multitude of doors had wiped me out.

As I stepped out of the bathroom, I froze in place as the unmistakable, distant howl of a wolf met my ears.

"Just a Cornish wolf," I told myself. "Which I'm just going to convince myself is a thing that definitely exists."

I crawled under the covers, pulled them over my head, and slept like the dead.

FIRST THING IN THE MORNING, I knocked on Desmond and Lachlan's door before proceeding to Olly and Meg's room.

"Get up!" I called out quietly. "We're going to Penzance."

"Penzance?" Meg asked groggily when she opened the door. "Why?"

"It's our only lead," I said. "We can get some breakfast there, then maybe do some exploring."

"Did I hear something about breakfast?" Desmond called out from the confines of his room. He pulled his door open to peek out.

"Hey, you're not dead!" Meg said.

"Not yet," he replied.

At that, Lachlan eased around him into the hallway and grinned. "There's still time," he said, which was enough to convince Desmond to leap back in and slam the door.

"I'll be in my room," I said with a laugh. "Don't take too long or I'll leave without you."

A few minutes later, the five of us were gathered together next to my bed, and I was staring at a photo of a restaurant called The Wharf House, situated along one of Penzance's main streets.

I summoned a Breach, which brought us to an alleyway about a block from the restaurant itself. Our small group made our way down its length, grateful when we arrived to find the place open and serving breakfast.

"I don't know why my appetite is so massive," Desmond said as he eyed the menu. "Seeking is hungry business, I suppose."

"You haven't even *done* anything," said Oleana with a yawn. "None of us has, except Vega."

"What did you find out about this place?" Meg asked. "Why are we here?"

"I'm not sure," I replied. "I mean, the bartender mentioned we should come here because of a news story from ages ago, but I'm not really sure we're looking for anything in particular. That's the problem with being a Seeker, though—you never quite know why you're doing anything until the answer stares you right in the face."

"You think we'll find answers in this particular place?" Desmond asked, looking around at the paintings and photographs of varying colors and sizes hanging along the walls.

"Who knows?" I replied with a shrug.

We ordered our food and ate it while carrying on a casual conversation about school, our social lives, and what had happened since we'd last seen each other at the Academy. It seemed Oleana had a new boyfriend back home in New York. Meg had a crush on a certain someone, and Desmond had no interest in anything other than finishing his studies and fleeing his parents.

It felt amazingly normal to talk like this. To just exist as regular human beings for once, talking about trivial things that didn't involve certain pain or death.

By the time we'd finished eating, I'd half forgotten why we were even there.

"How about if we go explore the town?" I asked when we'd settled up with our waiter.

"Sounds good," Desmond said. "But first, I just want to look at a photo by the next table."

We rose to our feet, lazily reaching for whatever bags we'd brought with us. As I put my jacket on, Meg, Olly, and Desmond got into a conversation about the photo he was staring at. It was a black and white shot of an old boat, and it seemed Desmond insisted it was a schooner. For some reason, Meg decided to dispute the fact.

"A schooner has two masts!" she insisted. "That's a sloop."

"It's a schooner! My granddad used to work on one. So I think I would know."

As I watched them bicker, Lachlan reached for my arm.

"Vega," he whispered. "Don't move a muscle."

"Hmm?" I asked. I looked at him, only to find his eyes fixed on something at the far end of the restaurant. I began to turn around, but he shook his head.

"What is it?" I asked.

"Three people just walked in."

"It's a restaurant, Lachlan. People have to walk in so they can eat."

"Well, these three particular customers are from the Otherwhere. And they're not allies of ours."

Very slowly, I turned to see three figures—two women and a man—seating themselves at a table right next to the restaurant's entrance. One of the women sat with her back to us, and all I could discern about her was that she had short, dark hair. The other had long red hair, pulled back at the sides, and high cheekbones. Something about her was beautiful and terrifying at once, and she brimmed with a hostile energy that made my skin crawl.

The man was tall and strong-looking, his arms as thick as most tree trunks. He, too, was frightening.

"Who are they?" I asked, pulling my chin down and pretending to rifle through my bag.

"The man is a member of the Kilairn Pack. You've met one of his kind before."

"His *kind*?"

"He's a mercenary. An assassin."

"A Sasser?" I whispered.

He nodded. "He's not the one who followed you that night on the beach. That one was more feral. But they were probably hired by the same person. The woman—the redhead—is a shifter from the Hinterlands, in the North-West of the Otherwhere. Another mercenary. Do you remember when you and I first met—when I warned you that the Usurper Queen isn't the only one in the Otherwhere with an interest in the Relics of Power?"

"Of course…my grandmother hinted at the same thing, but…"

"When I was still training with Lumus's forces, I heard a rumor that a wizard was contemplating defecting from his Order. That he was gaining strength and looking to build a force of rogue killers—ones who could move in the dark, take out their enemies quietly and quickly. I never expected them to show up in this world, though. Not until that night on the beach."

"Merriwether did mention a betrayal. You think it might be the same wizard?"

Lachlan nodded. "I'm afraid so."

"But who's the third member of their little party?" I turned to look again, only to see that the other woman—the one with the dark, short hair—was speaking to a waiter. For the first time, I saw her profile.

"Oh no."

"You know her?" Lachlan whispered as I jerked my head back around to conceal my face.

I nodded. "She—"

"What's going on?" asked Desmond, who'd given up on his debate about boats. "We ready to leave?"

"We're going out the back," I hissed. "Come on!"

"What? Why?"

"Shh! Not so loud. Just follow me."

As I led them down the back hall toward the bathrooms and the exit, Lachlan caught up to me.

"Who's the girl?" he asked.

I ground my jaw. "A Seeker," I said.

"*Who's* a Seeker?" Meg asked from behind us.

"Shh!"

I shoved the back door open and we emerged into a narrow alley. When the door had closed, I turned to face Lachlan.

"I haven't seen her in ages. She was at the Academy with us. She's a Pathic—someone who can control objects with her mind. She's very good at it."

"Wait—" Desmond shrieked. "*Freya* is here?"

"I'm confused," Lachlan said. "Why would a Seeker from the Academy be here with the enemy?"

"She *may* have been expelled after she tried to kill me with a very big rock during a training session."

"She would've succeeded, too, if you hadn't turned into a Shadow!" Desmond said cheerfully before shooting me a look of remorse. "Sorry. But the whole thing was kind of cool."

"It wasn't cool. I would've died if I hadn't disappeared."

"But you did, and everyone freaked out. She basically turned you into a superstar."

"Oh, okay. Should I go back in and thank her? Maybe she'd be kind enough to fling forks into all our eyes, for old time's sake."

"Now, now, children," Meg said with a stifled laugh. "Behave yourselves, or next thing we know, one of us will be impaled with a flying halibut."

"Guys, this is serious," Olly said. "They could get to the Lyre before we do."

"Merriwether did warn me about this a while ago," I replied. "That the other side might be recruiting help from disgruntled Seekers who weren't at the Academy for whatever reason. If she led them here…"

"It means they've found a clue, too," Meg said.

"We could follow them!" Desmond shot out. "Maybe they'll lead us right to the Lyre."

I shook my head. "No. We can't risk them getting to it first. It would be too dangerous."

They nodded.

"Okay. Follow me."

I turned to lead them down the alley away from the restaurant, only to be assaulted by a whiff of rotting fish and garbage.

"Man, that's foul!" Desmond said, cupping his hand over his nose.

"Let's just get back to the nearest street, and I'll open a Breach to Pevethy," I replied, hastily making my way down the alley. "The sooner, the better."

Lachlan was right behind me, with the others following. We'd only made it about twenty feet when I heard the squeaking of hinges and looked back to see Freya and her two companions coming through the restaurant's back door.

Freya stopped, crossing her arms over her chest and smiling, even as the other two kept going. "Hello, Vega," she called out. "So nice to see you. I'm honestly surprised you haven't disappeared on me again."

With that, she looked to a pile of metal garbage cans to our right, and slowly, their lids rose into the air, hovering as if they were slowly absorbing a flood of potential energy and waiting to slam into us.

The two assassins had already begun to walk toward us, chins down, eyes laser-focused on my own.

Freya may have been here for the Lyre, but as an added bonus, she seemed to be hoping to revisit attempted murder.

"Summon something, Vega! Block their way!"

It was Olly who yelled, jarring me out of my terror.

"Good idea," I replied, annoyed with myself for forgetting that my summoning skill was useful for more than just doors. I closed my eyes and pictured a brick wall rising between our stalkers and us, stretching as high and wide as the alley itself.

"Well done," Desmond said.

I opened my eyes and exhaled to see the strong-looking barrier protecting us from the two hostile agents. The trash can lids, which were on our side of the conjured wall, fell to the ground with a clatter.

We were safe for now.

Or so I thought.

After a few seconds, the wall began to fade and crumble, its conjured bricks tumbling to the ground one by one before vanishing.

"What's happening?" Meg asked. "Why's it falling apart?"

"I'm not sure," I said, panicking. "It felt so solid in my mind."

"They're coming through," Lachlan warned. "Come on! We need to get out of here!"

ESCAPE

"WE HAVE to get to the street!" I yelled as we sprinted full-speed down the narrow passageway. "They won't dare attack us with witnesses around!"

But what I'd thought was an opening at the far end of the alley turned out to be a tall chain-link gate. And to make matters worse, it was locked tight with a massive chain.

All but slamming into each other, we pulled to a stop just before we reached it.

I spun around to see what had become an all too familiar sight: two wolves skulking toward us, heads low, teeth bared. One red, one gray.

Freya was walking behind them, a series of objects rising from the ground to swirl around her in a menacing twister of potentially deadly projectiles.

We were trapped.

Next to me, a low, rumbling growl reverberated through the air. I didn't need to look to know that Lachlan, too, had shifted into his wolf form.

Fearless, he stepped forward to position himself protectively in front of us.

"He really *is* an ally?" Desmond said. "I must admit, I'm shocked."

"You really didn't believe me?" I retorted.

"No! I spent the night holding my sword against my chest, convinced I'd be called Mr. Stabbykins for the rest of my life!"

"Doesn't matter," said Oleana. "Ally or not, Lachlan won't be able to fight them both off. We're going to have to defend ourselves."

"Maybe not," I replied. "I can get us out of here. I can open a Breach."

But when I closed my eyes, I couldn't summon an image of the inn where we'd all spent the previous night. Someone—or something—was creating a block inside my mind.

"Vega?" Meg said, her voice shaking.

"Give me a second!" I insisted.

I tried to recall my house in Fairhaven. The Academy's library. Anywhere but here.

But all I could see in my mind's eye was a haze of mist, tumbling over rolling green hills.

It was like my powers were still active, still inside me...but some force was trying to draw my mind to a place I'd never been.

"I'm trying to get into the Waergs' heads," Desmond said. "But I can't. It's like I'm being held back—like someone's put a hand up and stopped me dead in my tracks."

"Whatever you're doing, Vega, you're going to have to do it now!" Olly said through gritted teeth. "I can't seem to use my powers either. There's something more powerful than just Waergs and Freya at work here."

"I'm trying!" I snapped. "I can't focus on any place I know. I'm only seeing...somewhere else."

I could hear Lachlan and the two enemy wolves snarling at each other, squaring off in preparation for the inevitably bloody battle to come.

If we didn't get away, Lachlan would end up wounded, at the very least. Or possibly killed.

I couldn't let that happen. I wouldn't.

"So let's go to the place you don't know!" Desmond cried. "Just get us *somewhere*!"

"I will. I see it now."

A pair of symmetrical doors sketched themselves in my head, turning more and more solid as I welcomed them to my mind's eye.

They were exquisite. Tall, narrow, rounded at the top. Carved of perfect, unmarred wood.

On one of them was a single rose, its stem coated in jagged thorns.

On the other was a half-mask, the kind one might wear to a costume party.

"What the hell…?" I said out loud as I opened my eyes to see the doors fully materialized in front of us. They were so tall and wide that they blocked off the alley entirely.

As I opened my mouth to speak, one of the Waergs smashed into the doors from the other side, sending them shaking as if they'd been clobbered by a battering ram.

Lachlan shifted back into human form, and along with the others, stood behind me, breathing heavily. I wondered if they could hear my heart pounding in my chest.

"Where does it lead?" Meg asked.

"I have no idea," I replied. "But we're about to find out."

"It could be a trap!" Desmond protested.

"Yes," I said, pulling the dragon key off its chain. "It could be."

THE REVELATION BALL

I DIDN'T KNOW what I was expecting when I pushed the doors open.

The rolling green hills I'd seen in my imagination, perhaps.

A rose garden.

A courtyard.

But what we walked into was none of those things.

It was a bright space, devoid of walls or ceiling—yet there was no sky. Visible air particles danced around us, reflecting light from some unknown source.

It was like we'd wandered into a world of light, with no discernible features. And yet it was one of the most beautiful things I'd ever seen.

"Do you hear that?" Oleana asked after a few seconds.

"What?" said Desmond.

Meg shushed him, and we stood silently, listening.

Then it met my ears.

Music.

Lilting, soothing, distant. Otherworldly and captivating.

I never wanted it to end.

"Where's it coming from?" Oleana asked from somewhere beside me. I turned her way, only to realize that she and the others looked…completely different.

She and Meg were dressed in floor-length gowns that looked like something out of a period movie, only they weren't from any period in history I knew.

Meg's was light blue, and Oleana's was a yellow so pale as to be almost white. The dresses were fitted perfectly to their bodies, yet looked light as air, their layers of fabric flowing as though an imperceptible breeze was teasing them. Their hair was pulled up over their heads in a series of intricate twists that would have made Marie Antoinette envious.

On their faces, they wore elegant masks of what looked like crepe paper, concealing all but their mouths and chins.

"What's going on? Why's everyone dressed up?" Desmond asked. I spun around to see that he was looking me up and down. He and Lachlan were both dressed in suits of deep red and dark teal, respectively. The jackets were tailored and long, and their pants were tucked into dark leather lace-up boots.

Their faces, like the girls', were mostly concealed behind masks. Desmond's was red and black, and Lachlan's was teal, to match his elegant suit.

"I…I don't know," I replied slowly, reaching up to feel that I, too, was wearing a mask that seemed to float a millimeter or so away from my skin, so that I barely registered its presence.

I could feel something tight around my ribcage, like someone had bandaged me into my clothing. Yet I didn't feel constrained.

"A corset," I gasped. "How the hell am I wearing a corset?"

I looked down to see that my dress was a deep, reflective gold —the same gold as Callum's dragon. The skirt was full and elegant, and as I reached for it, it moved like liquid through my fingers, flowing to the floor in luxurious, silken waves.

"What is this place?" Meg asked, spinning around. As she did so, the scene in front of us began to reveal itself in more vivid detail, and the music we'd heard upon our arrival grew louder and clearer.

"It looks like...a ballroom," Lachlan said from behind his mask. "Look!"

The air particles that had surrounded us since our arrival began to disperse and I started to make out shapes all around us. Couples dancing in swirling perfection over a checkered white and black marble floor. A full orchestra in the distance, and beyond it, a series of floor-to-ceiling windows that stood open to the outdoors, where I could make out sea and sky, but no other details.

The room was enormous, and spanning its length on each side was a series of marble columns that must have been at least thirty feet tall and five feet across.

"Have we traveled through time or something?" Desmond asked. "This is seriously insane."

"I don't know what time period had clothes like these," Oleana said. "I mean, corsets were a thing a couple of hundred years ago, but combat boots? And these dresses are beautiful, but they're not quite...right. This fabric doesn't exist. If it did, every fashion designer in our world would use it."

I looked down again, pulling my skirt up enough to see that I was wearing boots similar to the ones the boys were wearing. Leather and worn, lacing halfway up my calves.

Hardly appropriate for a masked ball.

But as I peered around at the rest of the partygoers, I could see that everyone wore similar footwear.

"Unbelievable," I said. "This is so weird."

"Vega, do you know where we are?" asked Desmond. "I mean, you brought us here. You must have done it for a reason."

"This must be what my grandmother was talking about. What did she call it—the Revelation Ball?"

"So, this is where we're supposed to find out about the Lyre?"

"Not sure. All I know is we're here, and as far as I can tell, Freya and her feral little friends aren't. That's a good start. So let's split up and see what we can find out. If there are enemies here, it's probably best not to draw their attention to a whole group of us."

The others agreed, and we each moved off in different directions. Desmond headed toward a table at the far end of the room that was covered in mouth-watering pastries. Lachlan roamed the perimeter. Meg and Oleana each made their way to a different corner to survey the partygoers.

Meanwhile, I started walking across the dance floor toward a familiar-looking figure. He was tall and dressed in purple, with a shock of gray hair and bushy eyebrows arching over his mask.

Merriwether?

I smiled as I approached, prepared to speak his name as soon as I was within earshot.

The man looked my way, but didn't appear to recognize me.

It's the clothes, I thought. *He's used to seeing me in my Academy gear.*

I pulled the mask up just enough to reveal my eyes, and was about to speak his name when he shook his head.

"Don't do that," the man said. "One must never, ever reveal one's identity at the Revelation Ball."

I pulled the mask down again, my smile fading quickly.

That…wasn't Merriwether's voice.

"But I wanted to…"

"I know what you wanted to do. But I am not who you clearly think I am."

I nodded. "Sorry," I said. "I just thought…"

"You thought I was someone else. Yes, yes, that happens a lot. We wizards tend to look alike. You thought I was Gerund? Or perhaps Laurelius?"

"Merriwether," I said with a disappointed sigh.

"Merriwether?" the man looked shocked.

Or at least as shocked as he could with a mask hiding half his face.

"He's not here. No. Not here. He cannot attend the ball."

"Why not?"

"Because he's a Guardian. A Keeper of Relics."

"I see. But what *is* this place? Where are we? I don't even know how we got here."

"Dear child, we are in the Ballroom of the Renaissance. You've been invited to the Unveiling."

"Unveiling? Of what?"

He turned to nod in the direction of a long wooden table that stretched out in the middle of the ballroom floor. I had no idea why I hadn't noticed it earlier; it must have been forty feet long, and I was *sure* I'd walked right across the middle of the dance floor.

At the table's center was an unidentifiable form, covered up with a long piece of silver fabric that cascaded all the way down to the floor.

"You will see," he said. "In just a little while. Now, if you'll excuse me, I need to find a friend of mine. See to it that you don't reveal yourself to anyone else, Vega Sloane."

"You know my name?" I asked.

But he was already halfway across the floor, headed toward another familiar-looking figure. Like everyone else, his companion wore a mask over his face. But it wasn't large enough to conceal a set of curling horns on top of his head. His legs bent backwards like the rear legs of a goat and tapered to an elegant set of hooves.

For a moment, my heart jumped in my chest. *Kohrin*, I thought. But I shook my head. No. This place was confusing me, deceiving my mind.

227

Making me see the people I *wanted* to see.

It wasn't altogether unpleasant, I had to admit.

Turning around, I hunted for my companions, who were scattered around the room now, each speaking to a different stranger.

Satisfied that we might be making some progress, I made my way quietly toward the table at the room's center.

As I approached, I reached out to touch the silver fabric that covered whatever top secret object was about to be revealed to the guests. But my fingers bent backwards as I thrust my hand out, slamming into some invisible barrier.

"Ow!" I cried out.

"You can't touch it." I turned to my right to see a young woman in a jet-black dress, a set of bright green eyes staring out at me from behind her mask. "No one can, except for the *Revelator* and *Revelatrice*."

I nearly jumped with joy.

There was no mistaking such a close friend.

Niala?

Yet she didn't take a step toward me, and I couldn't see Rourke anywhere.

I told myself my mind was playing tricks on me again. But when I nodded and began to walk away, she spoke again, this time under her breath.

"Vega. It's me."

I turned back to her, forcing myself to act casual for the sake of anyone who might be watching. But the truth was, I'd never wanted to hug anyone so badly in my life.

"Oh my God, I'm so happy you're here. Where's Rourke?"

"In my pocket," she whispered, nodding down toward her right hip. I looked down to see the tiny head of a black mouse poking out, its shining eyes staring up at me.

"How did you get here?" I asked, pulling up next to her and pretending to stare at the table.

"Merriwether sent me."

"But I thought he…"

"He can't come himself, but he can send his ambassadors. Those are the rules of Guardians. So I'm here for you. And for whatever might come after the Unveiling."

"The thing under the silver fabric," I said. "Is it…"

"Come with me," she replied, gently touching my arm. "We shouldn't stand here. We'll draw too many looks."

I followed her to a far corner, and we tucked ourselves into the shadows. "You already know what's under there," she said, nodding back to the table.

"If it's so close—if it's about to be revealed—can't we just take it?" I asked. "Or are they going to make us fight for it like a bunch of teenagers in a Dystopian novel?"

Niala laughed and shook her head. "The Unveiling is just what it claims to be: a revelation of the Lyre of Adair. The ball takes place once every fifty years. But the Lyre is not something you can just reach out and touch. Think of it as a projection of the real thing. A mere representation."

"Like a hologram?"

"Exactly."

"So what's the point? Why tease us with it?"

"Don't worry about the Lyre. Don't let its beauty mess with your mind. It's what the Revelator and Revelatrice will *say* that matters. So you and the others need to listen very closely, and decipher their meaning. It's very important."

"The final clue?" I asked. "That's it, isn't it? They're going to tell us where to look."

"Yes. And whoever figures out the meaning of their words will be the first to find the Lyre. I have to warn you—you have some competition here."

Niala turned and looked to the far side of the room, where a young woman in a green dress was standing alone. Her hair was short and dark, and she perused the room as if she was systematically contemplating which guest to kill first.

"She's here," I gasped when I recognized Freya. "She must have found a way through a portal of her own…unless my mind is screwing with me again."

"It's her," Niala said. "Don't ask me how she got here, but she did. To be honest, though, I'd be more worried about some of the *other* guests."

"What do you mean?"

"I mean the assassins."

She nodded toward a figure twenty or so feet from me. Dressed entirely in white, his shoulders were slightly hunched, his lips curled into what looked like a permanent scowl. Another man was walking toward us from the other side of the dance floor, dressed in a suit of mottled gray velvet.

In a far corner stood a woman with red hair, twisted into a thick braid on top of her head.

I tensed, fighting back the urge to reach out and squeeze Niala's hand.

"They won't hurt us here," Niala assured me. "They've been sent by someone to watch you and any other Seekers. It's the only way their employer can gain access to the location of the Lyre, if Freya should fail." With that, Niala turned her head and a slow smile crawled its way over her lips. "Of course, not *everyone* at this ball is hostile."

I followed her eyes to the far end of the room. Silhouetted against one of the broad windows was a young man—tall, with light brown hair.

I could have sworn he was staring right at me.

He was dressed in a dark gray suit, his lapels shimmering with hints of gold. An outfit that I would have found gaudy in my world. But somehow, it suited this strange place.

And it fit the man perfectly.

"Who is that?" I asked.

From the corner of my eye, I could once again see Rourke poking his small head out of Niala's pocket. He made a chirping sound as if telling me to go find out.

"All right, then," I said, beginning the walk. "I'll ask him myself."

A DANCE

THE YOUNG MAN stopped several feet from me, the slightest hint of a smile curling his lips. His chin was coated in a short layer of stubble, his hands clenched at his sides. I could see now that his lapels weren't simply speckled with gold decorations.

They were made of what looked like dragon scale.

It can't be, I thought. *My mind is screwing with me.*

A pair of bright blue eyes stared out at me from behind the young man's black and gold mask, beckoning me closer.

Winding my way between spinning couples, I slipped toward him until we stood only a few feet apart. Pulling my chin up, I studied his mouth, his eyes, assessing and wondering.

A girl didn't forget the first mouth she'd ever kissed passionately.

Nor did she forget eyes that made her melt each time they focused on her own.

"You're not real," I said. "You can't be."

"Oh, but I am," he replied. "Very, very real. More real than I've ever been, in fact."

He reached out, offering me his hand.

I took it.

In a swirl of motion, we began to dance to the music, pivoting and twirling between the ball's attendees in perfect synchronicity...despite the fact that I'd never learned to dance.

"How are you..." I said. "I mean, what happened? The Naming?"

"The Naming happened," he replied softly, leaning in close, his breath stroking my neck. "It was...difficult. But I promised you I'd find my way back to you, and I have. That's the important thing."

"It is," I said. "I'm shocked to see you—but in the best possible way. Are you...okay?"

He nodded. "I made it. I survived."

"You survived." I pulled back and looked into his eyes again, searching for any trace of the beast that had tormented him for weeks. But all I could see was the purest, most relaxing and inviting Mediterranean blue. Calm had finally settled into Callum's irises.

I could only hope it would last.

"Don't worry," he said. "I'm here now. I'm here for good, and I will not leave your side again. Whatever it takes—even if I have to leave the Otherwhere forever—I'll always find my way back to you, Vega."

"Promise?"

"I promise."

"I know I can't possibly hold you to that," I said, my voice threatening to break, "but I have to admit, I love hearing it."

I wanted to sob with joy. To bury my face in his chest and unleash the flow of bittersweet tears that was desperate to come.

But I couldn't. To do so would be to draw attention to us. And that didn't seem like a great idea.

"What was it like?" I asked, swallowing my emotions. "The process, I mean. The Naming itself."

Callum thought for a minute before replying. "It was like... like I was outside my own body, watching him from somewhere in the distance. He was in flight, moving toward a source of light that glowed like the sun. I was blinded—I shielded my eyes—but then I heard it. A voice, saying his name inside my mind. But it was different for him. The dragon felt it in his bones, in his blood. It changed him. Consumed him. It was as if that one word told him who and what he truly is. For the first time, he was whole. *I* felt whole, too…though I can't quite find the words to explain how or why." He let out a chuckle. "It's so strange. A name for a human is just that—a title, a moniker. Something we use to identify ourselves, to distinguish ourselves from others. But for a dragon…it's a revelation of one's soul."

I smiled. It sounded like the dragon was at peace at last. Which meant Callum might finally find some peace of his own.

"And you can't tell me his name," I whispered. "Because of the unwritten rule."

Callum stopped dancing. We stood perfectly still, the music still floating through the air around us, and stared at each other.

"I made my dragon a promise," Callum said. "And I don't intend to break it."

"So don't," I said with a smile. "Never break it."

He took my hands and pulled me into a frenetic waltz. It may have been minutes, or even hours, of blissful movement before we finally stopped. I had no idea where the rest of my party was, and for a while, at least, I didn't care.

All that mattered was that I had Callum back.

THE UNVEILING

AFTER A TIME, we were interrupted by what sounded like the clinking of silverware against crystal glasses. It came from all directions, delicate and aggressive at once. The music ceased, as did the dancing, and the crowd backed away from the long table in the ballroom's center.

Callum and I moved to one side, tucking ourselves behind members of the crowd in an effort to avoid being seen.

Some distance away, I spotted what looked like Freya and her assassin bodyguard, conspiring quietly, their eyes fixed on the covered object on the table.

One by one, Meg, Oleana, Desmond, Niala, and Lachlan approached us, tucking themselves into the crowd that surrounded us.

"Find anything out?" I asked the others in a whisper.

"It was so weird—I thought I saw my mother," Meg said. "So I went to talk to her. I couldn't understand why she was here... wherever here even *is*. But it turned out to be someone completely different. Still, I could have sworn..."

"I thought I saw my father," Olly said.

"Aunt," added Lachlan.

"Cousin," said Desmond.

It seemed everyone had deceived themselves into thinking they were seeing members of their close families. I avoided mentioning the wizard I'd mistaken for Merriwether. This was not the place to divulge the full truth about our relationship.

"Seems I'm the only one who actually ran into people I know," I said, gesturing to Niala and Callum. The others rejoiced quietly when they saw them.

All, that was, except Lachlan, whose jaw set in something approaching a grimace.

"What's wrong?" I asked him, but he simply shook his head and told me it was nothing.

"Shh!" Meg hissed as the crowd parted and two people made their way toward the table.

A woman, tall and slim and dressed in silver, glided along the floor next to a man dressed in cobalt blue. The elegantly dressed couple stopped next to the veiled object, smiled at one another, and turned to face the crowd.

"Something's about to happen!" Desmond said.

"Ya think?" Meg retorted with a snicker, drawing a sneer from Desmond.

"That's the Revelator and Revelatrice," Niala told us. "It's said that he's a wizard and she's a witch, though I'm not entirely sure."

"Every fifty years," the man called out, "at the Revelation Ball, comes the ceremony known as the Unveiling. Some of you know by now what is concealed behind me. You know its value. You are the ones who wish to claim it. The Seekers."

Members of the audience nodded in agreement, whispering excitedly among themselves.

"How many Seekers can possibly be here?" Meg asked.

"Too many," I whispered.

"Watch closely," the woman called out before she and her male companion each grabbed hold of a corner of the fabric. They pulled slowly, gently, until the silver veil slipped off, and the hidden object was revealed.

A collective gasp of admiration and shock arose from the crowd, followed by a round of applause.

I couldn't say I blamed them for being excited. The Lyre of Adair was stunning.

It hovered just above the table, and as we watched, the instrument began to rotate in slow circles as if proudly displaying itself for all to see.

Its body, and even its strings, were made of the purest gleaming gold. Its outline curved around in what looked like a delicate upside-down arch, slightly pointed at the bottom. Near the crossbar where the strings where attached, the instrument's frame curved outward to form the delicate heads of two familiar-looking golden dragons.

Shocked, I touched Callum's arm and he nodded as if to say, "I see it."

"Some of you gathered here today," the woman told the crowd, "wish to claim the Lyre. To harness its power and give it a home for the next half-century. And naturally, no one can blame you—the Lyre is a powerful relic indeed, laced with ancient magic and the power to protect entire realms. You would be foolish *not* to want to possess it."

"I claim it!" a voice called out over the quiet hum of the crowd.

Out of the corner of my eye, a sudden flash of movement startled me. Someone was pushing through the crowd, shoving people out of the way as he moved like a person possessed.

When he got to the table he stopped, his chest rising and falling in rapid pulses.

It was a boy about my age. I didn't recognize him. He was thin, average height, with brown eyes and bushy, dark hair.

He wore a mask, but as the man and woman stared at him, he ripped it off to reveal a young, innocent face. His eyes were locked on the Lyre, and something about his expression made me think of a Waerg just before it goes in for a kill.

"Who is that?" Oleana asked from behind me.

"I know him," Niala whispered. "He's a Seeker, rejected some time ago by Merriwether when he applied to attend the Academy."

"Why was he rejected?"

"He was found to have ties to the Usurper Queen. The Headmaster thought he was too great a risk. And now, he seems to be working for the other side."

"He's the queen's envoy?" I asked. "But if he gets the Lyre…"

"Don't worry. I have a feeling he's not going to succeed. Just watch."

The boy glared first at the man in blue, then at the woman.

"Give it to me," he said, reaching a hand out like a petulant child demanding a toy. "I claim it in the name of Queen Isla of the Otherwhere."

He looked determined, but his voice was strained, the tendons in his neck jutting out like he was fighting some force inside him.

"You know we cannot simply hand it to you, young Marek," the woman told the boy, her voice smooth and musical. "If you try to take it in this place, you will suffer for it. I'm sure the queen told you as much."

The boy shook his head. "I'm a Seeker. I asked for it first. It's my *right*."

The man in blue gestured to the room. "There are other Seekers here. Would it be their right, too, if they'd asked before you?"

The boy looked around, an expression of pure rage crinkling his features. "They don't want it badly enough. They haven't even *tried* to take it!"

"So go ahead. Try. But don't say we didn't warn you." The man gestured to the Lyre, backing away, a grimace on his face.

The boy ran at the table with a look of madness in his eyes. I glanced around at my party, wondering if any of them felt the same insatiable urge to reach out and grab the golden instrument.

I watched Meg clench her fists. Olly was pressing herself tight to Desmond, as if looking for some sort of support. Desmond, meanwhile, was grinding his jaw, his eyes narrowed.

They looked like they were fighting back inner demons who'd awoken to savage their insides.

And as I turned to the Lyre once again, I began to understand what it was that they were feeling.

Its gold sparkled and danced in the light, and a soft, sweet music began to waft from its strings, calling to me—tempting me. Asking me to claim it for myself.

Fighting off the strange desire, I edged closer to Callum, who put a hand on my back as if to say *Don't worry, I've got you.*

The boy, meanwhile, was now standing over the instrument, chewing on his lips. He looked like he wanted to take a bite of it. Like a hungry dog struggling to be obedient, he stared, his eyes going wide.

He shot one quick look toward the man and woman, then, with one final leap, he reached for the Lyre of Adair.

But the second his hands touched the Relic, both he and the instrument vanished.

Shocked, I pulled my eyes to the Revelator and Revelatrice. Both turned calmly to the crowd and smiled.

"Now you see," the woman said, "what happens when a Seeker does not follow the rules. Oh, don't despair—he's not dead. He has simply returned to his home, and been stripped of his abilities. He will no longer be able to enter magical realms. He is no longer a Seeker."

"What?" Desmond hissed. "They can *do* that to us?"

"Something tells me they aren't the ones who did it, Des," I replied in a whisper.

"But we—"

I put my finger to my lips, and we continued to watch.

The man in cobalt turned to the woman, who spoke loudly and clearly.

"*At low tide on the morrow shall the Seeker find the Face of Stone.*"

"*Two will enter Arthur's Lair,*" the man said. "*But the Lyre will go to one alone.*"

The woman continued. "There will be pain. And, in the end, there will be a great loss. Those who have sought the Lyre in the past remember. It has cost some their lives. Still others have lost their very souls. The Lyre does not give itself easily. It asks a price. Do not seek it if you're not willing to pay dearly."

I could have sworn she looked straight at me then, her eyes locking on mine as if she knew something I didn't *want* to know.

I shook my head. It didn't matter.

Nana had survived the search. She'd found the Lyre and brought it back to the Academy.

Which meant I could, too.

I threw Callum a sideways glance, but he didn't turn my way. Instead, he simply reached out and squeezed my hand before pulling away again.

"I don't like the sound of this at all," Meg said. "Is it too late to back out? There are other Relics of Power…maybe we don't need the Lyre."

"No," I said. "We have to find it. We can't let Freya get her hands on it and bring it to whatever awful person she's working for. We can't afford to lose this fight."

"Didn't the woman say it's cost some people a soul?" Olly asked. "Or their lives? I mean, is *anything* really worth that?

"It's just poetic language," Desmond said with a bat of his hand. "They're trying to freak us out before the big event, I imagine. Don't pay it any mind."

It was nice to see Desmond calm for once.

But something told me he was dead wrong.

"Go now," the woman said to the crowd, and one by one,

people began to disintegrate into the ether. "Seekers, rest tonight, for tomorrow will destroy one of you."

As I watched, the table, the room we were standing in, the woman, and the man all disappeared, until the only people left were my friends and me, standing in my room at the inn in Pevethy.

THE HUNT BEGINS

I LOOKED out the window to see that night had fallen on the eve of our final push to find the Lyre of Adair. The wind whistled through the inn's rafters. Across the road, I could see trees bending sideways, unable to fight back the gusts.

Everyone was once again dressed in their normal clothing: jeans, sweaters, sneakers.

I introduced Niala and Rourke to Lachlan, whose strange mood seemed to have improved. "Good to meet you," he told her, despite the fact that Rourke, now in his tabby cat form, hissed at him more than once.

Callum was wearing a red jacket with a white crest emblazoned on its sleeve, a white shirt, and a pair of dark jeans, as well as a pair of dark brown leather shoes. I had no idea where he'd acquired the clothing, but it didn't matter. Nothing mattered except for the fact that he was back in my world, and in one piece.

And as handsome as he'd been in his extraordinary ensemble at the ball, now he looked even more incredible.

"How long were we at that ball?" Olly asked. "It must've been hours and hours."

"Not sure," I said. "I don't think time passed the same way there as it does here."

"Well, what do we do now?" Desmond asked. "Where do we start? I'm so confused."

"The woman said something about a face," I replied. "A stone face. And the low tide. We have to find out what that means."

"Maybe it was a clock face?" Oleana asked.

"I guess," said Meg. "Or a carving—like a statue?"

"We need to ask someone," Callum offered. "One of the people who works here. If there's a face around the area, they'll be able to tell us."

I smiled, happy to see him take charge as he'd done so often at the Academy. I hadn't hugged him or kissed him yet, and I was aching to.

Unfortunately, any show of affection would have to wait until we were alone.

"It's entirely possible that anyone working in this place is on the enemy's side," Niala said. "They could lead us on a wild goose chase."

"Still," Callum said, scratching at his stubble, "it's worth asking, isn't it?"

"Fair enough," I replied. "Let's head downstairs and see what we can find out."

Without another word, our group proceeded to the welcoming pub and grabbed the large corner table—a massive slab of wood scarred by what looked like centuries of vicious assaults by the bottoms of pewter beer steins.

"Time for some more fish," Desmond said, rubbing his hands together as if he'd entirely forgotten what we were trying to accomplish.

"Really, Des?" Olly asked, laughing. "Food is what's on your mind?"

"Can't think on an empty stomach," he protested.

"He raises a good point," Meg said. "Let's grab something to eat while we strategize."

"You guys order something," I said. "I'm going to go talk to the bartender."

"I'm coming with you," Callum told me, and I nodded gratefully. Danger had begun to close in on us, and the thought of his protective presence was reassuring, to say the least.

We wandered over to the bar and had just seated ourselves on its comfortable wooden stools when the same bartender who'd served Lachlan and me the previous evening came over and grinned a warm greeting.

"What can I get you both?" he asked.

"Ginger ale," I replied.

"Same," Callum said. "Please."

When he handed us our drinks, the bartender leaned on his elbows and all but whispered, "Right. What can I *really* get you?"

"It's that obvious that we need help?" I asked.

"Let's just say you always have the look about you of someone who's either lost something important or is *about* to lose something. Either way, you have questions. So fire away. Do your worst."

"We're...looking for a face."

The bartender scratched his head and chuckled. "Well, I have one. There's a nose on it and everything. But I suspect that's not what you mean."

"No," Callum said. "This one's made of stone."

"I see. Do you mind telling me why you want a stone face?"

"I...we...can't," I said. "But I think it has something to do with low tide, if that makes any sense?"

"Low tide on which day?" the bartender asked.

"Does that matter?"

"It does," he replied, pulling himself upright and wiping the bar with a towel that had been draped over his shoulder. "It changes, you see. From day to day. Legend has it the tides shift to keep intruders at bay."

"Tomorrow," I said, wincing. It was more information than I wanted to convey. But it wasn't like I had a choice.

"First low tide will be around 6:30 in the morning," he said. "Much of the coastline is exposed at that hour. Bits that you would never otherwise see. Easiest to get a look at the shore if you're out on the water, if you catch my meaning."

He spoke the last few words slowly, looking straight at Callum as if hoping to convey some kind of tacit understanding.

All of a sudden, he was reminding me of Mrs. Robbins, our hostess at the Bed and Breakfast in Mabel's Cove. Did he—*could* he—know what Callum was?

"Thank you," Callum said. "That's very helpful."

We'd just begun to walk back to the table with our drinks in hand when the bartender called out, "Wait one second!"

Tense, we turned around to look at him, and he summoned us back with a flick of his hand.

"I just remembered something you might want to see," he said quietly, his eyes shifting from left to right like he was looking for eavesdroppers. "Near the ruins of Tintagel, on the coast. Be sure to get there well before the sun is up. There are sometimes shadows lurking in that place. Protectors, they say. They watch for strangers—for anyone who might be seeking the way."

"The way?" Callum asked.

"Into the tunnels."

"Okay, you've lost me," I said. "We don't know anything about tunnels."

The bartender sighed and draped the towel over his shoulder once again. "Tintagel is a ruin of a very ancient castle. But before it was there—before it was Tintagel—they say it was the site of King Arthur's home."

"I've heard that before," I said. "Some people think it's where the original Camelot was—the castle with the round table and all the knights."

"Right. Well, there's a legend that tells the story of Arthur's ability to move between worlds—from ours to the Isle of Avalon, and others, as well. Secret places. They say he found a tunnel he could pass through…a dark place, filled with dark memories. But on the other side, they say, was a dream."

"I see," Callum said, though he sounded skeptical.

"I know it sounds insane. I'm just telling you what the stories say."

"Do you know where the entrance to this tunnel is?" I asked.

The bartender shook his head. "No idea. But I'd be willing to bet if you find this face of yours, you'll know what to do."

I nodded. "Thank you again," I said. "You don't know how helpful you've been."

"I have some idea, actually." He pushed his left sleeve up and rolled his fist over to reveal the inside of his forearm, which was tattooed with a long, elegant sword.

"Oh my God…" I gasped.

I was staring at a perfect depiction of the Sword of Viviane. The sigil of the Academy.

"Hush, now," he replied, nodding toward a couple of men at the far end of the bar. "We wouldn't want to scare the locals."

"No, you're right." I threw him a grateful smile, grabbed Callum's hand, and walked back to the table.

"So? Did you two find out anything useful?" Meg asked as we approached.

"Yes," I said. "I think we did."

THE EVE OF THE QUEST

"TINTAGEL?" Desmond asked when I told the group what the bartender had said. "But I've been there. It's just ruins and rocks. There's nothing to see."

I pushed out an exasperated breath. "I still think we should take his advice."

"You know, I did hear once..." Desmond added. "Something about ancient, secret places underneath the castle."

"Underneath?" Meg asked. "But I've seen photos. The ruins of Tintagel are right on the coast. If there are places under the castle, wouldn't they be underwater?"

Desmond shook his head. "Not quite. There was a verse I learned as a child, once when my parents were telling me about the old legends. Let's see now, how did it go? *When the sea is low shall the searcher find the entrance to the lair...*"

"Wait. The lair..." I gasped. "*Arthur's* Lair?"

"I suppose," he replied with a shrug.

"Why didn't you tell me about this?" I asked. "This verse of yours is exactly what we need!"

"I didn't think of it until just now, honestly," Desmond said. "I haven't heard it since I was maybe six."

"Well, I'm glad you remembered," I said, pushing myself to my feet. "You know, I think I want some air. I feel like it's hard to breathe in here."

"Would you like me to come?" Callum asked.

I shook my head. "No, no. Stay here and catch up with everyone. I just feel like I need to clear my head for a second."

I headed out the pub's front door to hear the wind howling in the eaves. The trees that lined the road outside were bent and bowed, creaking as they threatened to snap in half.

Inhaling, I muttered, "Why do I still feel like something's missing from the equation? What don't we know?"

"Hey," said a gentle voice from behind me. "You all right?"

When I felt a soft, warm touch to my calf, I smiled.

"Better, now that you and Rourke are by my side," I said, turning to Niala. Rourke was in his Husky form now, his tongue lolling out in a happy pant. "You two have been very quiet. What are your thoughts on all this?"

"I don't know what to think," she admitted. "I can only say how I feel."

"And?"

"Apprehensive," she said. "Unsteady. Like something is coming that none of us could possibly have foreseen. I can't help thinking what happened the last time we went looking for a Relic of Power." She looked up at the rumbling, dark clouds that passed over the moon in diaphanous tidal waves. "A new storm is coming our way, and there's no telling which way the winds will shift."

"That's not exactly reassuring," I moaned.

"Vega. You have a small army of supporters around you. Four of you are Seekers. The other three of us—four, if you include Rourke as a separate entity—are skilled fighters. Hell, you even have a Waerg at your disposal. You have as good a chance as anyone at success."

"You're talking like I'm the leader here," I said. "I don't want to lead. I only want to make sure we bring the Lyre to the Academy."

"You don't want to lead, yet you're the one who literally brought us all to this place. It seems you're always the one who guides us. Like it or not, that seems to be your particular destiny."

"Ugh. Don't use that word," I said. "Destiny, fate. It all implies that I have no say in my own future. My own decisions. I have to admit, there's a part of me that wants to take Callum back to Fairhaven with me, hide under the covers, and hope someone else finds the relics. It's not like I'm the only Seeker."

"But you and I both know you won't run away. It's not who you are. Come on, Vega—you love a challenge, whether you want to admit it or not. Otherwise you would have fled this life ages ago."

I was trying to think of a retort when I heard footsteps in the gravel behind us.

I turned around to see Callum, his eyes fixed on Niala and me. "Everything all right?"

"All good," Niala replied. "Rourke and I are just heading in. We'll need to get some rest tonight if we're to get up before dawn."

"You don't have a room!" I said with the sudden realization. "Are you..."

"I'll be fine," she replied. "It seems our odd group of misfits are the only ones staying at this inn. And I have money, thanks to a certain generous wizard."

"Okay, good. We'll see you in the morning, then?"

"Bright and early."

With a nod, Niala slipped back into the inn, and Callum stepped over to stand behind me, wrapping his arms around my waist.

"What do you suppose our chances are?" I asked.

"Of finding the Lyre? I'd say they're pretty good."

"And our chances of surviving to see the end of the day tomorrow?"

He didn't reply.

"Callum."

"You're Vega Sloane," he said. "You're incredible. If anyone can find a way to live through this, it's you."

A shudder overtook my body, and I had no doubt Callum felt it. "This Lyre of Adair," I said, "...it feels dangerous in a way I can't quite describe. Like a trap waiting to be sprung."

"Your grandmother acquired the Lyre, did she not?"

"She did."

"And she survived, did she not?"

"She did."

"So I think you should have faith."

"Like I said, I can't describe it. I can't explain why, but I feel scared that we're about to lose something important."

"What say you let me panic, and you get some rest, Seeker?" Callum said, kissing the top of my head before nuzzling my neck. "Let's go to bed. And tomorrow morning, when the storm has passed, you'll see there was never anything to worry about."

"You've become very optimistic since your dragon got a name," I said with a snicker.

"I *feel* very optimistic. He and I are closer now than we ever were. We have a mutual trust—an understanding. He knows who I am now, just as I know who he is. So yeah—I'm optimistic. Whatever happens, I feel like I understand my purpose now."

"Good," I said, turning to face him. "Do me a favor and tell him to let you get a good night's sleep, would you? We're going to need his services first thing in the morning."

"Of course."

Callum kissed me then. A long, lingering kiss that sent the blood rushing through my veins in waves of silent pleasure. I could all but feel his joy as a new life took hold and filled him with excitement for what the future might hold.

I only wished I could share his bliss.

But instead, a new, insidious dread had begun gnawing at my mind.

I had no idea what the morning would bring. But I couldn't shake the feeling that tomorrow would be the worst day of my life.

"Come on," I said, taking his hand. "Let's go to bed."

SHADOWS IN THE RUINS

I COULDN'T SLEEP.

But every time I tried to pinpoint exactly what I was worried about, my fears evaded me, slithering away to jab at another part of my mind.

And so it went, for hours on end.

Callum, on the other hand, purred the night away in a deep sleep, and listening to his breathing soothed and calmed me enough that I finally drifted off around two A.M.

Which meant I slept less than two hours in total.

At precisely four o'clock in the morning, our groggy group congregated in Desmond and Lachlan's room.

It was still pitch-dark out, but the previous night's wind had died down somewhat, leaving an eerie quiet in its place.

"So, what's the plan?" Oleana asked with a yawn and a stretch.

"I'll summon a Breach," I told her. "We'll head to Tintagel. Callum and I will fly out over the ocean to get a good look at the coastline. We need to find this face, or whatever it is, as soon as possible, even if it's still dark out." I turned to Callum. "You're okay with being my transportation?"

"Absolutely."

"Good. All right, the rest of you need to keep watch on land for anyone coming. Stay together. Every living creature you see is a potential threat. Do you hear me?"

The three Seekers, Niala, and Lachlan nodded in unison.

"Once Callum and I figure out where we need to go, we'll gather everyone together and proceed to our destination. If all goes well, it will be a quick process."

"There's just one problem," Meg said.

"What?"

"The woman at the ball—the Revelatrice—said *Two shall enter.* Not seven. I don't think we can all go into this underground chamber, or tunnel, or whatever it is."

"She raises a good point," Niala said, fixing her eyes on mine. "You and Callum should be the ones to go in."

"Us?" I asked. "Why us?"

"He's the most powerful of us. You're the one who found the clues. It's the only reasonable solution."

"Sounds easy enough," Desmond said. "So why does everyone seem so bloody tense?"

He was right. Most of the faces staring back at me suddenly looked vaguely terrified, like everyone had suffered through a communal nightmare.

I was fairly certain my own face looked equally aghast.

"We don't know what we're up against," I told him. "I think we all remember what the woman said at the ball about loss."

"Yeah, yeah, something about losing our souls," he said, rubbing his hands together. "I'm not worried. I just want to go to the bloody ruins, get this elusive Lyre, and get home for some of my mum's buttered scones."

"With any luck, that's exactly what will happen," I told him. "But we need to start the search right now. Does anyone have a problem with the plan?"

When a chorus of head shakes met me, I said, "Great."

I summoned a door to the ruins of Tintagel. On its dappled

wooden surface was the image of what looked like a chunky medieval castle, banners waving from atop its stubby towers.

"Those aren't ruins," Lachlan said. "Are you sure this will take us to the right place?"

"They're not ruins, because that's Camelot!" Desmond said with delight. "I remember it from an old painting in a book my parents owned. So, the tales must be true. Tintagel really *was* built in its former location."

"Let's hope," I said. "Otherwise, I might be screwing this up big time."

Pulling the key off its chain at my neck, I unlocked the door and proceeded through, only to be greeted by a mist of light drizzle. A gusty morning breeze simultaneously threw my curly hair into instant disarray and cleared my head.

The others followed close behind, and in a matter of seconds, we found ourselves standing among the shadows of a shallow display of ruins.

The place was quiet, and as I pivoted around to survey the area, I was relieved to see none of the ominous shadows the bartender in Pevethy had warned us about.

"Everyone, this is the ancient castle of Tintagel," Desmond said. "Or rather, what used to be Tintagel. Very touristy during the daytime, though it's really just a pile of rocks."

"It's…a little uninspiring," Meg said, looking around. "Not much here."

I would have agreed with her, except for the fact that something about it felt strangely magical, like a wild energy danced around us, unseen and unharnessed.

"You ready for a flight?" I asked, turning to Callum.

"I just need a bit of space," he said, looking to the others to move back. "I don't want to hurt anyone when I shift."

They got the hint and backed away, leaving room for him to transform into his golden dragon.

I'd seen the beast a few times now, always blown away by his exquisite beauty, the elegant line of his neck, his incredible talons.

But something about him had changed since the last time I'd set eyes on him.

It took a moment to realize what it was.

"A crown," I breathed, staring at the circular rim of scales that was beginning to protrude from the top of his head. "You're wearing a crown!"

As if in response, the dragon shook out his head, then huffed out two small clouds of smoke.

"He is!" Desmond said with a grin. "A golden dragon with a crown. Not sure there's anything more regal than that."

"The heir of the Otherwhere is showing his true colors," Niala said with a smile, patting Rourke, who was standing next to her.

I walked up to the dragon and stroked a hand over his long, sleek neck. "You've changed in all the best possible ways," I said softly. "You know who you are now, don't you?"

A low rumble rose up in his throat, and I tried to tell myself it was a friendly sound rather than a hostile growl.

Hesitant, I heaved myself up onto his shoulders and peered down at the others.

"We'll be back as soon as we find what we're looking for. Keep an eye out, and stay low. There's no doubt in my mind that the enemy will come. The only question is how many of them there will be."

I shot Lachlan a look, tacitly asking him to protect the others. Much as they were skilled fighters, I knew none of them—not even Rourke—could match his sense of smell or his sheer power.

He nodded quietly, then shifted into his wolf form.

"I'm ready," I whispered, leaning down over the dragon's neck. "Whenever you are."

With that, the creature surged upward, taking me with him as I grabbed hold of his scaly mane and let out a cry of joy. I pressed myself down toward his body and we began the flight over the ocean, banking sharply after several seconds to turn back toward the coastline.

Straining against the darkness, I stared at the jagged, uneven series of rocky outcroppings that made up the northern coast of Cornwall.

"I'm seeing all kinds of caves," I said with dismay. "But I don't see a face."

Callum's voice danced in my mind. *Keep looking. It's here somewhere. I can feel it.*

—Now that you mention it, I can, too.

As we soared, I surveyed the coast, noting this and that curve in the rock formations. A boulder here, a pointy slab of stone there. But still no face.

"We should turn back," I told Callum after a few minutes. "The bartender said it was near Tintagel, and I think we've gone too far."

The dragon swept around, banking once again and turning back just as the sun threatened to peek over the horizon.

Just then, I saw something—a shape, reflecting the pinkish-orange of the breaking dawn.

"Wait, slow down!" I shouted. "Look!"

Outlined in the rocky cliff was the perfectly sculpted face of a bearded man.

"A nose. Two eyes. And at the bottom…right along the coast… a mouth."

The mouth isn't so much a mouth, though, is it? Callum asked.

"No," I laughed. "I think it's another cave. Makes the face look pretty angry. But it's *definitely* a face. Let's go tell the others, before the tide rises. The water's already lapping at the base of the cave."

Triumphant, we flew back to the ruins to let the others in on our secret.

With the rising sun, the ruins had become more visible. From the air I could see the surrounding landscape now—the steep curve of the coastline leading down to the churning sea. A series of partially standing walls, mottled with small windows, extended upward into the hillside, and a labyrinth of short, rounded walls sat to one side. They were coated in moss, and looked more like a series of shrubberies than the remnants of a noble palace.

Leading uphill was a long, zigzagging staircase, flanked on either side by railings.

But for some reason, I couldn't see anyone from our party.

When we landed, I dismounted, stalking quietly through the ruins while Callum shifted and let out a low whistle.

Figures started coming at us from behind the ruins to our right and left. First Desmond, then Niala and Rourke, then Olly, then Lachlan.

"What happened? Why were you separated?" I asked when we'd all gathered in one of the grassy areas.

"We decided to take a look around," Olly said. "That's when we heard Lachlan let out a warning."

"I picked up a scent," Lachlan added. "My kind."

I tensed. The way he said the words made it sound like it was no ordinary Waerg.

"Another Sasser?" I asked, swallowing.

He nodded, pulling his eyes to Callum for a second. "There's more than one. I picked up at least five separate scents."

"Okay, then," I said. "We definitely have to go down to the cave *now*."

"You mean..." Desmond asked. "You found it? The face?"

I nodded. "It's not far. I can take us all there."

"Wait a minute," Olly said. "Meg's not here."

My eyes widened as I realized she was right. I twisted around, frantically staring into the shadows around us.

"Meg!" I hissed. "Meg! Where are you?"

"I'll find her," Lachlan said. "You go ahead and summon a door. We need to be ready to leave."

I watched him go, then summoned a Breach that would lead us right to the cave's opening.

"We don't have much time," I told the others. "The tide will rise soon."

"Lachlan will find Meg," Desmond said. "Won't he?"

I shot a look at Niala and Callum, and a mutual understanding passed between us.

"He'll find her," I assured the two Seekers. But the truth was, I was losing hope.

Like Lachlan, I could feel a presence—a creeping threat, coming closer, stalking us from the shadows.

I pivoted around, my eyes catching every bit of movement around us—a swaying blade of grass here, a leaf moving across the landscape there—until I saw the unmistakable shape of a girl and a boy, sprinting toward us, darting in and out between the shattered ruins.

"Why are they running so fast?" Desmond asked. "Surely we have a few minutes before the tide rises…"

"I don't think they're running *toward* us," Niala said, drawing a shimmering silver blade from a thigh-sheath, "so much as running *away* from something."

At that, Rourke shifted into his black panther form and let out a snarl.

Beyond the two darting figures I could see now that a small army of wolves and humans were making their way toward us.

The wolves were enormous, their eyes glowing a horrific red.

Among the humans was a girl with short, dark hair.

"Freya," I growled.

But instead of coming our way, she and one of the Sassers turned to head toward a stony path that would lead them down toward the shore…and the mouth of the cave.

"Vega!" Lachlan's breathless voice called out as he and Meg approached. "You and Callum need to go *now*! You can't wait any longer. We'll try to cut them off."

"I can't!" I shouted back. "I'm not leaving you guys!"

Meg said, "Remember: *Two shall enter*...maybe it's code. Maybe the rest of us are meant to stay behind and fight."

Desperate, I glanced toward Freya and her companion. They'd reach the cave in a matter of minutes if no one stopped them.

"There's no time to argue about it," Lachlan said.

"He's right," Niala added, "If they get into the cave, Freya will find the Lyre first. You're the one who led us here, Vega. You need to get it. Bring it back to us. I promise, we'll be okay."

The Sassers were all around us now, eyes like rubies glinting in the growing light.

Indecision paralyzed me.

Merriwether would know what to do, I thought. *He'd find a way to send...*

Reinforcements.

"Damn it," I cursed. "I'm a Summoner. What am I doing?"

I closed my eyes and called out to an old friend.

"We need your help," I said. "Please, bring the others with you. It's a matter of life or death."

When I opened my eyes I looked to the hilltop high above us, where I saw twenty or so men and women dressed in red, green, and blue, making their way down the long, winding staircase. Even in the meager light, their weapons gleamed and shone like fire.

"Crow!" Niala cried when she saw the leader of the small military force. She turned back to me. "You called on the Rangers!"

"I did," I said. "There's no way I'm leaving you guys here without backup."

A moment later, the first of the Sassers fell when a series of arrows struck his side.

The battle had already begun.

My fingers shaking, I unlocked the door I'd conjured and turned to the others. "If anything happens to you..." I began.

K. A. RILEY

"Nothing will happen to us. It's not us the Sassers want," Niala said. "It's you. It's the Lyre. Our *only* job is to keep them from getting to it. And Freya's almost at the coast by now. We don't have time to talk about the pros and cons. Just go!"

"Come on, Vega," Callum said, taking my hand. "She's right. If we're to win this war—if we're to stay together and to keep the Otherwhere from falling—we have no choice but to go now."

Swallowing a cruel lump in my throat, I nodded.

Without another word, we leapt through the door, slamming it behind us.

INTO THE MOUTH

I FOUND myself standing on a bare patch of sand, the waves lapping at my toes. Staring out at the sea as if looking for guidance.

Where am I? What am I doing here?

"Vega…" a voice said. "It's time."

I turned around, shaking my head, my heart pounding as I recalled what had just happened.

Callum looked sad. Torn. Hurt.

Just as I felt.

He understood what we both might lose today. He knew as well as I did how crushing it was to leave friends in danger. It felt like a desertion.

"What if they die?" I said, my throat feeling like it was filled with jagged shards of glass. "Those Sassers are vicious. What if they die, and it's our fault?"

"If they die, it will be the enemies' fault. But something tells me they'll be just fine. What *will* be our fault is if the Lyre falls into the wrong hands," he added, pulling his eyes to two figures moving rapidly along the water's edge toward us.

I bit down on the inside of my cheek and nodded. I knew he

K. A. RILEY

was right, but I hated what he was saying. All I wanted was to go back up to the ruins, to fight with everything I had to keep the others safe.

Resigned to my cruel fate, I turned around, only to see the small, dark mouth of the cave awaiting our entry.

"Let's go, then," I said. "Let's find it."

Without another word, I stepped into the darkness with Callum by my side.

The cave was larger than it had looked from the outside, its floor sloping upward. The wet, curved stone surfaces inside the chamber reflected the limited daylight, guiding my eyes up to a narrow opening.

"You go first," Callum said. "I'll follow, in case anyone comes at us from behind."

Edging forward over uneven, loose stone, I climbed for several feet before reaching out to feel my way into the small, dark tunnel. I pressed my palms into the walls to either side as I went.

All of a sudden, I heard a loud crash and the ground under my feet seemed to shake.

The limited light that we'd had at our disposal had disappeared.

"What just happened?" I asked.

"The mouth sealed itself," Callum replied. "We're alone now. No one can get in."

"And we can't get out."

"Let's just follow the tunnel and see where it leads," Callum said, his voice soothing and calm. "Don't forget—we're meant to be here."

"Why do I not find that reassuring?"

With that, I turned and tried to feel my way along the tunnel. At first, engulfed in a thick, suffocating darkness, I couldn't see a thing.

Even the air seemed to grow thicker with each step, catching in my lungs and making me feel as if I was carrying a sack of boulders on my back.

The passage led upwards slowly but steadily, the terrain underfoot jagged and difficult to navigate without risk of a broken ankle.

But after several minutes of careful climbing, the walls of the tunnel began to take on an eerie, whiteish glow, and our surroundings became visible.

"There's a chamber up ahead," I said.

"Good," Callum replied. "Maybe that's where the Lyre is being kept."

"Let's hope."

I took another few steps until I emerged into a small cavern. There were no torches on the walls, no source of light that I could see. But as I eyed the space, the walls began to glow bright white, as though lit mysteriously from behind.

"There's nothing here," I said. "And I don't see any way out. I don't think—"

But as I spoke, the walls around me began to change, darkening and morphing into something else. The roundness of the cavern's walls and ceiling turned into sharp angles. The stone altered to dark wood.

I spun around, looking for Callum's reassuring face.

But he was gone.

I was alone.

"What's happening?" I asked out loud, drawing my dagger from its sheath at my waist.

Faded newspaper clippings began to appear along the surrounding walls, glued in place like ungodly, foreboding art.

Chains and hooks dangled from the ceiling, and the place smelled of rot and decay.

"The Murder Shack?" I muttered. "What the hell? How?"

I called out to Callum, but nothing.

"Why am I seeing this?" I asked the air. "Have I lost my mind?"

I stepped over to look at one of the newspaper clippings.

It was an article about a seventeen-year-old girl in Fairhaven, murdered by a local man.

I read it out loud.

Vega Sloane was walking home from Plymouth High on an autumn afternoon when the man known as Daryl the Psycho Killer...

"Hilarious!" I said, pulling back. There was no way I was going to read any further. Someone was playing mind games with me, and I had no patience for it.

I'd just begun to walk the room's perimeter when someone grabbed my shoulder from behind.

"Callum!" I shrieked. "Don't freak me ou—"

My words were cut off by a set of jagged fingertips digging into my flesh, pressing deeper and deeper until I screamed in pain.

Leaping free of the vice-like grip, I spun around, only to see a man standing in front of me.

He grinned as he examined me, his face creasing with the kinds of wrinkles that only years in the sun can inspire. His eyes were hollow and black, and he wore a plaid lumberjack's shirt.

He had exactly three teeth.

I'd never seen the man before. But I knew exactly who he was.

"You," I gasped, my heart pounding. "You're a fabrication. A fiction. You don't exist. Liv and I invented you when we were children."

His smile deepening, the man reached his arms out and grabbed me by the throat.

Gasping for breath, I croaked out a mantra.

You're not real.

You're not real.

With a burst of adrenaline-inspired energy, I thrust out my right hand, stabbing the blade at his chest. The apparition—or man, or whatever he was—shattered into hundreds of pieces and dropped to the ground in a delicate cascade of tinkling glass.

The room transformed once again.

This time, the cavern altered to dark gray stone. The ceiling rose high above me, and the walls pushed outwards, enlarging the chamber until it was large enough to hold several elephants.

High along the walls along the room's perimeter was a series of carvings of dragons and gargoyles. Several feet from where I stood were two large glass cylinders, each of which contained a sea of green ooze.

And floating in the cylinders were my brother, Will, and my best friend, Liv.

"No!" I shouted, running over and pounding on the glass as I'd done once before. "This already happened! Why are you making me relive it?"

I broke down, collapsing onto my knees, and stared up at Will's face.

"You're in California," I sobbed. "You're not here. You're safe. I know you are. Liv, you're at home with your family."

Why was this happening? Was I conjuring these awful scenarios, or was it the handiwork of someone incredibly cruel?

There was no way I was doing this to myself.

Which could only mean one thing.

"I know what you're doing," I growled, "and it's not going to work."

As if on cue, the glass prisons disappeared, and the chamber reverted to its former white-walled self.

But this time, a new tunnel opened up at the far end.

I called to Callum one more time, but there was no reply.

Wherever he was, I could only hope he wasn't suffering in the same way.

Terrified to see what the next few minutes might bring, I proceeded down the tunnel, my dagger clutched in my right hand.

I moved slowly along the passageway until I came to another glowing space. Fiery orange-red crystals lined its stone walls, giving it a horrifying glow that made me think of the depths of Hell.

As I stared, shaking, at its walls, a series of mature trees sprung up to my left and right, until a massive forest of pine and birch surrounded me on all sides.

I looked down to see that I was standing in the middle of a paved country road. Something about it was familiar—the way it curved up ahead, the shallow ditches to either side.

It was peaceful. Beautiful, even.

Yet it terrified me more than either of the two previous scenarios had.

Why did I know it so well? When had I seen this place?

When the sudden, horrifying screech of tires on pavement met my ears, I spun around to see a car careening off the road a hundred feet away and slamming at full speed into a tree trunk, its front bumper fracturing and its windshield shattering. Smoke billowed up from under the car's hood in awful, final gasps.

I raced over to the car, running as fast as my legs could take me.

I knew what I was going to see.

I knew.

Yet I couldn't pull my eyes away.

"Mom! Dad!" I screamed, my voice high and pleading.

My mother's window was broken. I hooked my hands over its edge, the jagged bits of glass tearing into my fingers, my eyes locked on her face. Her head lolled on her neck, her eyes filled with horrified confusion. Blood trickled down her forehead, and she was breathing hard.

"Vega," she said. "Vega…we didn't mean for this to happen…"

"I know, Mom," I said, tears streaming. "I know it was an accident. They should never have taken you from me. They should have killed *me*. It was me they wanted…"

"No," she said. "I'm glad they didn't hurt you. You're our treasure. You're our baby."

She reached a hand up and stroked my cheek, and I wept as I pressed my face into her palm.

"You're our treasure," she said again. "Our Vega…"

With that, she fell silent.

The image of my parents finally began to fade, and I backed away, horrified.

The woods around me shifted once again, reverting into a crystal cavern.

"Is it some kind of test?" I shouted, my throat hoarse.

"That's correct," an unfamiliar voice replied.

I twisted around until my eyes made out a shape—a tall figure, emerging from the shadows. He was wearing a hooded robe, his elbows bent, hands clasped in front of his chest.

"In order to acquire the Lyre of Adair, you must prove yourself worthy to possess it," the strange man said. "I am the Lyre's Keeper. I will not easily part with it."

"So you'll only hand it to someone you've tortured first?" I asked, wiping away my tears.

"I'll only hand it to someone who has proven themselves willing to suffer for it."

"That's *sadistic*."

"You may think so. I choose to see it as noble. It is wrong, after all, to surrender a Relic of Power to one whose nature is simply consumed by greed. Only a true Seeker understands what it is to give something up—just as you chose to leave your friends behind at Tintagel, Vega Sloane. You understand sacrifice."

Rage bubbled up under my skin. I failed to see how reliving my parents' horrible death proved anything, other than the fact that I was human.

"Where's the Lyre?" I asked.

"Only a little farther along. You will soon set your eyes on it."

"And Callum?"

"He's close," he replied. "You know he's close."

He was right.

I could feel Callum's presence. I could only hope this awful Keeper—whoever he was—wouldn't put me through any more torture before I got to see him.

"Is he being tested the same way I am?" I asked.

But instead of answering, the man turned and walked away, disappearing into the shadows until he faded away to nothing.

Where he'd once stood, the mouth of a new tunnel appeared.

THE OTHER SIDE

DESPERATE TO FIND CALLUM, I sheathed my dagger and ran down the tunnel, twisting my ankles this way and that on the jagged floor until I finally saw daylight ahead.

"Thank God," I moaned, limping toward the light, my mind addled and tortured.

When the tunnel finally came to an end, I stepped out into a beautiful green pasture. Idyllic, rolling hills surrounded me, the grass dancing along their slopes in a gentle breeze. I inhaled deep, taking in the scent of the strangely calming world where I found myself.

Nothing about this place was frightening. If anything, it felt like a calming drug. A sense of peace filled me, and I began to relax for the first time in what felt like hours.

"You made it," Callum's voice said from behind me.

I spun around to see him walking toward me. I raced over, ignoring the pain in my ankles and feet, and threw my arms around his neck.

"Are you okay?" he asked.

"Are *you*?"

"I'm okay," he said, but I could tell that something was eating away at him.

"Did he make you relive your worst fears?" I asked. "Because none of it was real—it was all just mind games. It's okay. We're through."

"You're right. None of it was real," Callum said, nodding toward something over my shoulder. "Until now."

I turned to see that the long table from the Revelation Ball had appeared in the middle of the field.

The Lyre of Adair hovered over it like a rotating, gleaming trophy.

"You think that's real?" I asked. "It's not an illusion, like at the ball?"

"It's real," he said. "I'm sure of it."

"How can you know?"

"I just do. Come on." He took my hand, squeezing hard like he was afraid of losing me. "Let's get this over with."

He began to walk toward the Lyre, but I stopped him.

"Why do I feel like there's something you're not saying to me?" I asked. "What happened to you back there?"

But he didn't answer the question. He simply said, "I knew there was a reason I came. A reason I had to be here. I understand now."

"Callum…you're scaring me."

"It's okay. I know how to make sure you get the Lyre. I know what I need to do. Just trust me, all right?"

I nodded, and we made our way over to the table.

That was when I spotted a piece of paper, folded in half, sitting on an elegant silver plate as if awaiting our arrival.

I stepped over and reached out to grab it.

"It's not for you, Vega Sloane," a deep voice said.

I twisted around to see the man who called himself the Keeper standing next to Callum. As I looked at him, he pulled his hood down, revealing his face for the first time.

And for the first time, I understood who he was.

I'd seen him once before, in the bonfire on the beach in Fairhaven. That night, I'd felt him prodding my mind, leafing through my memories. Searching for weapons to use against me.

His face was old and young at once. His skin was creased with age, but his eyes were bright and inquisitive.

He looked sad, like someone who was about to break terrible news.

"Who's the note for, if it's not for me?" I asked, my voice quaking.

The Keeper drew his eyes to Callum, who stepped forward and reached for the paper.

"What...what does it say?" I asked when he'd unfolded and looked at it.

The color drained from Callum's face. He turned away from me, reaching for the edge of the table, but said nothing.

"Callum?"

But he simply shook his head.

"Keeper!" I cried out, turning to the man who seemed to know my darkest secrets. "What is it?"

The man lowered his chin.

"It is the final test."

COST

"WHAT DOES THE NOTE SAY?" I asked again, desperate to understand. "Callum...you need to tell me."

He set his jaw and handed it to me.

Three little words were written on its surface:

Say his name.

At first, I didn't understand.

It was so random, so cryptic.

Say *whose* name? Why? Was this some kind of riddle?

But as I pulled my eyes up to Callum's again and saw the sickness setting in—the grim horror of his thoughts—a swirling feeling of nausea overtook me.

"No!" I shouted, turning to the Keeper. "This can't be the test. You can't ask him to do this. He's not a Seeker. He's..."

"I ask nothing of anyone. The Lyre is asking it of *you*."

"Of me?" I breathed as a sudden realization sank in.

The Lyre had already asked me to relive my worst fears, real or otherwise. To endure the horrors that came with their memories. Horrors I'd lived through in my mind a thousand times.

But each of those fears was based on a memory. An event that had already occurred.

So I knew they couldn't hurt me any more than they already had.

But there was one scenario I hadn't yet had to live through.

And it was the worst of all of them.

"This is *my* test," I gasped. "You've chosen it, because you know…you know that losing Callum is my one greatest fear. You saw it, that night at the bonfire. When you saw him with me. You know how much…how much I love him."

"I did not choose the test," the Keeper said, shaking his head. "*You* chose it."

"I didn't choose anything!" I shouted, lunging at him in my rage. "I would never have asked for this! You're a monster!"

Before I could reach the Keeper, Callum grabbed me from behind and pulled me back against his chest.

"We *both* chose this," he said softly.

"How can you say that?" I sobbed. "This is wrong. It's not fair!"

"We chose to love each other. We chose to be together. All along, we've known it would lead to pain and sorrow. We've always know this day was coming, Vega. We just didn't know if would be so soon."

"No, not like this!" I cried. His arms were tight around me now, protective and strong. But even he couldn't shield me from this pain. "We're not supposed to lose each other, not like this!"

I wanted him to fight. To transform into his dragon and burn the table, the Lyre, and the Keeper to the ground.

But instead, he just held me, saying nothing.

He'd already given up.

"Wait," I said, pulling myself free and turning to face him. "We can just leave. We don't *need* the Lyre. I can summon a door, and—"

"I'm afraid that isn't possible," the Keeper said.

"What? Why not?"

I closed my eyes and tried to call up a Breach back to Tintagel. But my mind was blank. An empty canvas, devoid of images or abilities. All I could see was blinding white, as if everything inside me had been wiped clean.

"Where *are* we?" I asked the Keeper. "Why can't I summon a door?"

"You are in the Beyond," he told me. "Both of you. The only way out is to pass the final test. To acquire the Relic. Or…to die."

I reached for Callum, gripping his arm to keep from falling in a heap to the ground.

"I'm so sorry," I told him, "I didn't know. I would never have come here if I'd known. I'd never have let you come with me…It's all my fault."

Callum smiled then, his sadness fading. For a second it gave me a dash of hope.

"Vega," he said, "do you really think there was a chance in hell I would ever have let you come here without me?" He pulled me close then for a kiss that almost made me forget how cruel fate really was, then pressed his forehead to mine. "I love you. Any pain I'm feeling is *because* I love you. I never, ever wanted to leave you, to say good-bye. But for you and for the Otherwhere, I'll do anything. I'll even die, if I must. Don't you see? This is *my* fate."

"No, it's not," I choked. "The prophecy…it says the heir of the Otherwhere will claim the throne."

"Prophecies don't always come true," he replied. "Besides, the prophecy also says the rightful heir may end up *destroying* the Otherwhere. Do you really want to take that chance?"

"You would never destroy it!" I cried. "You're so good. You deserve the throne. You deserve the life you were born to live."

"The throne was never mine," he said wistfully. "I was never king."

"But you were *meant* to be."

He shook his head. "Maybe I wasn't, after all." He gestured to the strange, lovely land around us. "Maybe this, right here, is what's meant to happen."

"I don't believe that." I turned back to the Keeper. "What will happen if he speaks the dragon's name?"

"I cannot know such things. No one can."

"Will he die?"

"I don't know. But he may well."

"Callum," I said, my vision blurred by the tears that wouldn't stop flowing. "You can't risk this."

"Well," Callum replied, "I have good news and bad news."

Choking back a sob, I asked, "What's the good news?"

"It's my choice."

"And the bad news?"

"It's my choice."

AN ENDING

I WANTED TO STOP CALLUM. To clap a hand over his mouth and mute him, so that saying the dragon's name would be an impossibility.

I even considered pulling out my dagger and wounding him enough so that he passed out.

But as always, he figured out what I was thinking.

"Vega Sloane," he said quietly, "I told you once I would go to Hell and back with you. I meant it. If this is Hell, then believe me when I say I'll find my way back. And so will you, if we're truly meant to be together."

"What if we're not?"

"Then let's be grateful for the good old days—the ones we got to share. Those were the best days of my life. The happiest. I'm the luckiest person who's ever lived, because I got to spend my best days by your side. But right now, there's something I need to do."

With one final kiss and a stroke of my cheek, Callum stepped past me and fixed his eyes on the Lyre.

"No…Callum, please…"

He took a deep breath, turned to lock his gaze on mine one final time, and breathed two syllables:

Caffall.

"*No!*" I screamed, leaping at him.

But I was too late.

The Lyre was in my arms, and Callum was nowhere to be seen.

I fell to my knees, sobbing as I clutched the Relic of Power to my chest.

"He's gone," I moaned, turning to look to the Keeper.

But he, too, had disappeared.

I was alone.

I fell down onto my side, sobbing as I held onto the Lyre—the item for which Callum had sacrificed himself—and wondered how I could ever go on.

I don't know how long I lay in the grass weeping. How long it took before my eyes lost the ability to produce more tears, and I finally rolled onto my back, destroyed.

As my eyes met the sky, my heart skipped a beat.

I could see something—a creature of some sort, flapping broad, elegant wings in slow motion high above me.

As I stared, a flicker of sunlight caught a wing and it glimmered an exquisite, metallic gold. The dragon banked and flew off into the distance, disappearing after a few minutes.

The joy I felt was unlike anything I'd ever experienced.

Callum had disappeared, yes—and maybe he was headed so far away that I wouldn't see him for some time.

But he was *alive.*

As I contemplated what it meant, the pastoral landscape surrounding me began to change. Suddenly I was standing in the ruins of a castle on the coast of Cornwall, the sea beating at the shore somewhere below.

The Lyre of Adair was still tucked safely in my arms. Behind me, I could hear voices.

"Vega?" someone called out.

I pivoted to see Niala and Rourke running toward me. Behind her were Meg, Oleana, Desmond, Lachlan, and Crow.

"You're all alive?" I cried out. "You did it! You fought them off!"

"We did," Niala said. "With a few injuries along the way." She nodded toward Desmond, whose shoulder was bleeding. In the distance I could see Crow's small company talking among themselves. A few of them seemed to have superficial wounds. "It's all right," Niala added. "I can heal them all."

"So tell me—what happened?" I asked.

"The Sassers are strong," Crow said, thrusting out his chest. "But *we* have ranged weaponry."

I laughed. "Did you find out who they were working for? Who hired Freya?"

"We did," Lachlan said. "I recognized a sigil emblazoned on a few of their cloaks. A staff with the head of a snake."

"The sigil of Marauth," Niala said. "One of the wizards in Merriwether's Order."

"We'll need to tell Merriwether what you saw," I said. "When we take the Lyre to him. But I'm sure he already knows."

"The Lyre!" Desmond shouted, pointing at the very obvious Relic of Power in my arms as if it was the first time he'd noticed it. "But what happened? Where's Callum?"

I chewed on my lip for a second before saying, "I don't actually know. But I hope he'll be with us very soon." I let out a sigh. "It's a long story, to be honest, and I'm not sure I can talk about it right now. Let's head away from the ruins. I don't want to summon a Breach to the Academy here and risk damaging this place. I can tell you about everything once we're safely out of here."

After Crow had gathered his small group of fighters, our

party set off hiking until we were standing in a gravel parking lot just outside Tintagel's borders.

I was about to conjure a door when Meg pointed toward something in the distance, and said, "What's that? Looks like someone's lying under that tree over there."

"Probably a tourist," I said.

I was standing behind two very tall Rangers and couldn't see what she was talking about. Not to mention that my mind was focused on other matters.

"Could be a Waerg," Desmond suggested. "If it is, we should most definitely leave him there."

"Wait. No—that's no Waerg," Niala retorted, even as Rourke let out a piercing howl. "I recognize that jacket…"

"Jacket?" I asked, my heart catapulting itself into my throat. "What does it look like?"

"Vega…" she said.

Panicking, I pushed my way between the Rangers until I could see what the others were looking at.

Some distance away, a young man was lying face-down in the grass.

He wore a red jacket emblazoned with a white crest, and a pair of dark jeans.

High in the sky, far above his lifeless body, a golden dragon flew in broad circles like a vulture waiting to descend and feast on carrion.

"It's Callum," I gasped, too terrified to move.

"That *can't* be Callum," Oleana said. "His dragon's in the sky. Shifters can't separate like that. Can they?"

I turned to Lachlan, who looked like he was about to be violently ill.

"They can," he murmured. "But…"

"But what?" I asked, frantic.

"Not without dire consequences for their human half. He…he can't survive for long. Not like that."

Niala turned to me, her eyes wide with terror.

"Vega!" she shouted, reaching out to grab me. "Don't! There's nothing you can do!"

But she was too late.

I was already running.

COMING SOON: SEEKER'S PROMISE

Things are not okay.

With a certain dragon missing, Vega is faced with an awful choice: Return to Fairhaven alone, or embark on a dangerous hunt in the hopes of saving Callum.

With the help of Lachlan, Niala, and Merriwether, she makes a promise that will lead her on a new quest...and this one may be her last.

Seeker's Promise is available for pre-order until its release in December 2020.

ALSO BY K. A. RILEY

Seeker's Series

Seeker's World

Seeker's Quest

Seeker's Fate

Seeker's Promise (December 2020)

Seeker's Hunt (Coming in 2021)

Seeker's Prophecy (Coming in 2021)

The Conspiracy Chronicles:

Resistance Trilogy

Recruitment

Render

Rebellion

Book Two: *Into an Unholy Land*

Book Three: *No Man's Land*

If you're enjoying K. A. Riley's books, please consider leaving a review on Amazon or Goodreads to let your fellow book-lovers know about it. And be sure to sign up for my newsletter at www.karileywrites.org for news, quizzes, contests, behind-the-scenes peeks into the writing process, and advance info. about upcoming projects!

K.A. Riley's Bookbub Author Page

K.A. Riley on Amazon.com

K.A. Riley on Goodreads.com

K.A. RILEY ON SOCIAL MEDIA

Website: karileywrites.org